FOR MADDIE WITH LOVE

For Maddie With Love

SHEILA YEGER

Based on the ATV series written by
Douglas Watkinson

NEW ENGLISH LIBRARY
TIMES MIRROR

A New English Library Original Publication, 1980
© 1980 by Douglas Watkinson
Novelisation © 1980 by Sheila Yeger

*

FIRST NEL PAPERBACK EDITION APRIL 1980

*

*NEL Books are published by
New English Library from Barnard's Inn, Holborn,
London EC1N 2JR
Set, printed and bound in Great Britain by
Cox & Wyman Ltd, Reading*

45004795 4

Chapter 1

The train was crowded. Looking round the compartment, Neil Laurie wondered briefly where everybody was going and why. He had always enjoyed train journeys, even as a child: the sense of adventure, of danger, the mystery of sitting anonymously in a crowd of strangers. When he was nine or ten, he used to pretend that he was a secret agent on a dangerous mission and that his mother was a spy carrying stolen documents in her bag.

Which reminded him, it was strange how she'd dropped that bag soon after they'd got in. She wasn't usually so jittery. In fact, she was usually so bloody calm it was enough to drive you round the bend. Not like his father, who was always a mass of nerves, as jumpy as a greyhound. They were chalk and cheese, his parents. Still, they seemed to be happy, as far as you could tell. What was it he'd read somewhere? 'Happy families are all alike.' He doubted that, somehow. At least, it was hard to imagine another family like the Lauries: first, his sister, Gilly, who kept trying to have babies and never quite made it – well, not up to now, anyway; then there was Nick, her husband – now, how did you tell your friends that your brother-in-law was a policeman? And Gordon, the eldest of the three – he was definitely what you might call an unknown quantity, a bit of a cold fish as far as one could make out. Then his father, Malcolm, in some ways more like a big kid than any of his children. And, of course, Maddie . . .

Neil looked at his mother with admiration. He had lost count of her age somewhere along the line, but thought she must be in her late forties. Not that you'd ever guess. She was slender, with the sort of discreet blonde hair that makes everyone else's look brassy, and amazing eyes which could change expression in a split-second. She looked like a woman who knew what she wanted out of life and was well on the way to getting it.

He was proud of her, yet slightly embarrassed that she had elected to come with him to Keele. It was, after all, his first term at University.

Maddie Laurie, hugging the window, was busy with her own thoughts.

It had begun quietly, undramatically. Nothing to get excited about. Well, nothing you could really put your finger on, anyway. Just a vague sense of something not right, a break in her body's familiar rhythms. So far, it had remained her secret, a private fear, barely acknowledged. As long as she could brush it away, laugh at it even . . .

That first time, at her daughter Gilly's house, it was lucky no one had seen her walk into the door like an idiot. She had told herself at the time she was just overdoing it a bit, getting herself into a state over Gilly's pregnancy.

Then again, that time in the restaurant – those wretched candles flickering, the light catching the knife, playing tricks with her eyes. She had probably had one too many – got a bit carried away with the occasion. Anybody could knock over a glass of wine – well, *couldn't* they? Specially sitting there practically in the dark? Malcolm said it was so you couldn't see what you were eating – or who you were eating with, for that matter! Well, she might be old fashioned, but she really didn't mind looking at her own husband. Those dim

6

lights! They were probably supposed to be romantic. Romantic, my eye! She and Malcolm, a boring old married couple with twenty-six years under their belts, and Jack Burrows and the surprising Angela – tough, shrewd, funny and, would you believe, his *fifth* wife! Now, two was sophisticated, three was greedy, four was verging on the ostentatious ... but *five!* Jack – her own gynaecologist and her husband's best friend. He had eyes in the back of his well-groomed head. After all, he *had* delivered all three of her children – Gilly, Gordon and Neil – and soon, with any luck, he'd be delivering her grandchild, provided Gilly made it this time. But Jack, damn him, in between bouts with Malcolm, Jack had, as usual, missed nothing.

Good thing he hadn't seen her today then, juggling with that wretched bag, dropping things all over the place. He'd have made something of that all right. Pompous idiot. She smiled.

'You know it's the first sign.' Neil's voice cut across the rumbling of the train. 'Talking to yourself, to say nothing of grinning like an ape.'

'No, it's the second. The first is hair on the back of your hands.' Maddie laughed, glad of the interruption to her thoughts.

'You all right?' Neil, she noted, was sufficiently concerned to want to make the question sound nonchalant.

'Like you said, it was only a bag.' Maddie gave him the answer she knew he wanted to hear; the rules of the game were satisfied.

They travelled on in silence. Neil immersed in his magazine. Maddie watched him surreptitiously, with affection.

'What are you staring at?' His voice was sharp.

'Fed up with me, aren't you?'

His 'nope' was hardly a convincing denial. She appreciated his honesty, aware that it was enough that he had 'allowed' her to accompany him. She could hardly expect him to enjoy her presence.

She took a thermos flask from the bag beside her.

'Coffee?'

Neil nodded.

She began to unscrew the top of the flask, then stopped. Suddenly, the simple, automatic action seemed fraught with potential hazards. She passed the flask to Neil.

'Pour the coffee, dear.'

He began to do so.

'What's the matter with me today?'

Her tone was light but Neil sensed that it was a serious question, demanding a reassuring answer. He side-tracked skilfully: 'Nothing . . . except you think your little boy's going out into the wicked world, never to be seen again.'

'What's she like, this girl?' Maddie asked, moving on smoothly, reprieved.

'Mmm?'

'The girl in the flat?' She had already elicited the information that there *was* a girl.

'Flat,' Neil replied succinctly.

'There *are* more important things.'

He handed her the coffee. She reached out for the cup, failed to make contact. He placed the cup squarely in her hand, as one might hand a drink to a child.

'These rattly old trains . . .'

He nodded agreement, entering into her duplicity.

She saw that he was not convinced, but it was still easier to lie, even to herself, to blame inanimate objects, brush it aside, laugh it off. There was always some pat explanation, someone else only too ready to collude with her evasion, some way or other of avoiding a head-on collision with all the sinister possibilities of the truth.

8

The train passed through a long tunnel. And, as it emerged into the light, Maddie became aware of a jagged kaleidoscope of clouds, trees, houses, images splintered and fragmented like broken glass; and, coming into gradual focus in the foreground, Neil's pale and terrified face.

'Mother, for God's sake, what's the matter?'

She found herself lying full length on the floor of the compartment. Other faces, voices, bobbed in and out of her consciousness like horses on a fair-ground roundabout – a blur of colours, a cacophony of discordant, ragged sounds. Cautiously, curiously, she touched her blouse just under her chin. It was wet.

'What happened?' Her own voice, too, seemed to come from a great distance.

'I don't *know*.'

Neil was afraid.

She spoke softly, carefully, treating each word as a fragile object: 'Don't be frightened. Just tell me what all these people are doing.'

Neil turned sharply to the onlookers: 'Go away!'

As they faded out of her field of vision she heard a man's voice, expressionless, and one word bounced back at her: 'Fit.'

'What did that man say?' she asked.

'A fit. You had a fit,' Neil replied quietly.

He had pulled her awkwardly to her feet. The floor of the compartment was filthy and her clothes were covered with dirt. She felt such a fool. Brushing at her skirt, she asked 'What does he mean, a fit?'

'Oh, nothing spectacular. Just frightening.' Neil replied as lightly as he could. Maddie reached out to grasp his hand.

'How do you feel, anyway?' he asked.

'As if someone pulled the plug out.'

There was a short pause.

'I want you to promise me something,' she said quietly. He knew what was coming.

'Not to tell my father?'

'Please,' Maddie said. 'It'll only worry him. You know what he's like.'

Neil agreed, but only on one condition. She must arrange to see a doctor immediately. Maddie tried to dismiss the suggestion as a waste of time, knowing all the while that Neil would pursue it relentlessly. Suddenly, everything had changed. What had been, up to that moment, simply an inward fear, her own private and personal property to dispose of as she wished, was transformed, in an instant, into something she and Neil owned in common. They had become unwilling partners.

A week later, Maddie stood in the kitchen up to her elbows in flour. The door opened and Neil appeared towing a bagful of dirty washing. Maddie had been expecting his arrival, knowing that it was only a matter of time before he would begin to apply pressure on her to take some action.

'Launderette closed down has it? Oh – and how's Judith? Not too keen on washing shirts, I see. Sensible girl. I mean, look at *me*, chained to the kitchen sink . . .'

Humour had always been her best line of defence. Delighted as she was to see him, she knew well enough that he had not come home just to get a clean shirt. Not this time.

And he, playing the game too, came back at her just as sharply.

'Now that's what I call a really warm welcome,' he joked. 'Positively glowing. Actually, I was thinking of going to the doctor – I'm suffering from a severe case of maternal deprivation. Talking of doctors—'

'Were we? I hadn't noticed.'

He reached out to kiss her on the cheek. She wanted to hold him, to reassure him and herself. Instead, she shrieked, 'Ouch! You haven't shaved! And if that bag is full of washing I've only one thing to say.'

'That makes a change anyway. You usually have at least half a dozen.'

Back and forth like a ping-pong ball, fooling neither of them.

Maddie placed a layer of pastry in the piedish and trimmed it off. At last, to her relief almost, Neil came to the point.

'Actually, I've come home specially to talk to you.'

'Have you now?' Maddie continued to attack the pastry, showing no reaction.

'When will Dad be back?' he asked.

'Tomorrow, I think.' She did not look up.

'That's good,' said Neil. 'Just in time for me to spill the beans about you. If necessary. You didn't see a doctor, did you? No – of course you didn't. You *wouldn't*. Well, that's that then.'

Maddie sighed. She had known what was coming all along. When Neil got something into his head ... Well, like mother, like son. It wasn't only her nose he'd inherited.

'You don't seem very worried.' He was almost shouting at her.

'Look,' she interrupted calmly, 'if you think there's *anything* you can tell your father which we can't somehow deal with between us, then you don't know either of us very well.' And, patting him on both cheeks in a mock display of affection, she left the room.

Catching sight of his dismal reflection in the kitchen window he saw that she had daubed him with flour so that he looked like a clown – which was what she had meant to do of course, make him feel a fool. He knew he had done it all wrong, blundering in like a ham-fisted idiot. He had chosen the wrong approach and she was too clever for him as usual.

But pride was an emotion he could not afford at present. So later, he came to her again, trying a different, gentler tack, and, this time, she listened, if not quietly, then at least with some acceptance of his fears. But even if she was prepared to discuss what had occurred, she was still reluctant to take the next step, to set in motion a chain of events over which she felt she would have no control.

'If I go to see a doctor,' she reasoned, 'what can he do? He'll send for the great British "test" ... then another test ... and eventually, because they always do, they'll find something wrong with me.'

But Neil refused to let go. 'Middle-aged women do not suddenly throw fits in a train for no reason,' he insisted.

'Singular,' she corrected. 'Fit. *One* fit,' and added with a casualness which he found thoroughly unconvincing, 'It can happen to anyone.'

He knew by her very refusal to acknowledge that the situation might be serious, how worried she was. He tried to persuade her that Malcolm should be told. She disagreed violently.

'He'll be less able to cope with it than you,' she insisted. 'If I think there's something wrong with me, *I*'ll do something about it.'

But Neil, one step ahead of her, had already made the next move. From the pocket of his jacket, like a conjurer who produces his white rabbit at the very moment when his audience seems to be losing interest, he drew a card.

'See,' he proclaimed, 'I have the name of a specialist – Mr Michael Pearson. He sounds ancient and reliable.'

Maddie tried to wrench the offending object from him

but without success. She was beginning to feel at a distinct disadvantage, but all that she could do was hope that he would have the tact and good sense not to upset the family apple-cart with scaremongering about her health – particularly not now, with Gilly about to give birth at any minute.

In fact, in some ways, it was just as well, she thought. Impeccable timing. Gilly's pregnancy and now the very imminent and longed-for birth of their grandchild was enough to occupy anyone's mind, even the volatile Malcom. Gilly was his favourite; he'd have no time to worry about anything – or anyone – else.

It had become a tradition in the Laurie household for the whole family to meet for Sunday lunch. It was not something they had ever consciously planned, but like many traditions it had gradually evolved over a period of time. They usually ate roast-lamb, which was Malcolm's favourite, Yorkshire puddings, which Gilly loved, cauliflower with cheese sauce, which was a concession to what they called Maddie's vegetarian tendencies, and potatoes in their jackets if Neil was home. And when Nick had become a part of the proceedings, they had to take into account his odd passion for custard with rice-pudding. It was far from being a conventional meal, but, thought Maddie, looking round the room, they were far from being a conventional family.

Gilly was helping herself to a fourth Yorkshire pudding, smiling at her mother as if to say, 'I know I shouldn't . . . but why shouldn't I?'

There was something of her father in her vivacious, rather than conventionally pretty face, her determined mouth, and her quick gestures. Whereas many women grow still and somewhat bovine in later pregnancy, she

13

had retained her usual quality of almost nervous liveliness.

As Nick took another jacket potato, Gilly's hand shot out almost automatically to try to stop him, but to no effect. He was a big man, well-built without being too solid, with a fine head of hair and the sort of face which would convince anyone of his good nature and honesty. Not a bad quality for a policeman, mused Maddie. He and Gordon must be much the same age, she thought and immediately registered, not by any means for the first time, the absence of her elder son from their family occasion. But Gordon, doing well as a solicitor in Herne Bay, was far too busy, she told herself, to keep popping home for Sunday lunch.

As her eyes rested last on Neil, he glanced up from his plate and caught her eye. He did not smile but slowly shook his head, as if silently reprimanding a recalcitrant child.

They were discussing possible names for the baby and he threw out the suggestion: 'If it's a boy she could call him Michael. Michael's a good name.'

The arrow found its mark easily enough, but still he was not satisfied. He had to give it a further twist, just to make sure. 'I know some very clever Michaels. Didn't you know a doctor once ... Michael somebody-or-other?'

He got up and walked towards the door. Then, pausing for maximum effect, he pointed at Maddie and blurted out to his father, 'She isn't very well, you know.'

Malcolm picked up the remark rather too quickly.

'What's the matter, dear?'

Maddie tried to gloss it in her usual way, turning it into an affectionate snipe at Neil.

'You know what he's like – tongue goes into first gear when his brain's in neutral.'

14

But Malcolm, remembering the night at the restaurant, was troubled by an impression – he could not quite put a finger on it, just something he had noticed, something strange, out of place.

Still Maddie was fighting to gain ground. 'Yes, I did have a bit of a headache last night and I made the mistake of telling him. You know what an old fuss-pot he is.'

'A headache? Is that all?'

Malcolm reacted with a violence which took Neil by surprise.

'Stop trying to create an effect all the time!'

Maddie tried to shield him a little. 'I don't think he meant any harm by it.'

Gilly picked it up immediately and could not resist taking it a step further, half-joking but serious enough to do some damage: 'It's only because he's left home. He thinks we don't love him any more, so to keep himself firmly in our minds, he throws in a little something for us all to worry about.'

Though Maddie again found herself grateful for any diversion, she knew how much Neil must have suffered from Gilly's remarks. Somewhat repentant, she allowed herself later to be drawn into discussion with him or, more accurately, she allowed him to harangue her, as he tried once more to force her to admit, if only to herself, that something was wrong.

Suddenly, she asked, 'Which of us is the more scared, you or me?'

She was surprised by the passion with which he replied, 'Look I *know* something's wrong. We know each other too well to play games.'

But Maddie was not yet ready in her own mind to face the possibility that he might be right.

Eventually, he saw no alternative but to take the law into his own hands. He had tried gentle persuasion,

strongarm tactics, teasing, threats. His mother had responded by making him feel alternately an overgrown
baby, an utter fool, a worrying old woman, or a bully. He
had exhausted all the reasonable approaches; now only
subversive tactics remained.

Neil rather enjoyed forcing his way past Dr Pearson's
tight-lipped secretary into the august presence of the
great man himself. The woman looked as if she had been
there as long as the deep-pile fitted carpets and probably
longer than most of the furniture. She reminded him of
one of his teachers at Junior School – formidable and
very easily offended. But a deep belief in the end justifying the means had propelled him through many similar
situations.

He fought back the impression that he was in the head-
master's office and launched into his carefully prepared
story.

'I was on the train last week and, to put it simply . . . I
had a fit.'

Once he had started, he was surprised by his own
confidence and skill in lying. He answered Pearson's
probing questions with ease, elaborating on a point here
and there, embroidering the simple facts to produce a tale
which was rich in descriptive detail and, he was sure,
entirely convincing.

When he had finished, Pearson quietly asked, 'Why did
you really come to see me? You describe the fit in precise
details, yet you say you were unconscious, and alone in
the compartment . . .' He paused. 'Perhaps there was
someone with you, on whose behalf you have come to see
me today . . . someone dear to you, someone who is
afraid to come themselves, someone older than yourself
. . . middle-aged . . .'

Neil's voice was little more than a whisper. 'My mother.' Then he added, even more quietly, 'I'm sorry.' Taking fresh courage from Pearson's unexpectedly gentle reaction, he asked, 'What could it be? What could have caused it?'

Pearson's reply was non-committal. 'I have no idea. There are many possibilities, most of them so trivial that both she and you would be amazed.'

When he told Maddie of his escapade, she was, as Pearson had predicted, strangely moved by his audacity. But she knew that now, more than ever, he had got her where he wanted her. It was her move. They had become, she thought ruefully, partners in crime, united in their conspiracy. So again she made a deal with him. She promised to go to see Pearson if he, in turn would promise not to tell Malcolm.

Chapter 2

Driving to the hospital through the late October afternoon on her way to visit Gilly, Maddie wondered, not for the first time, why the year did not begin in the autumn. Oxford, in particular, always seemed to her at its most subtly alive then, the pale light mellowing its old stone, new students gathering excitedly on corners like crows on bicycles, its streets gaudy with the turning leaves. Winter always felt like an ending, spring like a fresh start, but autumn was more complex – a time both of fruition and of exciting new possibilities. What was the expression? 'A time to live and a time to . . .'

She could not tell Malcolm. Not yet. Perhaps – just perhaps – there would be no need to tell him at all. She did not know whether she was protecting him from the truth or whether she simply could not face the crisis she felt sure the news would provoke. He was too highly strung. Stretched out so taut that you could almost hear him hum.

When strangers inquired what her husband did for a living and she replied, 'Oh – he's an accountant.' It always amused her to imagine what image the word might conjure and how far it would be from the truth. She had always thought of an accountant as being rather like a character from Dickens – dry and precise, all buttoned-up and unemotional. Until she met Malcolm, that is. He was as vulnerable and excitable as a child.

It was funny how Gilly took after him, but with subtle

differences. She had his quick temper and his vulnerability and she certainly knew how to get her own way, particularly with Nick. But Malcolm, underneath all the bluster, had a special sort of strength. While Gilly she wasn't so sure about. Sometimes she felt she knew all her children like the back of her hand, but at other times they could seem like strangers to her. All except Neil. She and Neil were definitely on the same wavelength; there was nothing they could hide from one another. Nothing ...

Waiting at the last set of traffic lights before the hospital, Maddie glanced at her watch. Ten to three. With any luck she should get there in time for the beginning of visiting. She could not bear the thought of Gilly, her eyes glued to the door, pretending not to notice if she was a few minutes late. Now that the birth was almost a reality, after all the long weeks of waiting and speculation, the poor girl was really beginning to show signs of strain. No wonder, with the endless examinations, the constant scrutiny, false alarms, tests and precautions. They would be enough to try the patience of a saint and Gilly was far from one of those.

Of course they were *all* worried sick about Gilly. They just had different ways of showing it. Jokes and explosions. Maddie smiled. Under stress, the family definitely divided itself into the jokers and the exploders. Neil, of course, always reacted to tension by taking humorous swipes at all and sundry; Gilly, Malcolm's girl in every respect, tended to go off with a loud bang when the going got rough. Nick – *almost* family – was definitely one of the humorists. Though sometimes, she had to admit, it was hard to tell whether he was joking or serious. Like that business with the washing-machine the other day. He'd come blundering into the conservatory and driven her mad for a full fifteen minutes, complaining about their temperamental washing machine. But what was he *really*

19

on about? Was it simply a gigantic hint – which she had not taken – for her to offer to do his washing in Gilly's absence? Or an even bigger hint that they would like a better-behaved machine for Christmas? Or perhaps it was just his way of telling her that he was worried sick about Gilly, hoping that everything would be all right this time, afraid to think what might happen if it was not.

What about Gordon though? Which category did he fall into? That was not so easy. She could not really say much about her oldest child. He had become a closed book to her recently. Or perhaps she should say an open and shut case? Since he *was* a solicitor. 'Oh you're one of the jokers all right, Maddie Laurie,' she sighed, 'the Queen of the Jokers, in fact.'

Malcolm, of course, the arch-exploder, was taking the whole thing as badly as possible and was giving everyone, Jack Burrows in particular, an appallingly hard time. You could not really blame Jack for banishing him from Gilly's bedside to his own office, where he could rant and rave to his heart's content, without causing undue havoc.

She found Gilly in a terrible mood, lashing out in all directions, in a vain attempt to find an outlet for her own tension and misery. And Neil, who was visiting her before returning to Keele, was, as usual, the main butt of her remarks. Strange how childhood rivalries cut so deep. They used to squabble a lot when they were children and somehow they had never quite got out of the habit. And, though Neil had a good tongue on him when he wanted to use it, it was Gilly who really knew how to wound with words. All the same, Maddie thought, it was difficult not to feel sorry for her, marooned in her bed like a beached whale, stitched up, wired up, plugged in – a miracle of modern science. It was enough to make anyone irritable . . .

At the end of visiting time, Maddie went to find Malcolm. He was prowling about the small room like a caged lion.

'Gilly OK?' He turned on her with the question as soon as she opened the door.

'Feeling blue.'

Her answer, innocent enough in itself, sparked off a burst of invective like machine-gun fire, with the much-maligned Jack Burrows as its main target: 'Not surprised ... Calls himself a gynaecologist! The man couldn't deliver the morning papers!'

'To be fair,' Maddie said reasonably, 'he didn't guarantee the baby'd come today.'

Exhausted by his own anger, Malcolm smiled and put his arms around her, relaxing for a moment against her. 'It's going to be all right isn't it? I mean, I can't get any sense out of Jack.'

'It is,' Maddie replied with some authority, 'I know it is. Third time lucky.'

On the way home, without knowing exactly why, Maddie was conscious of feeling vaguely depressed and rather tired.

Perhaps it was Gilly's mood which had infected her – or Malcolm's agitation. Or perhaps it was just the hospital, with its characteristic smell of antiseptic mingled with the scent of dying flowers. Or all those damn machines. Babies, she mused, ought to be born in a field full of poppies, in the sunlight, to the sound of birds singing. Not in a sterile hospital ward surrounded by flashing neon and to the accompaniment of some machine bleeping out a hymn to technology.

The journey from Oxford to Denton seemed longer than usual and Maddie breathed a sigh of relief as she finally drove through the white gates which led to the

Lauries' house. Parking the car in the drive, she noted with some satisfaction that the purple Clematis had finally reached the upstairs window. She had planted it two years ago and had almost begun to despair of it, but now it had obviously decided to surprise her.

The house could do with a coat of paint, she thought. Still it would wait for the spring. Perhaps they ought to branch out and try another colour this time, though it did look good in white. It was not a beautiful house, by any standards; it was too sprawling and untidy with bits stuck on here and there in different styles and at odd angles. Malcolm said it looked as if the architect had been constantly interrupted – or drunk.

Later that evening, Maddie was sitting alone in the conservatory. It had always been her favourite room, from the very first time she had seen it. It made her laugh to remember ... They had been shown around the house by the owners and she had found herself marooned in the kitchen exclaiming dutifully at the fitted cupboards and gleaming sink unit, while Malcolm had wandered off alone to investigate more interesting areas. Suddenly he'd burst in, grabbed hold of her hand and half-dragged her through the living-room.

'You've got to see this,' he enthused, as he pulled her along. 'There!' He triumphantly presented his 'find'.

He had been quite right, of course. She had fallen in love with that conservatory at first sight.

There was no furniture as such, just an old cane rocker and a functional rather than elegant armchair. Even the plants were crowded together in a pleasant jumble: chipped pots with geraniums, scarlet and sharp-pink, an optimistic attempt to grow an avocado, an old and much-revived palm, a pot-bound spider-plant. And, in a basket on the floor, a collection of oddments which might or might not one day find some function – scraps of material, old greeting-cards, some abandoned knitting.

It was here that Maddie always felt most relaxed, free to indulge in her own thoughts. And Malcolm knew enough to ask permission before intruding on this, her very private time and space.

'May I?' He hovered in the doorway.

'Mmm?' She looked up and smiled. She had wanted to be alone, but he was, nevertheless, welcome.

'I wondered if—'

'I'd fancy a game of rummy? I know!'

'Do you?' He had the pack of cards in his hand.

'Come on, then.'

He sat down and dealt the first hand. As they played they talked. Not, it might seem, about anything in particular: Neil and his first term at University, Gilly and the longed-for baby, jokes about the past, half-formulated plans for the future. But, as usual, the very things they hoped for most were the things they expressed most lightly, because this was their way.

Suddenly Malcolm broke off to look at Maddie sharply. 'So – don't tell me then,' he said. 'I don't care.'

There was a pause. Maddie pretended not to have heard or not to have understood. 'Pardon?' she said.

'What's wrong with you, I mean,' Malcolm continued.

Maddie did not look up from her hand of cards. 'I will if it ever seems important.'

'Promise?' Malcolm's voice was low but insistent.

Another pause, longer this time, then she replied, 'I promise.'

*   *   *

The next time Maddie saw Jack Burrows she casually asked him if he had heard of Pearson and inquired as to his professional opinion of him. She explained her sudden interest in the specialist by telling Jack that a friend of Neil's was due to go to see him and had asked her to investigate. Burrows praised him highly, but, remembering what he had observed in the restaurant, did not, for one moment, believe her explanation. Gilly had been asking about Pearson, too. He wondered what was this sudden obsession the Laurie family had developed for the man.

Maddie, oblivious of his suspicions, left his office with some Valium she had extracted from him for Malcolm and a firm belief that she had again been successful in her deception.

When she arrived home, she was relieved to find the house empty. Since Malcolm worked for himself, she could never be sure when he might arrive home unexpectedly. Just as well she did not have anything to hide. Well, nothing like *that*, anyway. He teased her about it sometimes: 'Come on then ... Where is he? Not in the wardrobe, surely!' And she would reply, grossly offended: 'At least credit me with *some* style. The wardrobe! He left by the French windows ten minutes ago!'

They did not have many secrets, she and Malcolm. Nor did they lie to each other. Not usually.

Maddie suddenly caught sight of her own face in the mirror which hung in the hallway. It did not *look* any different – one or two fresh lines perhaps – a hint of tiredness around the eyes. Surely there'd be some sign. Sign of what?

'You're a bloody liar, Maddie Laurie!' She suddenly spoke out loud. 'Something's wrong – and you know it. What in God's name are you trying to prove?'

She picked up the phone and made an appointment to see Pearson.

Afterwards, looking back on the events of those next few days, it seemed to her that her phone call to Pearson was the biggest step of all. In her own mind, but as yet unacknowledged, she knew the answer before the question was even asked; she had known it for a while. But, by voluntarily seeking expert professional help she was finally admitting to herself that she was ill – seriously ill.

When Malcolm returned that evening he found her sitting on the floor of the living-room, surrounded by photograph albums and piles of old photographs. She looked up, guiltily almost, as if surprised at some childish pursuit.

'Look at this one.' She held up a picture for his scrutiny. He peered at it and saw a much younger Maddie, squinting at the camera, looking like a startled rabbit and all dressed up in a neat little dress with a white collar.

'How unbearably sweet,' he said, pulling a face.

'Pig! Don't you remember that day?'

'Should I?'

'Well . . .' She enjoyed his dutiful attempt to place the photograph, then relented. 'Give in?'

He nodded.

'It was the day we had to tell my father I was pregnant with Gordon. Remember?'

'God – how could I have forgotten?'

Malcolm bent down to kiss the top of her head.

'What've you been up to day?'

It was an innocent question, but Maddie jumped apprehensively before she replied: 'Oh, nothing much. Well, I planted some hyacinths for Christmas.'

'Christmas?' Malcolm seemed surprised. 'But it's *months* away yet. I suppose the next thing you'll be telling me is that you've done your Christmas shopping and ordered the Easter Eggs!'

Maddie laughed. 'No, just the hyacinths. You have to give them plenty of time.'

Time ... There was always too little of it – or else too much. She had been so anxious about Gilly that she'd willed the time to pass quickly so that the hour of the birth would come and put an end to all the uncertainty. But now that very same hour, could, she knew, bring with it other, less welcome news.

Usually calm and unhurried, she had felt, over the past days, a growing sense of urgency, a need to see things *done*, completed. Hence the hyacinths.

'I thought you hated photographs,' Malcolm interrupted her thoughts.

'I do.'

'Why?' he teased. 'Because the camera always lies?'

'No,' and she replied with a gravity which took him by surprise, 'Because it always tells the truth.'

Suddenly she jumped up and caught hold of his arm. 'Malcolm, I want you to paint a picture.'

'Picture of what?' Malcolm asked.

'Me,' Maddie replied.

Malcolm, a Sunday painter, with no pretensions to being anything else, was struck by the incongruity of Maddie's demand.

'Strange request for you,' he remarked.

'Is it?' She busied herself picking up the photographs.

'Well – you don't even like having your photo taken.'

Maddie laughed:

'I just want us all to remember how I looked ... before I hit the rocky road to fifty.'

She thought she saw Malcolm's expression change

26

slightly, as if something had disturbed him, but it could have been a trick of the light.

'From the navel up then,' he joked.

'No, neck.'

'All right,' he laughed, pouncing on her from behind, 'if you insist.'

They subsided giggling into a heap amongst the photographs.

If Malcolm had been surprised by her request for him to paint her portrait, he tried not to show it or to investigate her reasons, but set to work the next day. He seated her in the conservatory – her natural habitat, he called it – and in her old rocking-chair.

Studying her face perhaps more closely than usual, as he mixed paints, attempting to find just the right shades to evoke her skin, her hair, her mouth, he suddenly gained a fresh insight into her particular beauty. Her features were irregular, but that was not important; she had a special quality – of calmness, stillness almost – but with those amazingly expressive eyes.

But, even as he watched, her face seemed to flicker momentarily, just a slight movement, like the ripple caused by a small pebble thrown into a smooth pond, and her eyes seemed to cloud over, losing their brightness. It was nothing much, nothing you could really be sure about. But strange, nevertheless. A couple of seconds passed, then it was over. She smiled, obviously unaware of any change. But Malcolm remembered the candlelight, was at once aware that there had been other, similar moments, and was suddenly afraid.

When Maddie took her first step into Michael Pearson's

office, she set in motion a chain of events over which she seemed to have little control. For a woman who had worked hard, if unobtrusively, to gain a fair measure of autonomy in her own life, it was a development she had anticipated with particular resentment.

At first it was a test – quite a simple one, it seemed, but one which, nevertheless, had to be performed the next day. Seated in a chair, electrodes attached to her head, she felt suddenly at the mercy of circumstances, caught up in a nightmare world of jagged lines and flashing lights. And, damn it, the only place she wanted to be was not here but at Gilly's side. She had a sudden crazy and almost comic vision of the two of them, mother and daughter, both wired up to their own private infernal machines, incapable of either escape or protest.

Then there were more tests: fluid drawn from her spine, X-rays, more electrodes ... Eventually, pushed beyond the limits of her patience she screamed out at Pearson: 'Plugged in, wired up, fed onto graph paper ... I can't drink, I've had a tent peg hammered into my spine, my head blown up like a football bladder, drugs that make me ratty and dopey. Just tell me what's wrong with me, for God's sake!'

But, while Maddie's time of uncertainty was not yet over, Gilly, at last, reached the final stage of all the long months of her waiting. And, at the end, she too, ironically enough, had her outburst. Feeling pressure build up inside her like a great stone rolling remorselessly through her body she screamed out hoarsely at Burrows, but Burrows, triumphant, knowing from her very abuse that the moment had finally come, goaded and coaxed her on to the climax of her labour.

Malcolm and Maddie, waiting at home for news, heard the phone ring. Malcolm answered, fighting, but not succeeding, to retain his composure.

'Oh to hell with it! Tell us—'

Nick's voice, breathless, strangely hoarse came back. 'It's a girl.'

For a moment Malcolm reeled, overwhelmed into silence by the sheer power of the realisation that the baby had actually been born, then the questions spilled out in a jumble of words. How much did she weigh? Who did she look like? And, most important, what would they call her?

'Eight six, but that's enormous! Beatrice Matilda? Yes . . . lovely!' Malcolm winced but lied convincingly. 'What *beautiful* names!'

Well, what did it matter really? Gilly had, at long last, given birth to her baby, their first grandchild. Who was he to quibble over a name. And Maddie, relieved that for Gilly at least there was a happy ending, felt a sense of quiet, if conditional, contentment.

The next day she called at Pearson's office for the result of the tests. Always finely tuned to the moods of others, she noticed at once that he seemed strained and ill at ease. She knew at once what he was going to tell her. She asked him if he was unwell. He replied that he was simply a little tired and changed the subject by inquiring brightly if Gilly's baby had been born.

'Yes, it was a girl,' Maddie replied, and added drily before he could comment, 'At least I lived long enough to see that.'

He tried to say something to divert her but she stopped him.

'It's all right,' she said in a matter-of-fact voice, 'I *know* I'm probably going to die. It hardly hurts at all if you say it quickly.'

Pearson watched her face for some sign that she might break and found none. His expression confirmed her statement. He explained her condition; as they had feared, she had a tumour on the brain.

'Is there anything you can do?'

'Nothing. I'm afraid it is completely inoperable.'

'You must help me,' she said quickly, as if struck by a sudden thought.

'Of course ... anything.'

'I must tell my husband.'

He nodded.

Her laugh, like so many things about her, surprised him. 'How's this for a hammy line: "Darling, I'm dying and I want you to be the first to know"?' Then she added more gravely, 'For the first time in my life I won't know what to say to him and he's bound to argue – he always does!'

They sat in silence for a moment, Pearson's eyes on Maddie's face.

'I'm going to die.' She tried the words again, to herself, experimenting with their sound. It was hard to imagine them coming from her own lips as part of everyday conversation, harder still to absorb their meaning, to understand fully what they might imply. She thought suddenly of the baby. Thank God, at least, that Gilly's baby had been born before ... And, more absurdly, the hyacinths! Lucky she'd planted them for Christmas. But Christmas ... She brushed away the unthinkable. The first problem was Malcolm.

With the first sharp hint of real despair, she blurted out helplessly, 'How do I tell him?'

Chapter 3

She knew that it was just a matter of time. That sooner or later he would have to be told, to be given a chance to have his explosion, to absorb the reality of it. It was finding the right moment that was difficult.

From the day when she had learned the results of the tests, Maddie had gradually grown more alert to each new sign of deterioration in her own body, so that things she might previously have dismissed as being of no real consequence – a severe headache, a sudden sensation of giddiness, a momentary loss of appetite, became instead sinister reminders that she must learn to regard herself as a sick woman, a woman who was about to die.

October had slipped into November. The trees were bare now, their leaves a sodden mass underfoot, their brightness a thing of the past. Walking through the Parks after visiting Gilly in hospital, Maddie felt the sharp, sudden hint of an early frost in the air and, turning up the collar of her coat, thrust her hand into Malcom's pocket for extra warmth. They instinctively quickened their step.

'You forget how small they are.' Malcolm's voice cut through the silence.

'What?'

'New born babies. You forget how much they cost you, how many things they prevented you from doing, how often they showed you up in public, how much food they stuffed up their nose instead of in their mouths.'

'How much fun they were,' Maddie added. 'They were, weren't they? Fun, I mean.'

'You know what they say?' Malcolm was not prepared to let her be *too* sentimental.

'No, what do they say?'

'Distance lends enchantment to the view.'

'Still, they *were* lovely, sleepless nights and all.' Maddie refused to be contradicted.

'You soft old thing,' said Malcolm and squeezed her hand in his pocket. They walked on.

'You always used to do that,' Maddie said, after a while.

'Do what for God's sake?' Malcolm was evidently thinking of something else.

'Squeeze my hand in your pocket. Remember?'

'Like this, you mean . . .' And he suddenly gripped her fingers tightly enough to break a few bones. She screamed out and withdrew her hand rapidly.

'Ouch! Gerroff you brute!' She nursed her sore fingers.

'Serves you right for saying 'remember' all the time. You're beginning to sound like a dowager duchess of ninety-three sitting in her rocking-chair and boring the hide off everyone with her recollections of the Boer War.'

'I *like* my rocking-chair,' Maddie reasoned.

'Don't be obtuse. You know what I mean. Perhaps it's being a grandmother! If I'd have known—' Malcolm pursed his lips with mock gravity.

'Yes? What would you have done? Go on, tell me!' Maddie stopped walking and stood full square in his path challenging him.

'I'd have . . . I'd have . . .' He searched for an appropriate retort. 'I'd have bitten your nose off!' And he lunged at her face, missing her nose by an inch or so as she turned her head, laughing, to avoid his attack. Then she ran ahead of him, dodging behind a tree for cover as he came after her whooping and bellowing like a demented Redskin. When he caught her, they wrestled together, she giggling, he breathless from the unaccustomed exertion.

'Grandpa!' She taunted him. 'Gramps! Grandad Malcolm!'

'Granny Nana Maddie' He came back at her. Suddenly she stopped struggling and looked at him, shaking her head.

'It doesn't seem possible, does it?' she said seriously.

'What? That we're actually grandparents? Well, it happens.'

'No,' she went on, 'I mean, inside my head I still feel like that girl in the photograph . . .'

'You mean old rabbit-features in her utility frock?'

'Yes,' she smiled. 'That's the one.'

'But that was taken years ago. When you were expecting Gordon.' Malcolm was puzzled by her mood, afraid where it might lead.

'I know. But I don't *feel* any different. I know I *am* – well I'm more than twenty years older for a start. But it still feels like the same *me*. Do you know what I mean?'

'I think so,' Malcolm replied slowly. 'Anyway,' he said, anxious to steer the conversation onto a more mundane level, 'You still look the same – apart from the false teeth, the wig, the corsets and the gammy leg, that is. Come on, I'll race you to that chestnut tree. Last one there can make the tea'

They ran laughing across the grass.

It should have been a happy time and in some strange way, it was.

Maddie, growing more troubled each day by unfamiliar

changes in her body, at the same time grew more aware of everything around her. It was as if the knowledge that her time had a boundary lent a new definition to each minute and, in particular, the hours she could spend with Malcolm became both intensely pleasurable and strangely painful. It seemed to her that they grew closer in those weeks, drawn together by fears they could not name, by memories they needed to share and by their very particular, robust and unsentimental kind of loving.

Malcolm was waiting, heavy with some undefined knowledge, conscious that there was *something* which would soon have to be said, terrified by what it might be. That day in the conservatory; the incident in the restaurant; something odd going on between Neil and Maddie – and Pearson. Everybody kept mentioning Pearson; his name had become a sort of secret password in the family. There were too many signs . . .

And, 'Do you remember?' That, too. How many times in the last weeks had he heard Maddie use those words? Why? She was not the sort of woman to start getting agitated about growing old. Then there were the photographs. She'd suddenly developed an obsession with old photographs. What was the point of delving into the past when the present was so full of possibilities and the future was . . . That was the problem, wasn't it. When you came down to it. You had the past, pinioned like a butterfly under glass, fixed, beautiful, immobilised. But the future was like mercury, the shining silver globules volatile, running in every direction, impossible to control.

Malcolm knew that he would not rest till he had gone to see this man Pearson and settled the mystery once and for all. There was probably a very simple explanation, as usual. He telephoned to make an appointment, and, finding that Pearson was obviously a very busy man, was surprised when he agreed to see him the next day.

'So,' Pearson said as Malcolm was shown into his surgery, 'you've come about your wife.'

'Have I?'

'Well, haven't you? I rather assumed . . .'

'I don't really know *why* I've come.' Malcolm was beginning to feel rather foolish

'Has she told you nothing about me? I find that very odd, you know.' Pearson sighed.

Malcolm floundered, struggling to gain some ground. 'She came to see you – she had a bad migraine. You gave her some pills.'

But Pearson was quietly remorseless:

'You didn't think it strange that she came to one of the best known neurologists in the country because she had a *headache?*'

Malcolm did not look up. Pearson's voice became more sombre. 'She came for a lumbar puncture. Do you know what that is?'

The news shattered Malcolm, but, even as he exclaimed in surprise, he remembered the day. 'I smelled it as I walked into the bedroom . . . But why?' His mind raced on now.

'Weren't you told? Mr Laurie, she stressed many times very forcibly to a point where I was . . . well . . . obliged to respect her wishes . . . she stressed that I was not to tell you.'

And with that tantalising, though, he sensed, incomplete, item of information, Malcolm was forced, for a while, to be satisfied.

He began to watch Maddie more closely than ever, while making a special effort to behave as normally as possible so that she would not suspect his vigilance. He did not tell her about his visit to Pearson. Time enough for that. There were more important things . . .

On Sunday evening they lit a bonfire, gathering all the fallen leaves off the wet grass, pulling down dead branches off the fruit trees, cutting back rose bushes so that they would bloom more abundantly the following year.

It was something they always did in November, before the evenings grew too cold to make it a pleasure rather than a chore. Maddie, wrapped up in an old duffel coat with an enormous pair of yellow Wellington boots, looked, Malcolm thought, like a rather glamorous Paddington Bear, plodding about happily amongst the garden rubbish.

He ran into the kitchen and emerged quickly with something in his hand. Neil, home for the weekend, was watching the scene from the kitchen door.

'What's that you've got?' He tried to grab his father's hand to see.

'Only honey. It's a pot of honey. Bears like honey, don't they?' Malcolm ran down the garden towards Maddie.

'Honey? The man's mad!'

He glanced towards the bonfire. He saw Malcolm grab Maddie round the waist from behind. She squealed and wriggled but he held onto her tightly. Through the misty half-light and the smoke from the fire, he was sure that his mother had her mouth open like a baby bird and that Malcolm was feeding her with honey.

Later, when the bonfire had died down to a pile of glowing ashes, Malcolm found Maddie sitting in the dark in her rocking-chair. She was crying. He came and knelt in front of her, his arms round her knees, comforting her.

'Hey. Hey. What's the matter?' he asked gently.

She almost threw herself against him, burying her head on his shoulder, sobbing bitterly.

'Hold onto me,' she said.

'Now come on,' Malcolm reasoned, 'This isn't the Maddie Laurie the shopkeepers know and fear.'

'Aren't I allowed to cry just once in a while?' she replied, defensively.

'No,' he said, 'It's against the rules.' Then, more tenderly: 'What's the matter?'

For a moment, she tried to offer possible explanations, but then she said softly, 'Malcolm, I'm not well.'

Malcolm sighed with relief and holding her quietly nodded, 'I know.'

'Do you remember the night you went to see Jack Burrows?' she asked.

'Do you remember, do you remember . . .' he chanted teasingly, if only to delay what would come next.

'No – seriously, Malcolm.'

Having decided to talk, she was not to be diverted. 'Something strange happened to me that night. I was downstairs, reading. I looked up at the clock; it was twenty to ten. The next thing I recall I was still looking at the clock, only it said five past. I'd fallen through time and consciousness. I had a wet patch on my blouse, just here . . . I'd had a fit.'

Malcolm was appalled. 'You did *what*?'

'Now I'll only tell you about it if you promise to keep calm,' Maddie replied. Glad to be free of at least part of the burden of her secret, she told him about the incident in the train and about the other occasions on which her body had behaved strangely. But that was all. She explained there was no pain, but it was obviously more serious than she was letting on. He listened quietly, knowing only too well that this must be only the tip of a far more terrifying iceberg and that he would have to wait a while before she was ready to tell him everything. But, still, it was a beginning.

When he went to see Pearson for the second time, it was at the doctor's request. Malcolm was immediately and forcibly struck by the change in the other man's demeanour since his previous visit. Then, he had been impressed by Pearson's urbanity and composure; now he found himself looking at someone who seemed as agitated and nervous as *he* was. He could not resist a comment: 'Why Mr Pearson, you're as nervous as my most irresponsible client,' he joked.

Pearson answered stiffly. 'I assure you this is very far from my natural state.' He paused. 'I'm afraid your wife is very ill.'

'How ill?' Malcolm asked, suddenly afraid.

'She has a large tumour on the parietal lobe ... two smaller ones—'

'Did you ask me here to tell me she's dying?' Malcolm heard his own voice rise, as if in anger.

'I most certainly did not.' Pearson's denial was adamant, but non-committal.

Malcolm grew exasperated. 'That doesn't answer my question,' he exploded. There was a moment's silence during which he looked searchingly at the other man, as if he could hypnotise him into giving any answer other than the one he knew he *must* give.

Pearson's voice was flat. 'The answer is yes,' he said. 'I'm afraid the tumours are inoperable.'

That night, after Maddie had gone to bed, Malcolm went into his study, telling himself that he must look at some papers before an important meeting he had the next day. The portrait of Maddie, now finished, hung on the wall, lit by the diffuse light of his reading-lamp. It was a lousy picture – it didn't look anything like her. Still, it wasn't surprising ; he was a lousy painter. He was just able to prevent himself from smashing into the canvas with his base fist.

'Why *me*?' he cried. 'Why *us*? Why pick on *us*? For Christ's sake what have *I* done? Maddie's heart goes out to all the scum of the earth and everyone loves Maddie in return ... So *why*? It's unfair, don't you think? It's just plain bloody unfair ...'

Then, he looked up at the painting and said more quietly, almost as if accusing it, 'What am I going to do without you? Have you thought of that? No, of course you haven't ... I have to think of everything, don't I?'

The explosion of anger and self-pity was characteristic and very necessary. Once it was over, Malcolm knew that he would be better prepared for what was to follow.

The next day, as they sat at the kitchen table, she told him, quietly, straight out, 'I'm going to die.'

Malcolm did not miss a beat. 'I know. I know ...'

Once it had actually been said, everything became easier. Maddie, who had carried her secret long enough, suddenly realised how many things there were in her mind that she wanted to share with Malcolm. Fears, which she had previously hardly admitted to herself, poured out in a torrent of words, explanations, speculation.

'I'm afraid – not of everything going black, I can't even describe it like that; black's a colour, implies that I can see it, and that around the corner are reds, yellows, blues ... But I'm frightened ... not of everything stopping, but of it grinding to a halt.'

Malcolm took her hand. 'Got an idea,' he said smiling. 'Let's close all the doors and windows. You and me against the world.' Then, remembering the one thing, the vital thing he had forgotten to inquire of Pearson, he asked in a quiet voice, 'When?'

'Not sure ... soon – I don't know exactly,' adding again, even more quietly, 'I'm frightened.'

Malcolm took her face in his hands.

'I want to ask a favour.'

'What is it?' she asked, and he answered,

'I don't want it hushed up – between ourselves, I mean – otherwise I'll never get to grips with it.'

Maddie agreed. They sat for a while in silence, then they both spoke at once:

'What do we do now?'

'Want another cuppa?'

They both laughed, breaking the tension.

'Well, there's your answer,' Maddie said. 'We carry on as normal, like the man said.'

'Man?' said Malcolm. 'What man?'

'Pearson,' she laughed, 'who else?'

'Oh *him*.' Malcolm endeavoured to sound scornful.

'Well,' she went on, 'What alternative is there? I've no great longing to see the Taj Mahal.'

'Me neither,' said Malcolm. 'But I bet you wouldn't say no to Loch Fyne.'

'You mean where we had ... I mean where we *thought* of having ... Gilly.' Maddie had no difficulty in remembering the occasion.

'There wasn't much *thinking* going on, not as *I* remember it.' Malcolm teased.

'Remember, remember. Now you're at it!' Maddie leant across to poke him in the stomach.

'OK, I give in. What about Christmas?'

But Malcolm had other plans for Christmas.

It was only natural that Malcolm's first impulse, once he had at last begun to absorb the reality of Maddie's condition, was to share his grief with his daughter. He had always felt closer to Gilly than to either of his sons; they reacted to things in the same way. He did not go to her seeking comfort but simply an affirmation of his own feelings. But it was difficult to shatter her happiness. She was still in that state of mindless euphoria which follows the birth of a longed-for baby; how could he go crashing in there with such news?

Each time he saw her he made an attempt to broach the subject, but faltered always at the last minute – or before.

He found himself visiting her even more frequently than usual, talking too much, about too little, until one morning she grew suspicious and challenged him.

'Something's bothering you. You came here specially to tell me, then decided against it. Is it family?'

There was his cue; he would never get a better one. But he could not do it. He side-tracked quickly: 'Are you coming to us for Christmas?'

Gilly was unimpressed. 'You never dropped by to ask *that*,' she snorted.

Suddenly Malcolm blurted out her name: 'Gilly . . .'

She looked up quickly. 'Yes?'

'There *is* something,' he began. But no. He couldn't do it; he'd tried and failed. 'We want to buy you a new washing-machine . . . and a drier. I'm worried Nick's the sort of bloke who might look on it as charity . . .'

But Gilly, wondering when he would find the courage to tell her, knew that there was something far more important than washing-machines on her father's mind.

Malcolm felt that the children should be told and that

41

this was an area in which Maddie should be prepared to help him. But she seemed reluctant to commit herself to any particular plan.

'We'll tell them soon,' she said vaguely. 'When I'm a little less frightened of the prospect.'

Malcolm, feeling vulnerable himself, pounced on her admission of weakness: 'You *said* you'd come to terms with it!'

'No, *you* said it.'

'Well, you let me believe it,' he retorted.

'Don't blame *me* for the mistake *you* made. You've been doing it for twenty-six years.' Maddie was not in any mood for letting him get away with anything. The conversation was beginning to develop into the sort of battle which, in normal circumstances they would both enjoy, each of them relishing any opportunity to indulge in a little verbal sparring with a worthy adversary. But this time it was sharper, more bitter. They let it go.

Malcolm had made up his mind to go to see his Uncle Sidney. When Maddie had learnt of this decision, she found herself resenting the thought of him involving an 'outsider' in their private grief. Malcolm, in turn, was impatient with her inability to appreciate how much he needed an outlet for his emotions at that time, a place to go where he would not have to behave like a responsible, controlled adult, but could indulge his more childish fears and give full rein to his feelings of pain and confusion. Maddie, he sensed, could not easily bear the thought of him losing control; it was easiest for her to imagine that he had been able to absorb the news of her illness without too much trouble.

On the way to Sidney's house, the peculiar bitterness of

his argument with Maddie stuck in his gullet like a fish-bone.

'Silly bitch,' he said aloud, 'Why does she always have to be so ... *obstinate*?' And then, after a brief period of calm he blurted out at a startled cyclist waiting alongside him at traffic lights, 'Pickle sandwiches! She knows I hate pickle sandwiches!' The cyclist, a rotund man wearing cycle clips and a Balaclava helmet, peered into the car.

'Mustn't lose my sense of humour,' Malcolm muttered. 'That would be fatal.' Now, there's a funny word. Fatally ill. I'm sorry, sir, there's been a fatality. A fatal accident. You used a word every day without giving it a second thought and then, bang, suddenly it kept jumping out at you all over the place. Like the other day – it was Maddie who'd said it – 'She'd have a fit.' That's all she'd said, then bitten her tongue. It was enough to make you laugh. To *die* laughing.

Trouble was, he hadn't felt all that much like laughing recently. In fact what he really felt like doing just at that moment was giving someone a good old earful. The first person that came to mind was Gordon.

He stopped at the next public telephone box, and dialled the number of Gordon's office in Herne Bay.

'Parkinson, Mills and Laurie. Can I help you?' The secretary's voice was prissy, clipped.

'I doubt it,' Malcolm barked. 'No one can, usually.' Then he went on quickly, 'I want to speak to Gordon Laurie.'

'Mr Laurie is with a client at the moment.'

God, the girl sounded as if she had a mouthful of dried peas.

'Excuse me,' he said, beginning in tones of mock-servility, 'but is that Parkinson, Mills and Laurie or is it bloody Fort Knox?'

'I'm sorry, I . . .' The poor girl was floundering. Served her right, the stuck-up bitch. '. . . He did ask especially not to be disturbed,' she bleated. She probably had red hair and bifocals. No – mousey hair and a Courtelle cardigan.

'What would you say,' he bellowed, 'if I told you it was a matter of life and death?' He waited for her confusion.

There was a slight pause. 'I'd get him to phone you back as soon as possible.'

'Well, don't bother,' he shouted, 'Just tell him his father rang. He may just about remember me!' And he banged down the receiver, kicked open the door, started the car on full choke and roared away, cursing at the top of his voice.

Ever since he was a boy, Malcolm had loved to visit Uncle Sidney. His house was a bit like a magic cave, every corner full of surprises, fascinating evidence of a million exciting and mysterious goings-on: bottles bubbling with some undefined and potent-looking brew, a pheasant hanging over the sink, and everywhere, cobwebs – not just a little something the duster had recently missed, but ancient, intricate and magnificent specimens, festooning the shelves and the corners of every room in wonderful profusion.

Uncle Sidney, needless to say, lived alone. But in his case it was impossible to think of it as a deprivation. Indeed it was hard to imagine him with a wife, though he had once had one. So complex and fascinating was his everyday existence, so full of little projects and pursuits, it was difficult to see how he could ever have made room for another person in his scheme of things. He was so utterly absorbed in his own life that he seemed to need no one and nothing else.

He greeted Malcolm as unceremoniously as ever, and

busied himself with one of the bottles on the kitchen windowsill. Malcolm watched him with affection. He was seventy if he was a day, but he was as robust and chipper as a man thirty years his junior. He was dressed in his usual fashion – tweed jacket, old flannel trousers, a collarless shirt. He looked like something from D. H. Lawrence, an eccentric old relic from another age, but his eyes pierced right through you and he missed nothing.

He listened while Malcolm calmly told him the news about Maddie. At first he continued to occupy himself with the bottles and the pheasant, but then he stopped what he was doing and looked at his nephew seriously. He had suddenly and instinctively realised that Malcolm had not only come to him with the news of Maddie's death; there was something else, almost more difficult to express, on his mind. But the boy was so tight, so full of pain. If only he could let go, take a chance and let it all out. It was like pus in a wound; you had to open it up, squeeze out the infection and let it bleed. It hurt like hell, but you had to do it. But Malcolm was all buttoned-up, holding himself in, using petty anger as the only outlet he knew and trusted.

Sidney spoke gently, reaching out to touch Malcolm's arm: 'Right, so don't tell me! I hate to sound old fashioned, but what you need now's a good cry.'

But still Malcolm held on. 'I can't,' he muttered. 'I'm sitting on a bomb.'

Uncle Sidney would not be satisfied. He held out his hand as if to take an imaginary object. 'Here,' he said, 'I'll take the bomb . . .'

Malcolm stood up. 'Uncle . . .' he began.

Sidney opened his arms wide and received him in a hard embrace as he began to sob, quietly at first, then more fiercely. When he had finished, he wiped his eyes and replaced his handkerchief in his top pocket.

45

'Thanks,' he said.

Uncle Sidney was munching away at Malcolm's sandwiches.

'Not at all,' he said, adding, 'Now I suppose you feel foolish.'

'Only a bit,' Malcolm laughed. It had, after all, been the main purpose of his visit. Now, he had to admit, he felt a lot better.

'Uncle,' he said, 'Have you ever tried coming to grips with a limited future? It's a contradiction in terms.'

'Only because you're a fool.' Sidney had no time or place for mere sentimentality. 'You're the kind of bloke who saw his whole life stretched out in front of him, some winding path up the mountain to a castle on top. Big fable – then *wallop*,' and he smashed his hand down on the draining-board, 'the mountain's about to fall into the sea and what's gone up there,' he tapped Malcolm's head, 'will float away. Good job! What are you left with? Day-to-day reality, not some vague notion of a future you're trying to pin down.'

Malcolm listened but was still not satisfied. But Uncle Sidney had not finished yet. 'Since it's going to happen, this tragedy, you might as well turn it to advantage. Take nothing about her for granted. Everything you do together will be vivid; nothing will be small; nothing will be ordinary – and it'll last forever. When a thing ends, in this case Maddie's life, it won't mean that she never existed. I don't believe in fairies, don't believe in God, don't believe in life hereafter. So what do I say is Maddie is but the sum total of everything people remember about her.'

Sidney paused. That was the end of that part, at least, but he knew that there was more. He made a loud hissing sound through his teeth, never taking his eyes from Malcolm's face.

'What the hell's that?' Malcolm asked.

46

'I'm lighting the fuse to that bomb. I want to see what's inside,' he answered and carried on hissing.

Malcolm looked at his uncle. He had gone so far; he might as well go the whole hog. The old man was as shrewd as a ferret anyway; he knew the score.

'I know she's going to ask me to kill her,' he began.

Sidney raised an eyebrow but did not interrupt.

'She won't slink off and do something violent herself, because that would terrify *us*, so she'll ask me to bump her off in the most civilised way I can find. The reason she hasn't asked me yet is because she knows I'm not ready for it.'

Sidney drew a deep breath. 'You should spare her the indignity of asking. Go home and make the offer.' He paused, watching Malcolm. 'Oh, you're looking for a scapegoat.'

Malcolm jumped. The man was amazing.

'It would be nice, yes,' he agreed.

'Someone to share the responsibility. Well, you can have me. Tell yourself that Uncle Sidney condoned it . . . that you yourself were in two minds and he forced you to make a decision. Blame it on me.'

That night, he returned home late to find Maddie, reading, stretched out on the living-room sofa.

'All right?' she looked up. He nodded. There was no need to go into details.

'What are you reading?'

'Well,' she smiled, 'It certainly isn't *War and Peace*.' He stood behind her, his hands resting lightly on her head.

'This question I'm supposed to be going to ask you,' she began, her eyes on her book.

Malcolm smiled down at her.

'You needn't bother. The answer's yes.'

'I hope we're talking about the same thing,' she laughed. 'It could be very embarrassing if we're not.'

Malcolm spoke quickly: 'You want some help to finish it.'

'That's right,' she replied. 'If you say no, I'll understand.'

'Don't worry,' Malcolm said, 'I won't let you down.'

'I'll pick the day and you'll give me something.' She wanted to have all the details clear in her mind.

'Yes,' he answered softly. 'I'll have it ready.'

Suddenly, to his surprise, Maddie jumped up, sending the book flying. 'I feel about two stone lighter already!'

He caught hold of her gently.

'Funny,' she added, 'when you shift the responsibility onto someone else . . .'

'I know,' he interrupted.

'Sidney.' She made the word a statement, rather than a question.

Malcolm nodded.

'He has ways of making you . . . brave. At least I'm looking forward to Christmas, now he's coming. I wasn't before.'

'Talking of Christmas,' Maddie began.

'Oh no, I've been dreading this. Don't tell me . . .'

'Since this is a very special Christmas . . .' Maddie began, laughing at him.

He completed the sentence: 'I know. I know . . . you want to spend a very *SPECIAL* amount of money.'

Chapter 4

'I've always liked these curtains.' Maddie was finding it difficult to concentrate on the book she was reading.

'Mmm.' Malcolm was engrossed in his newspaper.

'Especially in the winter,' she went on. 'I'm glad we didn't get the bluey-green ones, although I did like them better at the time. Didn't you?'

'Mmm. Mmm.' Malcolm turned the page.

'The bluey-green ones would have been fine in the summer but I think they'd have been a bit – well – cold for the winter. Don't you agree?' Maddie persisted.

'Mmm. Definitely.' Malcolm turned another page.

'I think we should paint this room purple with orange and red stripes and an emerald-green ceiling – and then we'll throw out all the furniture and sit on the floor. Shall we?' Maddie's voice rose a little in a last attempt to gain Malcolm's attention.

'Yes. Sounds a good idea.'

'You haven't heard a *bloody word!*'

'Temper, temper.' At last Malcolm put down the paper and looked up.

'Well, you haven't,' Maddie repeated accusingly.

'I thought you were supposed to be reading. I mean it was *you* that had a book you were dying to finish. If you'll pardon the expression,' Malcolm pointed out.

'I know. I just couldn't concentrate.'

'I know the feeling.' Malcolm made an attempt to recover the newspaper, but Maddie intervened.

'No. Let's talk.'

'What? About the curtains? Do me a favour . . .' Malcolm exclaimed.

'You haven't got the stuff then, have you?' Maddie's tone was light. Malcolm looked up sharply. A week had passed since they had first discussed the matter.

'No, I haven't,' he answered. 'How did you know?'

'Because you'd have told me.'

'Hmm. The *stuff!*' Malcolm folded his paper with an ironic smile. 'If you say it often enough it begins to have no meaning. It even begins to sound quite funny!' He held the paper over the lower half of his face to form an improvised mask and, looking with exaggerated caution from side to side, hissed in a heavy 'foreign' accent: 'You have ze *stuff*? No? Yes? No?' Then, laughing wryly at his own bad joke, added, 'Hilarious. Side-splitting. No, I haven't got the stuff, Maddie.' He could see her disappointment though she did her best to hide it.

'Well,' she began hesitantly, 'have you – er – spoken to anyone?'

He jumped up and wandered over to the bookcase, where he began irritably to arrange and rearrange a collection of small ornaments, his back to her. She watched him, sensing his unease, and waited for his reply.

'Well?' She was impatient for the answer.

'No,' he spun round. 'I haven't *spoken* to anyone. What the hell do you think . . . I mean do you think it's the sort of thing . . . Christ!'

'Don't let's hush it up, you said.' Maddie spoke quietly.

Her calm tone forced Malcolm to control his own outburst. When he spoke again it was a little more quietly. 'I thought I'd ask Pearson. And that's where it starts to get difficult. How do you ask a man . . . well . . . you know . . .?'

'You say, "excuse me, I'm looking for something to bowl the wife over with ... quite literally."' Maddie spoke in an affected 'Colonel Blimp' voice.

'Banana skin,' suggested Malcolm trying to enter into the spirit of the joke she seemed intent on making.

'Yes,' Maddie continued, 'but I don't want her to get up again.'

'*Exploding* banana skin, perhaps.'

Suddenly Malcolm brought his fist down with alarming force onto the top of the bookcase.

'Bloody hell, Maddie,' he shouted, 'I can't just turn it into a huge joke. I'm sorry, but I just can't!'

'I'm sorry,' she said in a quiet voice. He looked at her briefly, shook his head. She felt how hard it must be for him, struggling to convince her that he could cope with his pain, when all the time she knew the truth as well as he did. It was a game, really. An elaborate game. She seemed to be playing them all the time now, first of all with Neil, now with Malcolm. And yet she had always prided herself on being so straight – no devices, no subterfuge – and here she was learning to be as manipulative as the best of them.

'I'm the one who should apologise.'

She went over to Malcolm and touched his arm lightly.

'If I tell you something, will you keep it in perspective?'

'Of course, I won't,' he replied bitterly.

'Promise!'

He sighed deeply, 'Yeah, yeah. All right.'

'Well, sit down, and calm down. OK?' She led him to the sofa and sat him down beside her; then holding his hands between hers, she began to speak: 'Look, Pearson may have told me, and you, that I'm dying. But I don't think he actually *believes* it, yet. 'Thing is, he's almost convinced me as well ... He's still *willing* me to live. For his sake, as well as mine, don't go breaking that spell.'

Malcolm sat silent, looking down at his hands trapped between hers. She held them lightly but firmly. He could not move them away even if he wanted to. He looked up at her face: 'So – why bother with the stuff at all?'

'I'm afraid. That's why.' Her tone of voice startled him.

'Of course,' he said gently, 'Who wouldn't be?'

'Not of dying,' she continued, 'because no one can comprehend their own death. It doesn't exist. My fears are a great cloak of uncertainty, about everything: you, the kids, the cat, the house . . . But the strange thing is the power of that uncertainty diminishes when I think of being able to time my own death – when I know I have the means to wipe out all my fears.'

They sat in silence as he absorbed what she had said. Suddenly it all seemed clear to him. He really had no option. If he had not been sure of that fact before, he was sure of it now.

'OK,' he said slowly, '*not* Pearson.'

'But somebody.' Her voice was urgent.

'Jack Burrows?' Why hadn't he thought of Jack before. He'd be sure to want to help. Maddie was less certain.

'But,' she hesitated, 'he's a friend . . .'

'Precisely.' Malcolm replied with conviction, 'What else are friends for?'

Malcolm and Jack Burrows had known each other for years. As Jack, with typical panache, liked to put it, what could bind two men more closely than a mutual interest in money and a woman? Malcolm was his accountant and he was Maddie's gynaecologist. The two men also shared a tendency to quick anger, an innate resistance to personal criticism and an annoying habit of airing their grievances in public.

If there was one task which Malcolm dreaded each year, it was sorting out Jack's finances.

As Jack came through the door of his office, a briefcase in hand, Malcolm groaned audibly and braced himself to face the inevitable. Jack banged the case down on the scrupulously ordered desk, then opened it with a flourish. It was full to bursting point and the very act of opening it was like taking the lid off Pandora's box. Bills, old cheques, accounts, receipts flew everywhere, creating an atmosphere of instant and total chaos.

Malcolm held his head in utter despair. Every year it was the same. Would the man *never* learn? It would take him three times as long as necessary to sort it all out. He was dealing with a lunatic – a man who wrote cheques and forgot to fill out the stubs – who gave away money and forgot who he'd given it to – who ran up bills and neglected to pay them . . .

'For a man so skilled, so gentle in many ways,' Malcolm burst out, totally exasperated, 'you're a disorganised *monster*!'

'But fascinating,' Jack insisted.

'Is that what Angela says?' Malcolm asked cruelly. He had already heard murmurs about Jack's latest marriage.

'Mind like a dripping tap,' Jack mumbled.

'You'll lose her just like the others,' Malcolm warned, laughing.

'Nonsense! She worships the ground I walk on. I've seen her on her hands and knees.'

Maddie, entering the room at that juncture with three cups of coffee, grimaced with distaste at the remark.

'Anyway,' Jack continued, smooth as hot chocolate sauce. 'It's all right for you to talk! Best wife a man could wish for.' And Maddie, knew that he was, sadly enough, being serious for once, and almost forgave him.

Malcolm spent the next few hours wrestling with Jack's accounts. God, the man grew more chaotic by the minute! If he didn't have an accountant who understood – one who was prepared to turn a blind eye, to bend the rules . . .

'Jack,' he said suddenly, though he had been preparing the question in his mind ever since Burrows' arrival, 'if I wanted to kill myself, how would I do it?'

There was a long pause. Jack had been suspicious for some time now, ever since that night in the restaurant. He'd seen Maddie's eyes become cloudy, lose their sharp gaze in the flicker of candlelight; he'd watched her lurch and waver on the way to the Ladies' Room. She'd pretended she'd had too much to drink, but he knew her better than that. She wasn't a woman to lose control. He'd watched her closely after that. And then all those questions about Pearson. Putting two and two together, you didn't have to be a genius to see what was going on. You didn't even have to be a doctor. He'd known she was ill all along – and he'd been afraid it might come to this.

'Forget the last ten seconds, Malcolm,' he began stiffly, 'and remain my friend; proceed and you become a dot on my horizon . . .'

Malcolm smiled. 'I do believe you have a speech prepared.'

But Burrows was not in a joking mood. 'This loud-mouthed teddy-bear image I project hides a set of principles which you, as an accountant, will never appreciate. Your ethics lie somewhere between debit and credit, no doubt.'

Malcolm was surprised and offended by Jack's tone, but Jack, refusing now to be diverted, launched into his main argument. 'In the body business one must distinguish between the living and the dead. There is no such person as one who is almost dead, or barely alive. The dividing line is clear, but fragile – so fragile that *some* of my colleagues have been known to break it.'

'But there's no hope for her, Jack, except to choose her own time,' he reasoned.

Jack responded with an icy smile. 'No hope? I didn't realise you were God or I'd have spoken more politely to you. No hope? She doesn't believe that . . . and I doubt if you do.'

He stood up and began methodically to pack all his scattered papers into his briefcase. Malcolm watched him miserably but said nothing. He had always thought of Jack Burrows as a man devoted to a life of cheerful excess, steam-rolling his way happily through relationships, going under temporarily only to bob up again with relentless good humour, striding through life with an almost enviable flair and a profound disregard for its more petty restrictions. Now it was as if he had been brought face to face with a totally different Jack – a stickler for principle, a narrow-minded, rigid, observer of the rules. He had always known that this friend had a selfish streak. But whereas usually he ran roughshod over everybody without even bothering to justify it, now he was wrapping the whole thing up in a mass of high-sounding claptrap.

'Selfishness had made you afraid of everything, Jack,' Malcolm blurted out, 'real or imagined. Hence your gown of principles. Not so with me. I come into my own when my back's against the wall.'

Jack looked at him coldly. 'Principles transcend everything; that's their definition.'

'Pompous bastard,' Malcolm murmured.

Jack clicked his case shut and walked from the room.

He did not, however, leave the house immediately.

Instead, he went looking for Maddie. Finding her sitting alone in the conservatory, he came straight to the point.

'I can't do it, Maddie. Yes, you know what I'm talking about.' His voice had lost the cold tone he had employed in his conversation with Malcolm.

Maddie nodded.

He went on, 'I won't do it and I can't condone it. If you want to know my reasons, Malcolm will tell you.'

'Right.' Maddie replied with one word.

Jack walked to the door but turned, his hand on the handle. 'There is one I didn't give him . . .'

'I know.' Maddie sighed. 'But it's a bit late in the day for that, isn't it?'

'But it is true, though . . . I've wanted to—'

Maddie cut into his declaration sharply, her voice bitter. 'Not true enough. Otherwise you'd help me.'

He shook his head.

'When I'm dead, Jack, he may need you.'

'Oh, I'll be there, you can count on that.'

But she knew from his uncompromising tone that he was not offering her any easy comfort.

That night in bed Malcolm found himself going over and over the incident in his mind. Maddie, oblivious, was engrossed in her book beside him.

'Who'll help me fight the Jack Burrows of this world when you're gone?' he asked miserably.

'Mmm?' She refused to be distracted.

'Jack Burrows. He's a pompous idiot.'

'What?' She murmured, not looking up. Suddenly he snatched the book from her hands.

'Hey! I was reading that!'

'You don't say! I'll keep the place for you.' He put the

book down on the floor beside the bed. 'I've been thinking,' he said, putting his arm round Maddie's shoulders.

'Makes a change anyway!'

'About chucking in the business.'

'Seriously?' The idea took her by surprise.

'I've decided, really,' he went on.

'You'll need it to fall back on – to lose yourself in,'
Maddie argued.

'And that's precisely why I shall sell it,' he insisted. 'I
don't want propping up. I refuse to the swamped by grief.
Just think about it. Someone dies, so you tear your own
hair out as if they'd never existed. Grief always seems
such an insult to the dead.'

'Joy's a bit out of place too,' Maddie added gravely,
but not without humour. 'I will not have people being
happy at my funeral.'

Funeral. It was another of *those* words, the ones you
tried not to mention. They looked at each other, said
nothing, waiting for the moment of fear to pass.

'Sorry,' Maddie's voice was subdued.

'It's all right,' Malcolm replied.

'I'm looking forward to Loch Fyne,' said Maddie,
after a moment.

'I should bloody hope so,' said Malcolm. 'And do me a
favour, will you.'

'What's that?' she asked.

'Finish this book before we leave or I'll end up talking
to the sheep.'

It was that same night. Maddie had read a little longer,
Malcolm had dozed. They turned off the light. Malcolm
lay for a while listening to the rain against the window.
Maddie usually fell asleep first; he needed a little time
these days. But it had been a tiring day. He slept. Sud-

denly he was awakened by a rhythmic banging and a series of hoarse, animal-like grunts. Appalled, he turned on the light and jumped out of bed. He watched with horror as Maddie thrashed from side to side, her mouth open, an extraordinary, primitive sound emitting from her throat.

'Maddie! Maddie.' He called her name, hoping to be able to rouse her, but the rhythmic thrashing continued. He watched helplessly, until the grunting stopped, she clenched her jaw and her whole body shook with a violent and uncontrollable convulsion. He waited until it subsided, climbed shakily back into bed and almost weeping with fear, gathered her spent body into his own trembling arms.

But still, even with that most alarming and conclusive proof of Maddie's condition to haunt him, he was no nearer to finding a solution to his dilemma.

That winter, following the birth of Beatrice Matilda, Malcolm and Maddie had fallen into the pleasant habit of spending Sunday afternoons with Gilly and the baby. Conversation was usually inhibited by the constant necessity to pick up, coo over and generally worship the latest addition to the Laurie family. If anyone did talk it was usually only to remark on some aspect of Beatrice's progress which had hitherto escaped comment, to utter some apparently appropriate inanity in her miniscule ear, or to voice an urgent request for a fresh nappy, a Kleenex or some other essential item of baby-ware. Gilly was therefore surprised, in this context, to see her father reading a letter from Jack Burrows. She strained her eyes to see what it said.

'Dear Malcolm,' she read, 'I do not think my decision

to seek financial help elsewhere will come as any great surprise to you . . .'

'Why's he done that?' she asked.

Malcolm waved a cheque in the air. 'Well, he's settled his account – all of it. That makes a change, anyway.'

'No but why?' Gilly would not let it rest at that.

'I made an assault on his principles . . . in broad daylight,' her father answered, and holding the cheque aloft triumphantly cried. 'Still, this'll pay for our holiday!'

'But what was it all about?'

God, the girl was as tenacious as a limpet! 'Oh, your mother, what else?' And he bent down to kiss Maddie on the forehead, thus signalling an end to the discussion.

But Gilly, as Maddie had so often had cause to remark, was her father's daughter. Once an idea had entered her head, she would worry away at it with almost irritating persistence, shaking it this way and that refusing to be side-tracked till she had reached a satisfactory conclusion.

Maddie, who had found her only daughter intractable and obstinate as a child, could not help admiring her tenacity now that she was an adult. Malcolm, too, comfortably unaware of any similarity between Gilly's behaviour and his own, had frequently declared himself defeated by her foot-stamping and tantrums in childhood, but now found himself enjoying the occasional duel of wills with her.

The day after Malcolm and Maddie set off on their journey to Loch Fyne, Gilly was in her kitchen wrestling with a large pile of nappies. She was glad her parents had taken themselves off for a few days. They could do with the rest. Her father had been behaving in a most peculiar manner over the last few weeks. Gilly cursed under her breath as she hauled a bundle of dripping nappies from one tub to another. And her mother – now that *was* strange. She was usually so cool. But even she had been a bit jumpy recently, and *looking* rather peaky too. Then there was all that business about Jack Burrows. They'd been doing business together for years. Gilly smiled to herself, remembering how she had abused Burrows at the end of her labour.

Something else was at the back of her mind but she couldn't quite put her finger on it. Then she remembered. It was that day, weeks ago, when she'd come into the kitchen just in time to see her mother walk full-tilt into the door, crashing into it as if it wasn't there. And then, to cap it all, she'd tried to pretend it hadn't happened, to make a joke of it. It was almost as if she wanted to hide something – as if she knew *why* she had done it and didn't want anyone else to cotton on – as if . . . no, surely someone would have said. Who, for instance? What if no one else *knew*? But Daddy – surely *he* . . . Of course, he had been trying to tell her something for weeks, popping in at all hours then disappearing without saying anything much. As if he couldn't pluck up courage.

The washing-machine rattled and spun to its conclusion. Suddenly coming to a decision, Gilly went into the hallway and picked up the phone. She dialled a number and waited for someone to answer.

'Parkinson, Mills and Laurie.' Good – at least it wasn't engaged.

'Morning,' she said. 'I'd like to speak to Gordon Laurie, please.'

Of course, Gordon was busy. That was more or less inevitable. Cost a pound to speak to him these days. Stuck-up prude.

'Look,' she said with as much authority as she could muster, 'it really *is* important that I speak to him.' But the girl – well-trained, of course – refused to give in.

'May I have your name please,' she insisted, 'I'll get him to ring you back.'

Gilly pulled a face at herself in the hall mirror. What the hell! He *deserved* it! 'Lady Caroline Lamb,' she replied.

The secretary was suitably impressed and put the call through to Gordon. He, too, was surprised and flattered by the possibility of talking to the aristocracy, and answered in his most pleasant voice. Gilly stifled a laugh, paused for full effect, then hissed, 'You *bloody* snob!'

'Go away, Gilly. I'm busy.' He'd reverted to his normal, offhand manner.

But she would not let him get away with it *that* easily. She began to shout down the phone: 'If you put the phone down, Gordon, I'll catch the next train to Hernia Bay and take your office apart brick by brick. Now you know I would, so don't risk it.'

Gordon sighed and resigned himself to a wasted minute or two.

'What is it?' he asked.

'I'm worried about Mother,' Gilly replied. 'I don't think she's very well. I've got a feeling it's something quite serious.'

'Then you should be calling a doctor, not a solicitor dear.'

'Neil knows all about it, but he won't say,' she continued regardless.

'Then beat it out of him. You always used to.'

Suddenly Gilly had had enough. 'I'm asking you to come and help me, you great lout,' she shouted.

'Truth to tell, Gilly, I'm a bit pushed right now,' he began testily, but Gilly, in no mood whatsoever to be thwarted, came right back at him.

'Now listen to me!' she bellowed. 'You do damn all with your weekends. Forget the rugby club Friday night, wake up fresh and alert Saturday morning and zoom up here. Otherwise Monday I'll be in your office making a scene. How does that grab you?'

And Gordon, who at least knew when he was beaten, agreed that he would be there.

Neil, on vacation from Keele, had come to stay with Gilly and Nick while his parents were away. It was an arrangement which suited neither party particularly well. Gilly had never really hit it off with her little brother, as she still liked to call him. They were just too different.

Gilly was sure that Neil knew more about Maddie's condition than he was prepared to say and decided to force the issue. Catching him unawares in the midst of a light-hearted slanging match one evening, she asked, 'Did Mum and Dad go off all right?'

'Suppose so,' Neil replied. 'Took enough rubbish with them to set up house!'

'Let's hope the change puts her back on her feet again,' she remarked casually. Neil jumped.

'Why?' he asked. 'What's been the matter with her?'

'I was hoping you'd tell me,' Gilly replied, sitting down next to him.

'Nothing, as far as I know.' Neil was not prepared to give up any secrets – well not *that* easily anyway. He picked up a newspaper and tried to appear interested in it. Gilly snatched it from him and put it down where he could not reach it.

'Are you absolutely sure?' she asked.

'Well,' he replied, in as casual a tone as he could muster, 'there were some headaches ...'

Gilly pounced on the word immediately. 'What headaches?'

But Neil still refused to give much away. He obviously

knew far more than he was prepared to divulge, especially to her, but all he would concede was that Maddie had suffered a spate of headaches and had gone to see someone who had 'fixed her up'. And with that Gilly would have to be satisfied.

Gilly knew she had no alternative but to go to see Jack Burrows and to ask him point-blank about the argument between himself and her father.

Jack Burrows was waiting for her visit. He watched her stride purposefully through the door of his drawing-room, with the baby on her hip, looking, he thought, just like one of those appalling Amazon women, going forth into battle.

Gilly handed Beatrice Matilda over for his appraisal. He eyed her with interest. A fine specimen – good pair of legs, lovely eyes – just like her grandmother . . .

'You'll have guessed what I'm here for.' Gilly's tone was terse, businesslike.

'No. I'm not as clever as everyone thinks,' he replied, handing the baby back to Gilly.

'The argument you had with my father.'

Jack sighed again and gestured to Gilly to sit down. This *could* be tricky. Gilly arranged herself on the green chaise-longue and continued.

'It was about my mother, yes?'

'What does *he* say?' Jack was boxing clever.

'He muttered something about insulting your principles. And now I want to know what he was talking about,' said Gilly, determined to break through his reserve. But, like Neil, he was not easily prepared to divulge what he knew.

Suddenly, hoping to shock him into some response, she blurted out, 'I think she's very ill,' and watched Jack's face as she spoke. He remained quite impassive, but improbably so, she thought. That, and his shrug of denial was all the proof she needed. 'And now I *know* that she is,' she said triumphantly. 'Your reaction was too callous, even for you.'

'So,' Jack's voice was resigned, 'I must be hiding something. Well, if I am, that's how it's going to remain. Where did they go?'

'Mm?' Gilly's mind was elsewhere, trying to absorb what she had learnt.

'For their holiday?' Jack asked.

And she replied, with a wry laugh. 'Memory Lane. They've taken a trip down Memory Lane.'

Gilly was not Jack Burrows' only visitor that week. But, whereas she had arrived as an uninvited, though not totally unexpected, guest, Michael Pearson came as the result of a specific summons from Jack himself.

Pearson was someone whom Burrows had, for some time both admired and, in some undefined way, envied. The man was so calm, so organised, so successful, yet still he had that nice manner about him that kept the patients flocking in. People often remarked how *human* he was, as if being an eminent specialist would automatically make you into some sort of monster. Jack wondered, idly, whether his patients described *him* as human. He doubted it somehow. Not that he cared, really. He got the work done; that was all that mattered, in his book anyway.

Pearson accepted the drink Jack had poured for him, and sat down on the chaise-longue. 'I don't usually respond to a summons you know,' he said with a trace of irritation.

Jack knew that the man did not like him and for some

reason the fact bothered him more than usual. Still there were more important matters to discuss.

'Well,' he said smoothly, 'I do think the niceties can be put aside for the particular problem, don't you?' and, his eyes on Pearson's stony expression, he produced the words which, he felt, were bound to evoke some response: 'Maddie Laurie.'

But still Pearson appeared unmoved.

'What about her?' he asked, without giving any indication that her name had any particular connotations to him.

'Did I mention that her husband and I are old friends?' Jack asked.

'You did,' Pearson replied. God – however long would it take the man to come to the point! 'Well spit it out!' Pearson said as patiently as he could, 'I'm a busy man.'

'Put simply, he tried to back me into a corner last week. He wanted my advice on how to kill her.'

Pearson, though not unduly taken aback by the information he had just received, needed a little time to absorb its full implication. He refused to give Burrows the satisfaction of seeing any surprise or shock on his face. Wasn't that, after all, what the wretched man wanted? Some endorsement for his own reactions perhaps, a sense of self-righteous comfort in knowing that he had done the right thing?

'Do you tell me this out of concern for the wife?'

Burrows nodded and added sagely: 'Backed by a clear definition of right and wrong.'

'Such a piece of information is a mighty burden, Jack.' He smiled, his eyes sparkling with amusement. Jack knew the man was making fun of him.

'Feel free to laugh at me,' he said pettishly, then, after a pause, added, 'You condone the idea, do you?'

'What idea?' Pearson asked.

'He was quite clear,' Jack answered. 'He says it's her wish. She has a notion to choose her own time.'

Pearson was interested to see how far Burrows could be pushed.

'Sounds reasonable to me,' he said, and waited for Jack's explosion. It came at once.

'What's happened to you, Pearson,' he shouted, thumping his fist down onto his desk. 'Have you been sucked into this laissez-faire stew? The kill-and-let-kill school?'

But Pearson would not give him the satisfaction of so easily categorising his behaviour. 'I never followed a body of opinion in my life,' he sighed. 'I'm world-famous for it. I'm like a bag of beans. I refuse to settle into one shape so that you can bombard me with righteousness.'

Jack, offended and thrown off-balance by Pearson's response, played his best card. 'When she dies,' he pronounced, 'I shall demand a thorough post-mortem.'

'And you carry such weight?' Pearson asked scathingly.

'Enough,' Jack muttered.

Pearson's last words, spoken with precision, were calculated to inflict a deliberate and well-aimed blow at Jack's professional pride. 'You're good, yes,' he said slowly, as if weighing every word, 'you're *very* good. But you're not *special* because you know nothing of the people you treat. You're a fool, Burrows,' he said. 'He's your friend, you say. He comes to you for help. You send him away and no doubt you threaten him as you've done me.' Pearson stood up and approached Burrows, leaning across the desk to deliver his statement with as much force as he could. 'And where does he go? Straight to a chemistry book? Hmm? Straight onto the street perhaps? Because if he means to kill her, the likes of you won't stop him. So you, his friend, cause him to shop around in a very dirty market. And maybe he'll find something, and maybe it won't work.' He began to shout for the first time. 'And maybe he'll come back and break your neck!'

'We're talking about *murder*,' Jack answered. He refused to be swayed by such emotive arguments. 'To which you sound more than willing to be an accessory,' he added primly.

Pearson smiled. He had been right, the man *was* a pompous fool. 'Is that how you see it! *Some* of us might call it, rather, a supreme act of selfless love.'

He finished his drink and handed the glass back to Jack with exaggerated politeness, then stood up to leave. Jack watched him in angry silence.

'By the way,' Pearson's voice was low, 'I take it you *did* refuse him. Only you never said.'

'I did,' Jack replied. 'Will you?'

Pearson shrugged his shoulders.

'Who knows,' he said, walking to the door. 'I won't have you make up my mind for me, though, that's for sure. And I advise you not to set the dogs on me if she dies. *If* she dies. You wouldn't be the first to try it.'

Jack was about to answer, to defend himself, in some way to redeem his dignity, but Pearson, turning in the doorway, did not allow him to.

'Thanks for the information,' he said, 'I lift the burden of it from your shoulders and place it on my own.' And with a slight but disparaging mock-bow to Burrows, he left the room.

Pearson, however, had one more confrontation in store for him. He was reading up some interesting cases in the Bodleian, perusing the upper shelves, when he looked down the ladder into the upturned face of an anxious-looking young woman.

'Yes?' he said pleasantly. She probably wanted the book he was reading. They usually did.

'My name is Gillian Puxley,' she began. He sighed, replaced the book.

They shook hands and he waited to hear what she had come for. Though it was not hard to guess.

'I've seen Mr Burrows,' she began.

'So have I.' He smiled faintly.

'He knows but he won't tell me,' she blurted out. But Pearson refused to be drawn.

'I know *exactly* what you want,' he said quickly, 'but I hardly think I'm the person to tell you, do you? Your parents are on holiday, aren't they?'

Gilly replied that they were expected home that night.

'Well,' said Pearson cheerfully, 'that's only a few hours. Your last wait was nine months.'

'She won't tell me,' Gilly burst out, 'and nor will my father ... and your diffidence is making me suspect the worst. Can I assume that I have an answer and that it's yes?'

'To what question?' Pearson inquired, admiring her tenacity but unwilling to be coerced.

'Is my mother gravely ill?' she asked, watching his face closely.

He paused just long enough for her to know the answer but said, 'Mrs Puxley, I can't break the confidence of my patient, but I will ensure that they tell you themselves exactly what is going on.'

'Thanks,' Gilly said, knowing that she could go no further with him.

'Oh, one more thing,' he added, turning to mount the ladder again, 'would you be kind enough to give your father a message for me. Tell him to call on me. I've got something he's been looking for.'

And he climbed upwards, looking, Gilly thought ruefully, for all the world like a rather approachable but nevertheless firm god, ascending to Olympus.

What Gilly had described as a 'trip down Memory Lane' had not proved to be an unqualified success for Malcolm and Maddie. The old haunts they had set out, with such enthusiasm to rediscover, seemed a good deal less enchanting in reality than nostalgia had painted them. And, with nothing to do all day but remember, Maddie found that memories can be painful as well as pleasant. Actually, it was not the memories which hurt; it was the process of remembering. It made her too aware that the past was full of colour, of incident, while the future . . .

The long journey to Scotland had proved surprisingly and annoyingly taxing – another reminder that her body was now refusing to respond in its usual way to the stringent demands she had always made upon it. She slept badly in the unfamiliar surroundings, waking dry-mouthed, unrefreshed, and somewhat daunted at the prospect of the long walks which Malcolm had in store for her.

For a while she feigned enjoyment, rather than risk hurting Malcolm who had organised the trip expressly for her benefit. But eventually the effort proved too much for her and she began to feel the mask slip, just a little at first, but enough to allow Malcolm, watching her every move, to notice and to comment.

The weather had been dreadful. Surely, Malcolm insisted, it had been better last time. But, as Maddie wryly observed, last time they had not even noticed the weather. It was not the landscape that had changed; it was them, the people in it. And what else could you expect, after all that time. The mistake was in expecting everything to stand still, remain the same.

At last, with a sort of dogged determination to extract the last ounce of nostalgia from the occasion, they set off, through driving rain to have lunch at the old pub which had been their favourite haunt many years before.

As they struggled along, they comforted themselves with the thought of the ploughman's lunch waiting at the other end.

'Home-made bread, still warm from the oven, wasn't it?' Malcolm drooled.

'Yes, and a hunk of cheddar so big it was like a door-stop,' Maddie added.

'And the jar of pickled onions on the table so that you could take as many as you fancied.'

'Mmm, am I looking forward to *this*,' Maddie sighed.

They walked eagerly into the tiny bar, shedding their wet anoraks with relief. Malcolm ordered a beer for himself and a tomato juice for Maddie.

'And two of your amazing Ploughman's please,' he added, rubbing his hands with anticipation. He thought that the barman gave him a strange look but made nothing of it till he called, 'Ploughman's twice,' and gestured to him to collect their lunch.

Malcolm eyed the two portions with undisguised dismay. 'Amazing' wasn't the word for it. In fact, the only amazing thing about it was that they had the cheek to charge you for it at all, let alone the exorbitant £1.80 he had just surrendered. It was nothing but a small slice of cut-loaf, flanked by a barely visible morsel of mouse-trap perspiring in its cellophane wrapper.

'No pickled onions?' he asked more in despair than expectation, but the barman shook his head dolefully.

'Got no call for them, you see. It's all salt-'n'-vinegar crisps these days.'

Puzzling over the logic of this remark, Malcolm made his way dismally back to his seat. Poor Maddie.

But Maddie was in a dream – nothing unusual these days, he'd noticed. She kept drifting off, looking into space, as if she had things to think about which were more vital than conversation. He placed the two pathetic offerings on the table in front of her and coughed slightly to attract her attention. She looked up, saw the meagre platefuls, caught his eye and smiled.

'The wind of change,' she joked, catching his hand. 'Still, it *is* more than twenty years. We couldn't really expect everything to have stayed the same. Remember that bit in "The Go-Between", what was it?'

' "The past is a foreign country",' Malcolm said quietly.

'It is, isn't it?' Maddie insisted, 'That's what we've been finding out. Look, I thought I was longing for my whole life to start again, from about 1950. Well, I'm not. It's like having a fairy story read to you as a kid. There comes a very special day when you have to admit that the prince doesn't exist, the princess is yourself in an elegant pose and the castle's a council house.'

'Well,' Malcolm said, 'don't think back, then.'

'Then what the hell are we doing here?' she reasoned. 'I don't mind memories popping up of their own accord but I'm through with chasing them.'

'I'm enjoying it,' Malcolm said quietly.

'It's morbid,' Maddie went on, 'It's an archaeological dig: here's the bench we sat on, here's the house that was painted tangerine . . . I want my *own* house, my *own* kids. I want to do boring things like wash up and vacuum carpets because for the first time in my life I know I'll enjoy it. Do you mind?'

'You haven't hoovered a carpet for years,' Malcolm pointed out gently. But he understood what she was saying only too well.

'We'll go home,' he said.

'When?' she asked eagerly. He promised they would set out early the following morning.

They arrived home in the late evening, after a long and exhausting journey. Malcolm lifted their cases out of the car while Maddie searched for her key. Having located it at the bottom of her bag, she was about to unlock the front door when she found that it was already opened. Gingerly she pushed it with her foot. She could see a light burning inside the house. Burglars? No – who would want to burgle THEM? Squatters? With a dramatic flourish, which looked a good deal bolder than she felt, she flung open the door of the living-room and turned on all the lights.

There, framed in the fireplace, stood all her children – Gilly, Neil and Gordon – even Nick – posing like a Victorian family photograph. For a moment she was speechless, then flying across the room at the speed of light, she flung her arms around Gordon's neck in a positive ecstasy of surprise and excitement.

Of course Malcolm had known all along. Wasn't it just *typical* of him. She looked at him with affection as he walked past her, carrying a suitcase, but did not loosen her hold on Gordon. It was good to be home anyway, but *this* . . . well, this was in the nature of a bonus!

After that Gilly took charge. She had put a chicken in the oven ready for their return; now she persuaded Malcolm to go out and buy a bottle of wine.

Maddie, watching with amusement from the side-lines, observed with interest and a certain wry satisfaction, that her daughter was beginning to take control of the situation.

During a lull in all the rushing to and fro, Gilly spoke

quickly to Malcolm: 'Your friend Mr Pearson would like to see you,' she said, her eyes on Maddie's face.

'When?' Maclolm's reply was guarded; he could not be sure how much Gilly knew.

'Now,' she answered.

'He can wait,' Malcolm said with a nonchalance she found quite unconvincing.

'He's got something you've been looking for,' she added.

'I'd better go then,' said Malcolm.

Malcolm found Pearson a very easy man to talk to and told him so. Pearson, who set great store by his personal contact with patients and their families, accepted the compliment with pleasure. Taking a dusty bottle of Scotch from the bottom drawer of his desk, he poured two drinks and sat back in his chair.

'You must forgive Jack Burrows if you can,' he said, after a while.

Malcolm looked up surprised, wondering how Pearson knew so much of his private affairs.

Pearson continued, 'He's an old man at fifty, never changing, never asking himself the vital question, "I was right yesterday but am I *still* right today?" '

Malcolm looked at the other man with respect.

'You – er – believe in ... pulling plugs out?' he asked carefully.

'Nothing so abstract,' Pearson replied. 'I believe in your wife and the fact that she's dying.'

Malcolm jumped. Somehow the word sounded more final coming from the lips of a man who inspired so much confidence in his own ability.

'I also think it's cruel,' Pearson added quietly, 'to hide the fact from your children.'

At the mention of the children, Malcolm felt his throat constrict with fear. 'No! I can't, not yet . . .' he muttered.

Pearson leant forward, as if to give special emphasis to his words. 'They must have the chance to make amends, to pay back her love where necessary.'

He gave Malcolm a moment to absorb what he had said, then turning to open the top drawer of his filing cabinet, he took out a small brown bottle and placed it, without ceremony, between them. He then pushed it across the desk towards Malcolm.

'I live in hope you won't use it,' he said quietly. 'The weight of such an act could break you in two, but in ten minutes she'll be deeply asleep, dead in twenty.'

Malcolm took the bottle, and without looking at it, put it in his pocket.

'Thank you,' he said simply.

Chapter 5

'If God exists,' Malcolm thought bitterly, turning up his collar as meagre defence against the driving rain, 'He must be a ruddy comedian.' He looked at Maddie, standing next to him at the bus-stop and wondered how she managed to appear so *calm*, in spite of everything. Not only, he thought angrily, was she just about to snuff it, but the blessed car had broken down into the bargain – just when they needed it most.

'It would have to be today of all days,' he muttered. 'The car, I mean. Bloody French rubbish! Held together with a bit of string and a prayer, if you ask me. Food – that's what they're good at – oh, and the wine's not too bad either, I suppose. That's what they should bloody stick to. Leave the cars to people who know one end of a crankshaft from another.'

Maddie smiled with infuriating sweetness, but said nothing. She'd heard it all before, of course. Still, it did give Malcolm something to rail against at a time when he desperately needed a legitimate outlet for his feelings.

She had really pitied him these last few days, wrestling with himself, tossing and turning by night, distracted, nervous and bad-tempered by day, as he tried to come to terms with what must be done. She looked at him, wishing that there was something she could say that would make it easier.

Maddie had long since accepted that she could not, *must* not, attempt to penetrate the unusual and special relationship Malcolm enjoyed with his only daughter; but now, as they set out to tell Gilly the news of her illness, that very specialness only made things worse.

The meeting with Pearson had provided Malcolm with a solution to one problem, only to make him more painfully aware of another. Of course, he reasoned with himself, he had known all along that the children had to be told; it was simply a question of how and when. But how *did* you tell a child that their mother was dying? What words existed in the English language which could make it seem less terrible? He found himself trying out various ludicrous opening gambits, like a salesman looking for ways of introducing a product which he knows has little appeal: 'Sorry to bother you, but I thought you'd like to know . . . your mother's about to kick the bucket,' or, 'I know that this is going to come as a shock to you, but your mother's going to die.' But no matter how you said it, Maddie was going to die and *that*, Malcolm thought bitterly, was a fact – an icy, incontrovertible and appalling fact.

Of course, they had argued about which of the children should be the first to know. Maddie felt that it should be Gordon since he was the eldest, but Malcolm wanted it to be Gilly. For a start, he was sure she almost knew anyway. After all, she had gone to see both Pearson and Burrows of her own accord, so she was bound to have more than an inkling of what was going on. But, he was forced to admit, there was another reason. Gilly was going to be the hardest to tell and, because of that, he wanted to get it over with before he lost his nerve altogether.

'How are we going to put this?' he asked suddenly. 'I mean the actual words? What are they going to be?'

Maddie shrugged, 'No idea.'

Malcolm was immediately struck by another problem.

'Nick won't be there,' he pointed out. 'Is that a good idea? He's involved, too.'

Maddie smiled. Having Nick as a son-in-law had proved an unexpected bonus to her. It was one thing to be able to tolerate your daughter's husband, quite another to find him both a good friend and an amusing contributor to the family dialogue.

'He's very special as a son-in-law – none of the aggravation one expects,' she said happily, but Malcolm could not resists a sly dig.

'He does as he's told, that's why . . . by both of you,' he laughed.

'There's more to old Nick than that,' she said, shaking her head. 'It's an illusion your Gilly creates for everyone's amusement. But I've seen him make her jump!'

Gilly had been waiting for her parents' visit. She guessed that it would take them some time to pluck up the necessary courage, hoped that they would not leave it *too* long. It was beginning to be an effort to keep up the pretence that she knew nothing.

Returning, drenched to the skin, from a shopping expedition to find them installed at her kitchen table, she knew instinctively that this was the moment she had been anticipating and dreading. It was hard to look at their faces, harder still to find any words which would ease the tension which hung in the air like electricity. Instead, she clattered about the room, putting away tins and packets, pausing only to give Beatrice Matilda, blissfully asleep in her pram, the occasional rather violent rock.

'Why didn't you hang your coats up? Aren't you stopping?' she snapped suddenly, but, almost as soon as she had spoken, she put her arms around her mother's shoulders in an attempt to apologise. 'Sorry Mum, I don't know what's the matter with me. Everything seems to hurt these days, no matter what . . .'

Malcolm looked up, surprised and dismayed by this statement. It was no good, he couldn't do it after that. He jumped up brightly.

'We're just off,' he said. 'Only dropped in on our way. Come on, Maddie.'

But, as his courage had diminished, Maddie's had grown. She took his arm and made him sit down. Then, turning to Gilly she inquired quietly.

'You haven't asked me how I am. Does that mean you know?'

Gilly felt herself go hot and cold. She touched her own face, sure that it must reveal her fear.

'N-no,' she said.

'Then why did you visit Mr Pearson and Jack Burrows?' asked Maddie.

'They wouldn't tell me anything,' Gilly answered, but her mother cut across her words with absolute authority.

'Wouldn't tell you that I'm going to die soon,' she said.

'No . . . no . . . why should they?'

'Because it's true,' Maddie replied simply. 'And Pearson knows it even if Jack doesn't.'

She pulled the pram towards her.

'Hello, Beatle,' she whispered.

Suddenly Malcolm, oblivious of what had been said, burst out, 'Can't beat about the bush, Gill. I thought I could . . . thought there was a way to make it sound like a positive advantage . . . but there isn't . . . Your mother's going to die.'

He had hardly paused for breath, nor looked at Gilly once while he spoke; now he raised his eyes to her face.

'I just said that,' Maddie exclaimed.

'When?' he asked.

'Just now,' Maddie replied.

'I didn't hear.' He shook his head, bewildered. 'She say that?' he asked Gilly. She nodded her head in confirmation. Trust him, she thought lovingly. He'd managed to turn even *that* pronouncement into a sort of fiasco. She swallowed hard, resisted a sudden temptation to grab hold of her father and squeeze him till it hurt.

'Well,' she said, after a long pause. 'What do you say? Thank you for telling me? Do the others know?'

'Not yet,' Malcolm replied.

'Want any help?' she asked.

'No, no.' Maddie answered for him, 'It wouldn't be fair on them.'

Her father's eyes seemed to be burning holes in her face. She turned away, finding his scrutiny too difficult.

'How do you feel?' he asked.

'I don't,' she answered simply.

It was true. She kept searching around in herself for some reaction, but could find none to fit. She had seen people laugh at bad news; she'd even seen someone laugh at a funeral. Now she knew why they did it. What else could you do? It was simply too big to absorb on any serious level, and anyway, you just did not have the mental equipment necessary. It was not something you just heard and registered like the weather forecast or the Test score. Even the words sounded peculiar, inappropriate. You just could not make sense of it. Not all at once.

'What's wrong with you?' she asked Maddie after a while. Might as well get all *that* over with at least.

Maddie touched her head.

'Tumour,' she said.

'How long have you known?' Gilly asked.

'Couple of weeks.'

Right. That was all the information out of the way. Now what? She sat looking at her parents, waiting for someone to make the next move. They watched her.

'Right ... right,' she said when the silence became unbearable for all of them. 'I shall probably burst into tears in a minute. Don't worry about it, will you ... I seem to have this delayed reaction to everything these days.'

But she was afraid to cry, in case, once it began, it was impossible to stop. Suddenly she thought of something else. 'Nick'll be flattened, Mum. He thinks you're gold,' she said.

'Maybe I should tell him myself then – alone,' Maddie volunteered, but Gilly disagreed.

'No ... I'll pick a time,' she said.

The baby began to cry, fitfully at first, then more insistently. Gilly picked her up, holding her small warm weight against her.

'Got to feed the baby,' she muttered.

Maddie jumped up. 'I'll come with you,' she offered eagerly.

Nick Puxley was sitting in a clapped-out-looking van with his friend and colleague, Detective Constable Pete Harrison, watching a house opposite. It seemed to Nick that they had been there for weeks, rather than days. His body was stiff with tiredness and inactivity, and his eyes ached from peering through the binoculars.

Harrison, not a man to ask personal questions or dwell too much on psychology, could sense his friend's agitation. Your first murder, it got you like that. And your second. After that you pretended to get hard – made out it was all routine, like booking a man for parking on a crossing. You never got over it, though. Just like you never got over pulling people out of cars. You just *acted* cool, that's all. But inside it was like a rat was eating your guts. And anyone who said otherwise was a liar.

Harrison put down the binoculars, stretched and yawned noisily, then nudged Nick with his elbow. He pointed to the glasses to indicate that it was Nick's turn to watch the house, but Nick didn't make a move.

'How do you shoot a girl of twelve?' Nick was asking the question as much of himself as of anyone else.

Harrison's patience was waning. 'You pull the bleeding trigger,' he answered, then went on. 'You do it because you don't think, you can't see past the end of your neck. All this wallah could see was a row of silver: silver ... money ... want ... gun ... get. Then someone disturbs him. Pop!'

Harrison pulled an imaginary trigger. Nick watched him with growing dissatisfaction. It was all very well, explaining it away like that, making it sound like a game of cowboys and Indians. It was all very well ... unless you started thinking – what if it was *my* child he shot, what then? That was when it started to get complicated. Because in a way, it *was* your child – just because it *could have been*. It was enough to drive you mad just thinking about it. It was all right for the Harrisons of this world – somehow they didn't let it get them down – but it wasn't for him, that was for sure, and he didn't care *who* knew it. He leant back in his seat, his eyes closed, as if that might help to shut it all out.

'I've no stomach for this work. No head. I can't see it as a file in a tin cabinet. Helen Spender is my girl ... me and Gilly are her parents.'

Harrison shot a glance at Nick, then looked rapidly away. He'd had it – he could see that. He'd seen it coming for some time. Now it was as plain as the nose on your face. And in this job once you'd had it there was only one way to go, and that was *out*.

'I should move up country if I were you,' he said

quietly ... 'Find yourself a decent job ...' and before Nick could begin to protest, he added, more in his usual tone. 'But meantime lean over into my bag and get us two beers.'

Chapter 6

Afterwards, when it was all over, Nick sometimes asked himself when the decision was made. Perhaps in a way Harrison made it for him. It had been on his mind for ages, of course, nagging away behind everything like a bad toothache.

One minute there he was sitting in the van eating his heart out over that poor kid and half an hour later he was walking into his own house with the news. But it was not the kind of news he could impart straight. Specially not with little Helen Spender still on his mind. So he had hit on the ludicrous idea of pretending he was drunk. That way he could get away with murder, to coin a phrase – and somehow, in the middle of keeling over and talking a load of eyewash, he could spill the beans and it wouldn't hurt at all.

As he propelled himself into the kitchen, he was taken aback to find, not Gilly, but Malcolm and Maddie sitting in silence at the table. They looked up, obviously surprised to see him home at that time of the day. He lurched towards them, banging into a few chairs just for good measure. Maddie raised her eyebrows but said nothing. Funny, that! She didn't seem as lively as usual. In fact, they both looked as if they'd lost a fiver and picked up sixpence.

'Nick, you shouldn't be here,' said Maddie.

Nick raised his finger to his lips in an exaggerated plea

for secrecy, then leant over to plant a clumsy kiss on her cheek.

'Let that be our secret,' he whispered. And seeing Malcolm's bemused expression, added, 'and yours.'

'Anything wrong?' Maddie asked.

Trust her to be the first to catch on. She was a bright lady *and* a bit of all right into the bargain. Thank goodness she was there – thank goodness they were both there, come to think of it. He didn't fancy facing Gilly's wrath alone.

'I have news for your daughter that will send her into an apoplexy of reproach ... i.e. she'll splatter me over that wall with a single splat. But since you're here, and which of us can say that the great policeman in the sky didn't preordain that, she may satisfy herself with a quick rolling-pin to the bonce. Not that I don't love her. I do. Where is she?'

Maddie replied that Gilly was upstairs feeding the baby. She was finding Nick's performance a considerable strain, not least because he so obviously was *not* drunk, but, for some obscure reason, simply pretending to be. Whatever news he had to impart, it must be pretty alarming to merit such an amazing display. And whatever it was, he had certainly chosen the wrong moment.

'What's your news?' she asked, hoping, perhaps, to be able to defuse the situation before Gilly appeared. But Nick refused to tell her. Instead, he began to shout up to Gilly at the top of his voice.

'Hallo my treasure, my box of doubloons, my cup which runneth over!'

Then suddenly breaking off, he turned to Maddie and Malcolm and asked, 'Did you ever hear of Helen Spender?'

They said they had not. He did not know why he had asked them anyway. Or rather he *did*. As if talking about

84

it all the time would make it go away. Exorcism by excess.

'She was only twelve,' he said, almost under his breath.

'Childhood sweetheart?' Maddie asked.

'What a clean mind you have,' he joked. 'Tell me,' he went on, almost seriously, 'do you reckon young Gilly bean will wear as well as you've done down the years? Or does she take after your husband here?'

Maddie looked at him and shook her head slowly. 'Yes,' she said.

'Yes what?'

'She'll last you out . . . in the image of her father,' she replied.

'Only married her cos I thought she'd end up looking like you,' Nick said ruefully. As he spoke, he could see Gilly out of the corner of his eye. She had come in without him noticing.

'What are you doing home?' she asked. There was no need to inquire whether she was glad to see him.

Maddie, seeing Gilly's mood, got up as if to leave, but Nick's face made her sit down again.

'You're pissed!' Gilly's voice rose in amazement and anger. 'Eleven o'clock in the morning and you're pissed!'

But Nick, committed now to his performance, had nowhere to go but forward. 'I return to you my sweet,' he declaimed, 'bearing news that will throw the world off its axis . . .'

Gilly looked at him in total disbelief, then without warning she began to lash out in an absolute fury of incomprehending anger.

'You bastard,' she screamed, 'you bastard. What's *your* news then, eh?' She flung the words at him. 'You've got news . . . *you've* got news! Well, so have *we* . . . only it didn't take half a bottle of Scotch to shape it!'

Maddie watched helplessly, knowing the necessity of

Gilly's rage, but sensing how inappropriate was its target. 'Leave him alone, Gilly. He's obviously not feeling too good,' she pleaded.

Nick looked at her in grateful surprise. Of course, she *knew*. She would.

'Takes a real lady to know the truth behind these things,' he observed quietly, then, more grandly, 'Your news or mine, who shall speak first?'

'I will,' Gilly spoke quickly.

'We'll toss a coin,' he suggested and threw an imaginary coin into the air. 'Heads. I win. Cos yours will be good news. Mine is bad . . . all bad, nothing but bad.'

Gilly looked at him as if she might murder him.

'Shut up,' she growled, but he was not to be deterred.

Standing up, he opened his arms as if addressing a vast audience and began: 'I have this day—'

But Gilly could not bear it a moment longer. 'Your pin-up girl's dying,' she said with conscious cruelty.

'. . . decided to . . .' he went on, not fully absorbing Gilly's remark, then, seeing Maddie looking up at him, he suddenly realised what he had heard. 'Oh no,' he whispered, shocked.

And Gilly, witnessing his instant return to sobriety, turned and ran from the kitchen; Malcolm followed her.

Nick stood awkwardly, unsure of his next move. God, if ever a man had put his foot in it! He'd come barging in full of his own troubles when all the time . . . He sat down heavily opposite Maddie, his head bent.

'You've not had more than two pints or I'm a Dutchman,' she said gently.

He looked up. 'Pretending to be drunk is even better than the real thing,' he explained, 'you remain in control of what you want to forget.'

She leant across the table to take his hand. 'Poor Nick,' she whispered.

'Poor Maddie, Poor Mac,' he said, almost to himself, then lapsed into an uneasy quiet as he began, slowly, painfully, to absorb the full implication of the news.

Suddenly the silence was broken by the insistent ringing of the doorbell. Nick, too far away in his own thoughts to be disturbed, did not move. The bell rang again. Maddie extricated her hand and, gently touching him on the head as she rose, went to open the door.

Harrison had decided to chase up young Nick before he got himself into more trouble. It was one thing to get a bit fed up on the job – but you didn't just go skiving off home. Not if you knew what was good for you.

As the door opened, he was surprised to see not a dishevelled or embarrassed Nick but an attractive lady he had never seen before.

'Nick?' he asked. 'Is he home?'

She smiled and asked him to come in; he followed her into the kitchen.

Nick was sitting there at the table, looking as if he had been pole-axed. He nodded at Harrison and introduced him to Maddie. So *this* was the famous mother-in-law. Some blokes had all the luck!

'Heard a fair bit about you,' he said, laughing. 'Which brings me straight to the point. What the hell is he up to?'

Nick hardly looked up but muttered, in a voice that was barely audible, 'Came home, didn't I?'

'Now listen, you can't just walk off the job when the mood takes you,' Harrison began, irritated by Nick's manner. He turned to leave the room. 'Up on your hind legs, son, and we'll be off.'

Nick did not move an inch. Instead he motioned to his friend to sit down. Harrison did not comply. This was beginning to get a bit silly.

'Nick . . .' he pleaded.

'I'm needed here for a bit,' Nick said.

Maddie intervened quickly, 'He's had a bit of a shock, actually.'

Harrison appeared not to react to this information with anything more than routine sympathy. 'Oh dear,' he said calmly, 'I'm sorry to hear that.' Then, looking at his watch in a business-like way, took hold of Nick by the sleeve of his anorak in a last attempt to encourage him to leave. 'Come on, mate,' he said cheerfully.

Nick shook him off with a surprising violence. 'You have to crash into everything! You're one of the big-footed who kick their way in at the worst moment in everyone's life.'

Harrison refused to take Nick's outburst seriously but continued to try to persuade him to go.

Finally, Nick looked at Maddie and, in a cruelly casual voice, said, 'She's just told me she's dying.'

Harrison was not sure at first if he had heard him correctly. He hoped he had not. But Maddie's face gave him the answer. She looked first at Nick, then at him as if her main concern was that *he* might be upset by the information he had just received. He turned to her and asked quietly, 'Is it true?'

'I'm afraid it is,' she answered.

'I'm sorry,' he said with dignity. 'He's right, I certainly have picked my moment!'

Maddie found his reaction surprising. He looked such a nervy character, yet, when other men would have gone all to pieces, he had remained calm. And his presence, in the midst of what was obviously to be even more of a crisis than she had anticipated, was strangely reassuring.

In the living-room Gilly was drying her eyes, comforted still by Malcolm.

'What will you do?' she asked in a quiet voice.

'I'm tougher than you think ... but I've got to tread a fine line, Gilly. Your mother'll think if I get too independent that I never needed her in the first place.'

Gilly snorted scornfully. Fat chance of that!

'She's not *that* daft,' she retorted.

Suddenly Malcolm turned to her.

'Shall I tell you something slushy?' he asked.

'Go on then, embarrass me,' she said encouragingly.

'I've found out what love is – no, don't laugh. So you think it's weird ... Your parents aren't supposed to love each other as far as I remember, they sit at opposite ends of the table and pass the marmalade. I was never able to imagine my parents in bed.'

Gilly looked up, surprised. 'Why should you *want* to?'

'Oh I didn't,' Malcolm laughed. 'But they were the only people in the world who never made love!' He paused, then added, 'Gave it all to me.'

'We used to listen to you two.' Gilly threw the remark in casually.

Malcolm forced himself not to react.

'You know that perpetual truth about never knowing how much something means to you till you've lost it? In a way, I'm lucky ... I've recognised it a few months in advance. It isn't the ability to iron shirts, save money, raise kids; it's being surprised by the fact that she *still* doesn't bore you.' Suddenly Malcolm slapped his own face hard with the palm of his hand. 'You'll have to stop me getting sentimental, Gill.'

Gilly took his hand from his face.

'It doesn't matter,' she said softly.

'You'll keep an eye on me?' He caught hold of her hand and held it just for a moment, surprised at how good it felt.

'Will you need it?' she asked. She did not move her hand away.

He nodded.

'I'll stand guard then,' she replied, adding with a glance towards the kitchen, 'other people's problems always make your own seem small.'

Malcolm sighed. He had wondered when they would get round to Nick.

'Old Nick,' he began tentatively, 'you do tend to shout at him ... sometimes.' His voice tailed away. Gilly gave him a fierce look.

'Yes, I do.'

'Now, he knows you don't mean it. Well, of course, you don't—'

'I *am* beginning to mean it,' Gilly broke in emphatically.

Malcolm tried to brush away the possibility that she was serious, but she was not to be deterred.

'You can wish as hard as you like, it won't go away. He moans – not like most people, a solid bout of cursing for ten minutes and then forget it – he goes on like a wasp in a bottle, a continuous drone of dissatisfaction.'

It was obviously worse than he had realised. He had been so wound up over Maddie that he just had not noticed that there was another problem, and now poor Gilly had to contend with the two things at once. It was something to do with Nick's job, of course. He should have had the sense to guess – to see beyond all the jokes and bravado, and realise that the man was in trouble. Of course he'd moaned to Gilly. Who else could he moan to?

'Look,' he began gently, 'he may be moaning lately, but he's a good man.' He paused, noting her surprise, then continued. 'Now if Beatrice suddenly woke up and cried, you'd go and pick *her* up ... Why not him?'

Gilly looked at him as if seeing him for the first time.

90

'Anything else I should know about myself?' she asked very quietly.

'You waited three years for that baby,' said Malcolm; 'and by God you were hell to be with. He never complained once.'

'So,' Gilly admitted, 'I shout at him.'

'When the going gets rough, yes,' Malcolm agreed, and added, 'but with your mother's death to cope with, you may start screaming.'

He had finished what he had to say. At first he thought she might argue, jump, as she usually did, to her own defence, but instead she got up slowly and made for the door.

'We'd better go in,' she said. 'And find out what it's all about.'

He stood up and followed her into the hallway. Just before they reached the door of the kitchen, she turned and touched his arm.

'Thanks, Dad,' she said simply.

He nodded, realising how much the remark would have cost her. 'Best go in and join the others,' he said.

Nick's news had been shattering, but afterwards, as Malcolm and Maddie sat at home talking over the events of the day, Malcolm pointed out that in one way at least, his timing had been impeccable. In the furore that had followed his revelation, the news of Maddie's death had been forced out of the limelight. But the scene that followed between Gilly and Nick had been ugly.

'Are they going to be all right – Nick and Gilly?' Maddie asked.

'Course,' he answered blandly, 'He's only changing this job, you know. He's not going to Mars.'

Maddie did not seem convinced, but the last thing he wanted was for her to start fretting about *that*.

'Maddie,' he reasoned, 'give them a chance, for God's sake. They just fell out for a bit.'

'I hope so,' she said. 'You spoilt that girl . . .'

'Just like *you* spoilt Neil.' Malcolm could not resist the opportunity.

Maddie was about to protest, when she saw Malcolm turn away and perform an elaborate mime of unsteadily opening a bottle and pouring a drink.

'Well,' he said apologetically, 'it seemed to work for Nick!'

Maddie, smiling, held out her hand as if it had a glass in it.

'Same again please,' she said.

Chapter 7

The following day, Maddie and Malcolm set off for Herne Bay to see Gordon.

Maddie had risen earlier than usual, leaving herself ample time to prepare for the journey. It was strange and disturbing to note, however, that the most mundane things seemed to be changing, moving out of her control. Before, she had always prided herself on being able to dress and leave the house within ten minutes of waking, but now, dressing had become an ordeal. And brushing her hair, which had previously been a pleasure, now made her head ache even more than usual.

But worst of all, was the struggle to perform these tasks calmly – to behave as if nothing was different, while all the time she could feel Malcolm's eyes watching her every move.

The weather was surprising for that time of year – brilliantly sunny and, out of the crisp wind, it was almost warm.

Looking out with enjoyment at the Kent countryside, Maddie could not help smiling to herself at the absurd irony of the situation, though a confrontation between Malcolm and his elder son was never any laughing matter, whatever the circumstances.

It was, after all, the first time they had made the journey since Gordon had become a partner in Parkinson, Mills and Laurie. She had lost count of the times they had suggested driving down to visit him – just for fun one summer afternoon, or to have lunch with him one Sunday. The sort of things parents did with their children. But there was always some reason why he could not manage to see them.

Sometimes it was an important client who couldn't be put off; at other times he had to study for exams, decorate his flat, look at a new car. He did not come home very often either.

Families were strange: you were handed a role early on – a niche that was carved out for you – and afterwards you had God's own job to find another, however much you might want to. It was usually the middle child of three who was supposed to feel the outsider, but in their family, it was Gordon who had suffered. She and Neil, of course, were as thick as thieves and Malcolm and Gilly the same, while Gordon, for all his brains and good looks, was always out on a limb. It must have hurt a lot, Maddie thought – it must *still* hurt a lot, she corrected herself.

Gordon's office was on the ground floor of a modern block. It was not, Malcolm noted as they pushed open the door, the sort of solicitors' office he was used to – where you were greeted by a seedy old clerk with a big ledger under one arm – where every available surface was covered with comforting-looking legal tomes and documents tied up with tape. You could feel safe in a place like that – secure in the knowledge that you were being looked after, that a combination of years of experience and a good layer of dust would be bound to safeguard your best interests. For a start, everything was spanking clean and new-looking: acres of polished teak with not a spot of dust in sight. The only tomes he could see were an up-to-date Egon Ronay and a pile of telephone directories. This looked the kind of place where they'd take your money with one hand and stab you in the back with the other. Trust Gordon! Still the girl behind the desk was certainly an improvement on Bob Cratchit. She was, he realised, the girl he had harangued on the phone the other day.

'I'm Malcolm Laurie,' he said. 'We're Gordon's parents.'

The girl drew in her breath anxiously. 'He's out,' she said.

Malcolm got up and opened the door which apparently led to Gordon's office. The room was empty. The girl continued to eye him with a mixture of fear and mistrust as if he were some unpredictable species of wildlife or a dangerous criminal.

'When will he be back?' he asked irritably, pacing up and down the room. The girl said she did not know.

'All right,' Malcolm said, pulling up two chairs in uncomfortable proximity to her desk. 'We'll wait.'

One of the things Gordon Laurie hated about being a solicitor – and there were several – was having to speak nicely to jumped-up bastards like Simon Anstey.

Anstey wanted to buy a house and he needed Gordon's help. It was not just *any* house, but an elegant and lavish mansion known as Wentworth, built in the eighteenth century, set in acres of rich farmland, with its own lake, and its own deer. It was, Gordon thought with more than a little bitterness, a gentleman's house, not that Anstey was a gentleman, of course. Far from it. He was, on his own admission, a 'grass-roots yob', born and bred in Leytonstone. But he had worked hard to acquire just the right clothes, just the right accent and just the right aura of wealth. Now all he needed was the house to go with it. But, typically enough, he did not want the house to live in. No, he had far more elaborate plans for it than that.

He wanted to convert it into what he himself described as a 'kind of space-age brothel', a conference centre cum health farm where he could easily persude people to part with their money in return for a little luxury in peaceful and beautiful surroundings.

Gordon was a good-looking man in that slightly urbane way which speaks of too many expense account lunches. But there was something else, thought Anstey. Something which spelt 'loser', in spite of the carefully chosen tie, the good suit. It was like animals: you could smell it a mile off. The man was running scared; he just couldn't relax. Always had to be saying something, agreeing. He was as twitchy as a kid who's been caught helping himself in Woolworth's. Still, business was business, and Laurie was in a position to do him a bit of a favour.

Gordon had been summoned by a brief phone call at particularly short notice to meet Anstey 'on site' to discuss the purchase. First of all they had looked over the house, then they had walked across the fields to view the home farm. Gordon, uncomfortably cold in his thin suit, waited to hear what Anstey had to say. It was, as he had suspected, a case of bending the rules. The man wanted the house – but he wanted to purchase it on his terms and at his price. He'd done his research well, of course. His sort always did. He had found out that the vendor was in the package tour business and had deduced from that that March would be his most vulnerable time financially. He planned, quite simply, to corner the man, then make him an offer he would be in no position to refuse. With Gordon's help. The whole scheme depended on Gordon's help – and, of course, Gordon would be amply rewarded for his pains. Rewarded, in fact to the very pleasing tune of twenty-five percent of the saving.

They were leaning on an old five-bar gate, their conversation punctuated by the grunting of pigs. Gordon looked briefly at his companion and wished he had the guts to say what he really thought. Anstey might *act* the gentleman with his sheepskin coat and tweed cap, but underneath it all he was just a ruthless operator who knew what he wanted and had a pretty shrewd idea of how to get it.

'You're joking!' he exclaimed.

Simon shook his head. 'That's your target,' he reiterated, 'and twenty-five percent of what you save me is yours, plus your fee.'

Then, turning to Gordon with a slight smile, he added, 'I think it could be set to music, don't you?'

'I'll write the tune here and now,' was Gordon's reply.

Back in the office, Malcolm was growing tired of waiting for Gordon to return. It was all very well for Maddie chatting away to the secretary, who, it seemed, also had the misfortune to be the long-suffering girlfriend, about the boy's eating-habits and whether he got enough clean shirts. But that was hardly the purpose of their visit. Suddenly, the mere thought of *why* they were there at all made it impossible for him to wait any longer. He jumped up, folding the newspaper he had been idly reading for the last hour.

'Tell Gordon,' he said, 'that we have some news that will disturb him greatly.'

The girl looked up sharply, but said nothing.

'Where are we going?' Maddie asked.

'Lunch,' Malcolm replied, and added firmly, 'We'll be back this afternoon. Ask him to wait for us.'

The restaurant where Anstey chose to entertain Gordon

to lunch was the most expensive in Herne Bay, which did not necessarily mean it was the *best*, but, as Gordon observed cruelly, simply that a man like Anstey would assume it to be.

They had finished their first course, effortlessly disposed of a bottle of over-priced wine, and were waiting for the sweet-trolley with its usual array of sickly conconctions which Gordon would try, without success, to refuse.

Anstey was in an expansive mood, and was treating Gordon to an excerpt from his somewhat predictable life story: another classic tale of rags to riches.

Gordon listened without great interest, knowing it was simply a preamble to the inevitable questions about *his* family, *his* private life, and knowing that today, as ever, he would have to improvise a little with his answers.

He couldn't remember when he had first started deviating from the truth – probably at school, where he'd told his friends his father was a pilot and they'd duly clamoured to meet him. At University he'd trapped more than one unsuspecting girl with tales of a private fortune and a country estate. The fantasy had always provided a happy alternative to the truth – the hostile family and the mixed-up childhood. He'd learnt to disguise his feelings, too. But little by little, he had committed himself further, until what had begun as a relatively harmless game had become a snare in which he was more viciously trapped than his victims.

He had just made a difficult decision to forego the profiteroles and cream in favour of the more innocuous fruit salad when he looked up and, to his vast surprise, saw Malcolm standing beside their table, and next to him, looking a little self-conscious at their intrusion, his mother.

'Father! Mother!' he exclaimed.

'What happened to "Dad" and "Mum"?' asked Malcolm wryly.

Maddie, conscious of Gordon's intense embarrassment, tugged at Malcom's sleeve. 'Don't let us disturb you,' she said. 'We've got a table somewhere.'

'As he so rightly says,' Malcolm continued in the same bantering tone, 'we're his parents.'

But Anstey insisted that the Lauries join them at their table. Gordon prepared himself for a very awkward five or ten minutes. After that he'd have to get rid of them somehow. He couldn't have his father blundering in and fouling up a deal like this. Trust him to appear like the bad fairy, just when his presence was least welcome.

'Well,' he said without enthusiasm, 'What a surprise!'

'We were just talking about you,' Anstey remarked, and added to Gordon, 'You neglected to say that your mother was beautiful.'

'What are you doing in Herne Bay?' Gordon asked, ignoring Anstey.

'We know someone who lives here,' Malcolm answered drily, but Maddie, trying to keep the conversation at a civilised level, interrupted: 'We've come to see you, dear.'

'Why, what's wrong?' Gordon inquired, as if questioning a client.

'Not in your professional capacity,' growled Malcolm, becoming more and more incensed by his son's manner. 'As your parents! Remember us from the old days?'

Sometimes, Gordon thought bitterly, I wish he'd drop dead. Sarcastic bastard. Today of all days! Just when he'd got Anstey all nicely sewn up. Trust *him* to come pushing his way in with his big mouth.

And his mother, bless her, twittering on about Simon being a 'first-time buyer', talking about his house purchase as if he were thinking of getting a £10,000 mortage on a semi-detached in Cowley. One's parents could be such a liability sometimes – such a bloody embarrassment. And whatever it was he'd come to tell him, surely he could have waited at least until he'd got Anstey out of the way. Instead of which he'd made him look an idiot, as usual, and worse, made him *feel* an idiot.

'So, what is it, Dad?' he asked irritably.

'Rather talk to you alone, later this afternoon,' said Maddie quietly.

'Got a fair bit on this afternoon,' he lied without effort.

'No you haven't,' Malcolm insisted. 'We checked. And if you had, you could drop it.'

'It's my life,' Gordon shouted, unable to control himself any longer. 'Take your nose out of it! I left home five years ago!'

'My congratulations on producing such a courageous son, Mr Laurie,' Anstey said nastily. 'I would never have had the nerve to speak to *my* father that way!'

'He would've had the sense to brain you,' Malcolm countered in a sullen voice. He was in no mood for Anstey's slick humour or clever banter. He was not too fond of the way he kept on flattering Maddie either. But as for Gordon, that was a lost cause, as far as he was concerned. He'd come to see him because it was his duty to do so, and as usual the boy had kicked him in the face with his insolence, his coldness, his bloody nerve – and to top it all he had to listen while this other idiot smarmed his oily way round Maddie and while she lapped it all up as if there were no tomorrow.

'Why?' he shouted at Maddie, suddenly losing control. 'Why should we sit here suffering while he keeps skiving away from the subject – with your help!'

He glanced round to see that most of the other diners had paused in their conversations, eager to hear what he would say next. But he was past caring.

'I don't give a toss for how many conventions get broken!' He banged the table with his fist, causing a half-full glass of wine to tip over, the wine soaking rapidly into the laundered cloth. 'He sits there,' he continued, taking the emptied glass to point at Gordon, 'wishing we were a thousand miles away – well, he's got a few home truths coming!'

Anstey, who by now was thoroughly enjoying himself, egged Malcolm on. 'Do tell,' he begged, 'He simply *can't* be the saint Parkinson believes!'

But Malcolm rounded on him fiercely. 'And *you* sit there with all the charm of a greasy comb, flashing your dough in quiet glimpses.' Then, turning to Maddie, he delivered his final blow: 'While *you* sit here on the secret to end all secrets . . . Tell the bastard.'

Maddie paused, embarrassed by the scene, and particularly by Anstey's presence, then resigned herself to the inevitable. 'I'm going to die, Gordon,' she said quietly, as if the words had no special significance. 'That's all . . . that's all we came to tell you.'

The silence seemed to go on for hours. The other diners, forks held halfway to mouths, glasses frozen in mid-air seemed in a state of suspended animation, like mime artists immobilized in some absurd tableau.

Suddenly Malcolm turned and shouted to the on-lookers, 'Oh, get on with your grub, all of you,' and, as if released from a spell, knives and forks began to clatter again and the buzz of normal conversation was resumed.

'Why didn't you say earlier?' Gordon asked Maddie.

'You didn't give us a chance,' she replied.

'Well . . .' said Gordon, and his voice was gentler than before, 'No doubt you'll handle it with your usual grace and elegance.'

Maddie was surprised and moved by Gordon's unaccustomed eloquence. 'Why, Gordon,' she said, 'that must be the nicest thing you've ever said to me.'

Gordon looked straight at Malcolm and replied, 'I don't get much chance to speak, either.' Then, after a pause in which Malcolm found himself fiddling with the remains of a bread roll, he added, 'Do you know when?'

'After Christmas,' Maddie replied, 'I refuse to miss Christmas.' Her voice was light, as if she was talking, not about death, but about a tiresome engagement. She turned to Simon and apologized for the conversation; he shook his head.

'I shall come home of course,' said Gordon, but Maddie quickly assured him that it would not be necessary.

'Well,' said Gordon calmly, 'whenever you say. My affairs aren't that urgent that they can't be ... junked forever.'

'Come home for Christmas then,' said Maddie and he quickly assured her that he had intended to, anyway. Malcolm raised his eyebrows in wry disbelief and muttered under his breath. But Gordon, with a dignity with which he surprised even himself, failed to rise to the familiar bait. Instead he said quietly, 'Anything I can do, you let me know.'

'I'll leave a message,' said Malcolm sarcastically, but still Gordon did not respond in kind.

Instead, using an unaccustomedly stern tone of voice, he said, 'perhaps we can forget our differences for ten minutes, Father.'

Malcolm nodded without speaking and looked away. If it were anyone but Malcolm, thought Maddie, you would have said he looked ashamed.

Maddie had just one more matter to settle with Gordon before she left for home. It was something which had been bothering her for a while and now, in the wake of the day's events and revelations, she felt able to ask him to make a revelation of his own.

'It's a bit short notice to ask you to go all the way,' she began cautiously, very conscious that Gordon was not in the habit of disclosing personal details, 'but at least tell me the score so far. Are you thinking of getting married, yet?'

He smiled, knowing the answer she wanted to hear.

'Yes,' he said, almost immediately, but not quite.

When Malcolm and Maddie arrived home that evening, Maddie's first task was to arrange the large bouquet of red roses with which Simon Anstey had surprised her that afternoon. She decided to put them in the hall in an elegant white vase which would set them off to their best advantage. It had been a curious gesture from a total stranger, but a touching one, nevertheless. She sighed to herself as she stood back to admire the perfect blooms. Malcolm had treated Gordon abysmally – even more so than usual. And he knew it. He had been silent and morose throughout the journey home and now he was wandering around the house just behind her all the time, like a miserable little dog who has misbehaved and expects to be whipped. But she would not give him that satisfaction. She sensed that even now Malcolm was standing watching her with the flowers and, out of a sort of irritation with him, she continued to arrange and rearrange them, even though she was already satisfied with their appearance.

'I thought Gordon took it all too smoothly, didn't you?' he volunteered after a minute or two.

Suddenly she felt tired and very angry. 'What do you want from them?' she asked, '*La Boheme*?' and, turning to face him, added, 'I hate you right now. I never thought

103

I'd hear myself say that. Everything, every object in the room, every word that's said, is an excuse for you to be foul. Even to me. And poor Gordon – you made him look dreadfully small.'

'I wonder if that's how he responds to everything,' said Malcolm. 'As if it were mildly inconvenient, but tomorrow's another day.'

Maddie wondered if Malcolm would ever understand Gordon.

'If I do one thing before I die,' she began to her own head, but, remembering, abandoned the protestation in mid-sentence. She *had* tried – she had lost count of how many times, to create some sort of bridge between them. But it was as if they spoke different languages and refused the services of an interpreter. Both of them were hurt by the lack of communication; they just had different ways of showing it. While Malcolm lashed out cruelly, hitting anything in sight, Gordon simply withdrew more and more into his shell. But she knew it was simply a form of defence, that it was by no means impregnable. Faced with Malcolm's aggression and sarcasm, he had clearly been unable to risk any unusual display of emotion, but that was not to say that he had felt nothing.

'*Really* hate me?' Malcolm's voice sounded small and she had to resist an urge to say she was sorry, that it had all been a mistake.

'Wearing off,' she said brusquely and added, 'He'll turn up soon, you see if he doesn't.'

'Gordon? Here?' Malcolm's voice was incredulous.

'Tomorrow at the latest. Maybe even tonight . . . and you won't recognize him.'

'Pigs might fly,' he scoffed. But he wished that Gordon *would* appear, if only to vindicate Maddie's faith in him. She had made herself so vulnerable to him, he could not bear to see her disappointed. He sat for a long time alone, rocking himself gently back and forth in the rocking-chair by the window watching the apple trees gradually disappear into the early dusk of the late November evening. He could hear Maddie in the kitchen, then upstairs. He wondered if she was waiting for Gordon, and hoped that she was not. It had been a long day, a difficult day, and the gentle rocking motion of the chair was making him drowsy . . .

Suddenly he was jerked awake by the sound of car tyres screeching on the gravel outside. He jumped to his feet and almost ran into the hall.

But Maddie was there before him, framed in the doorway. The car door opened and Gordon, his face taut with anxiety, stepped out. He saw his mother, and, without a word, stumbled towards her.

Malcolm waited just long enough to see him catch hold of Maddie as if he would never again let her out of his sight, then he turned, unnoticed by either of them, and walked soberly back into the living-room.

For a moment he stood by the window, looking out over the wintry garden, then, without switching on the light, he sat again in the rocking-chair, waiting. As Gordon came through the door, uncertain, as ever, of his reception, Malcolm drew a white handkerchief from his pocket and shook it out in the time-honoured gesture of surrender.

'Truce?' he said, his eyes on Gordon's face.

'If you like.' If he was surprised, he fought not to let Malcolm see it. But then it was *bound* to be difficult; there was so much to undo.

Ever since that appalling moment in the restaurant, Gordon had felt his carefully maintained defences crumbling, all the games and strategies by which he had locked out his true feelings suddenly useless. He had tried to fight against it, to carry on as if nothing had happened. But the damage had been done. In an agony of self-analysis, he realised that somewhere amidst the deceits and the disguises he had lost himself – and in so doing he had lost touch with all those he cared for. The time had come for a change. First, he had to talk to Malcolm.

But in the event, that was easier said than done. In spite of the 'truce', he found it was still as difficult as ever to approach his father. There was, after all, a whole lifetime of misunderstanding between them, which would not so easily be erased. Each time he tried to make the move, the courage deserted him.

At one point, he despaired and started back towards Herne Bay, but three miles on he turned the car around and drove back to the house.

'I was thinking about going home,' he explained to Malcolm.

'*This* is home,' Malcolm said, gesturing him to sit down.

'Herne Bay,' Gordon said firmly, declining the offer.

'It's unimportant,' said Malcolm magnanimously. 'But there's something you want to say to me?'

Suddenly Gordon felt nervous. There was no going back now. 'Yes, yes,' he said, and added. 'You won't like it.'

Malcolm raised his eyebrows and waited for the first blow. It was, as he had expected, a hard one.

'Just what *have* you done for Mother?'

Malcolm drew in his breath sharply but controlled his anger. 'If I were you,' he said very quietly, 'I'd think very carefully before I went on.'

'Why,' said Gordon, 'It's not just a battle of wills about whether I go to law school or become an engine-driver. I'm saying you've taken the word of one aging neurologist and accepted it. Totally.'

'These tests were irrefutable,' replied Malcolm, but Gordon would not let it go as easily as that.

'The world does not begin and end at Radcliffe, Father, excellent though it may be. Geneva, Toronto, New York ... There are neurosurgeons in these places who *have* performed miracles, yet you haven't even considered them.'

Suddenly Malcolm felt a sense of desperation. It was a losing battle with Gordon – always had been, always would be. He had tried, Christ knew he had tried to meet him halfway, and what did he get for his trouble. He got kicked in the face – lectured, criticized, by his own son – by his own son who never deigned to come home more than once in two years, and only then when he wanted to borrow money, who nearly broke his mother's heart with waiting for him to phone or write. What *right* had he got, barging in!

'Do you think I haven't looked into all the possibilities?' He kept his voice as calm as he could, not trusting himself to control his anger. 'Do you think I *want* her dead?'

But Gordon ploughed on relentlessly. 'I thought, generously,' he said, 'that the shock had narrowed your vision, that maybe money was the —'

Malcolm interrupted him: 'No shortage of vision, no shortage of money. We have tried everything. Your mother is going to die.'

'I don't believe it,' retorted Gordon. 'I came home to force you to do something and—'

'You're a liar,' Malcolm cut him off. 'That isn't why you came home at all, though you wouldn't admit to it.

'I've never told you a thing in my life,' said Gordon.

'Why should I start now?' Then, after a moment, he added, 'Maybe I will . . .'

But first he had to speak to Maddie.

It had been a hard thing to decide to do, but he knew that it was necessary. Once he began, she made it run smoothly for him, as she would, and the words fell into place.

'I've lied in my time about just about everything,' he began, 'except you . . .'

'Perhaps I didn't need a gloss to make me bearable,' said Maddie gently. Gordon nodded in agreement.

'And nothing else around quite matched you,' he went on quietly. 'All looked tatty in your presence, even myself.'

Maddie reached out and touched Gordon's face.

'Don't worry yourself,' she said. 'You'll be all right.'

Gordon shook his head. 'All my life I've run away from reality. The only thing I ever believed in, amongst the lies and the deceits, was *you*. Now you're going and everything is going to fall apart.'

He looked down at her.

'Simon Anstey was about to pay me a small fortune,' he went on. 'I'd have used it to shore up the myth I was building about myself.'

Maddie took a deep breath. He did not want to be comforted; that was not why he had come to her. He wanted to tear down what he had so painstakingly built up so that he could start again, from scratch. So that the only thing she could give him which would help him now, was the truth – however hard or uncompromising.

'You've had everything too easy, Gordon, only don't tell a soul that I know,' she began gently.

He nodded, but was silent.

'And it wasn't us who made it easy; it was you. At every turn of the way you've picked the most convenient route onwards. And you've been incredibly lucky. But a combination of brains and good fortune haven't done a lot to help you with reality.'

She watched him closely as he struggled to absorb what she had said.

'If I was five years old,' he said. 'I'd ask you not to die. I'd beg you ...' he began, then suddenly his eyes filled with tears and the words caught in his throat.

Maddie stood up. It was enough. She knew that she dare not allow him to go on, for his sake and for her own. She caught hold of his arms and gripped them in a gesture both of comfort and restraint.

'I can't do anything to help you,' she said, her voice almost hard, 'I can't change it, can't alter your view of it, can't set the clock back ... for myself, let alone the rest of you. You *aren't* five ... and I can't blow away the nightmares.'

'Afterwards' had become a new and strangely potent word in Maddie's vocabulary – a word which described a frightening and uncharted territory, fraught with terrors, not for *her*, but for everyone she cared for. The thought of 'afterwards' lent a fresh urgency to everything in the present. There was no time to waste; everything must be resolved.

The hours she spent with Malcolm were full of strange contradictions. On the one hand they found themselves almost consciously savouring every moment, trying to draw the last ounce of pleasure from the time they had together. In some ways, they were like young lovers again, newly excited by each other, jealous of time spent apart, highly responsive to each other's moods. But for

Maddie it was more complex even than that. It was as if, knowing that they had little time left, she felt that they must always be working on various levels at once: relishing the present, drawing comfort from the past and laying down the foundation for the future for Malcolm which would help her to be able to leave him, if not without regret then at least with the minimum of anxiety about his well-being. There were so many strands to it and they must all be woven together.

But what Maddie wanted most of Malcolm just then was for him to resolve his difficulties with Gordon. She could not bear the thought of consigning the two of them to a lifetime of unnecessary loneliness and isolation, when it would take so very little for them to become instead a source of comfort and support to each other. Gordon had at least made a move in Malcolm's direction, but Malcolm, with his customary recalcitrance, had refused to meet him even halfway.

But the worst part was that they were *both* injured and confused – retiring silently to their lonely corners to lick their wounds, each unable to understand the other's behaviour. Gordon, as usual, had reacted by retreating, while Malcolm, in *his* fashion, had found the best form of defence was to attack rather than show that he had been hurt. Maddie had seen it all before. It had all the predictability of a bad but familiar play. But this time was different. This time they could not be allowed to let it happen.

When Gordon left for Herne Bay early next morning, she listened to Malcolm's predictable complaints through breakfast, watching him gradually work himself up to a crescendo of all-too-familiar abuse against his elder son. Suddenly she was prepared to endure it no longer. Grabbing hold of Malcolm with a violence which took him by surprise, she forced him to look at her.

'He came home because, contrary to your views, he is *terrified* of me dying. I'm the one thing in his life which is constant. He's given up on you because he never knows what you want of him next ... He's a liar about insignificant details, but he's never unkind about his family, even you! And when I die, he'll grow up overnight. And if you want to see him thereafter, you'd better do something about it, fast!'

On the way back to Herne Bay, Gordon was surprised to find that he was feeling, if not happy, then certainly a great deal less unhappy than he had felt for ages. It was as if his talk with Maddie had lifted a huge weight which had been lodged in his chest. Suddenly everything seemed so much clearer. There were things to deal with in Herne Bay that were long overdue, just as there had been things in Denton. But the only difference was that now he felt stronger – more positive and more able to do what must be done.

First, there was Sue. He found her sitting behind her desk, opening the morning's mail. As usual, she was pleased to see him, and as usual, she dared not let him see *how* pleased. He had hurt her too often with his indifference. He perched on the edge of her desk, and caught hold of her hand. She looked up, surprised, but still holding something in reserve.

'There is no manor house, no horses, no Rolls-Royce.' he said softly. She smiled.

'I know,' she said. 'Your father told me. She smiled. 'Who cares?'

Gordon took a key from his pocket and handed it to her. 'That's a spare key to my flat. Will you keep it?'

'Right,' she said, amazed, but still containing her pleasure.

The relationship was sealed. It had been easy. And he had done it, not to please his mother, who was going to die, but to please *himself*, who was going to start living, really living, instead of just going through the motions.

Next came Simon Anstey. Anstey was a man who liked to have things his own way with as few obstacles as possible. He wanted to tie up a deal and, having made the basic gestures required of him when he had heard of Maddie's illness, he had soon reverted to his usual practice of putting business before everything, even the personal feelings of a man whose mother was about to die. He had rung Gordon several times at Denton, without success and when he eventually made contact, he had shown little sympathy or patience, but had tried to frighten him with warnings of Dick Parkinson's wrath should the deal fail to come off. But there was, as Gordon had suspected all along, more to this deal than met the eye. Simon Anstey was not the only fly customer around by any means, it seemed. For behind all the machinations, the frantic phone calls and the talk of percentages and incentives, lay one simple but shocking truth: both he and Anstey had been set up – made fools of by Parkinson himself, who had thought nothing of tying them both in knots so that *he* could purchase Wentworth for his youngest son. It was a dirty trick, but then it was a dirty business; Gordon had known that all along. He picked up the telephone and asked to be put through to the poor devil in the middle of it all – the owner of Wentworth. First he would put him in the picture; then, he would go and tell Anstey the deal was off. And, while he was doing that, he thought with some satisfaction, he might as well tell Parkinson a few home-truths into the bargain. After all, what did he have to lose?

The next morning Gordon was surprised to find his father waiting for him at work. He must have left home at the crack of dawn!

He invited him into his office, but Malcolm said that he would prefer it if they could talk where they were, in front of Sue.

'As you wish,' said Gordon stuffily, finding his father's unaccustomed good mood almost more difficult to handle than his usual aggressiveness.

'I don't *want* an apology, you know,' he added. 'I nipped off without saying – you must have thought—'

'Typical, I said ...' Malcolm smiled. Then he grew more serious. 'Look, I know you're scared of her dying. For lots of reasons. So am I. When something like this happens, you realize how much you love the kids. While she's around she can make up for any offhand word or action on my part. When she's gone, it'll be down to me.' He looked straight at Gordon. 'I've treated you like a pig and I'm sorry. I meant to say much more, but I can't really think of anything.'

Gordon could hardly contain his astonishment. 'You drove all the way to say that?' he asked.

'Reckoned that way you'd think I meant it,' Malcolm replied gruffly and began putting on his overcoat.

Gordon knew he could not let him go. 'What about lunch with us?' he suggested enthusiastically. But it was only 11 o'clock. 'Hell,' he said, anxious to provide an alternative, 'we'll shut up shop and go for a walk.'

'It's freezing,' Sue pointed out.

'Go for a drive, find a pub – let's do that.'

'OK,' said Malcolm. 'Let's.' He paused. 'Gordon ...' Gordon stopped, caught by Malcolm's tone of voice. 'I've been thinking, on the way down. We've fought all your life about one thing – supremacy in Maddie's eyes.' Gordon nodded in agreement as Malcolm went on. 'Daft

113

really, because neither of us had it. That belonged to Neil.'

Gordon stood for a moment acknowledging the simple truth of it, then turned and went off into his office to get his coat.

Malcolm and Sue stood quietly looking at each other, finding no necessity to comment on what had happened. Then Malcolm, catching hold of her hand warmly asked, on the spur of the moment, 'Would you like to spend Christmas with us? We have a fabulous time – and this'll be extra special.'

Sue nodded. 'Thank you,' she said, 'Thank you, I would.'

Chapter 8

It was December, and Maddie, with perhaps even more enthusiasm than usual, threw herself into all the last-minute preparations for Christmas. There were Christmas cards to be bought and written, presents to be chosen and the dress, which she was knitting for Beatrice Matilda, to be finished.

If she was conscious of being troubled a little more often by blurring of her vision or if she was forced to accept that the familiar tasks seemed to tire her more quickly than on previous occasions, she simply registered these facts as unwelcome but immutable signs of the relentless progression of her illness and refused to let them interfere with her excitement and anticipation. But one thing was on her mind perhaps more than her own disturbing symptoms: the fact that Neil was still to be told the news that she was about to die.

The thought of his reaction terrified her. They had been so close all through his life, and she had always made things so easy for him. How would he ever be able to cope with the knowledge that she was about to abandon him? It was her own fault, of course. She had kept him too long as her 'baby', not allowing him to grow up, unwilling to let him be exposed to the harsher realities of life.

In fact, Malcolm knew different. Untroubled by guilt or rose-tinted spectacles, he identified in his younger son a certain quality of toughness which Maddie could not detect. Neil, he maintained, was not the dependent boy Maddie imagined to be, but a natural survivor, who knew how to use his vulnerability to get what he wanted out of life and out of other people. It was a characteristic for which, somewhat in spite of himself, he could not suppress a certain degree of admiration.

Neil himself was looking forward to Christmas: to gorging himself on his mother's mince-pies and crispy roast-potatoes, to wallowing in the deep baths, to the colour television and the central heating. Home comforts – they were worth a compromise or two. Independence was one thing, but by the end of term he felt that he had earned a short respite from the temperamental water-heater, the take-away curried mice, the wind whistling through the empty refrigerator – and Judy's cooking.

Whatever else Judy had to offer, it certainly wasn't home-made cakes and Yorkshire pudding, he thought ruefully, as they tried, without a great deal of success to hitch a lift in the direction of Denton. He stood by the roadside, abusing the drivers of half-empty vehicles who sped by without a glance.

Judy sat miserably on her rucksack, not even bothering to watch the road, a picture of abject misery. She was one of those women, thought Neil with a sort of intense pride, who look interesting even when they look their worst. Her face was not beautiful by any standards, but it was alive, always changing. It was a 'lived-in' face, a face which told stories. It was also a strong face. One look at her and you could see that she knew what she wanted out of life – that she didn't mind fighting to get it. That she *had* fought, hard, and would fight again if necessary. But sometimes, like now, when she was tired, or the day had been a little too long, you could see that once something had hurt her, and that occasionally, that hurt was hard to forget.

He looked at her. 'We'll have a *real* Christmas,' he said.

She nodded, smiling. He liked it when she smiled more than anything, especially if it was because of something he had said. 'The next one'll stop,' he said, holding out his thumb with renewed vigour. A car drew to a halt.

'Oxford?' said Neil. The driver opened the passenger door.

'Jump in,' he said.

'See,' said Neil, taking Judy's hand.

She kissed him lightly, just behind his ear, and smiled again.

Malcolm and Maddie were sitting up in bed when the doorbell rang. They looked at each other, puzzled. They weren't expecting any visitors, and it must be getting on for eleven o'clock. Neither of them moved.

The bell rang again, this time more insistently.

'You go,' Maddie said, reluctant to abandon the interminable knitting which threatened to be the one thing to defeat her before Christmas.

Malcolm jumped out of bed, grabbed the nearest garment, which had happened to be his raincoat, and ran downstairs. He did not take the chain off the door but opening it gingerly just a few inches, was surprised to see a bedraggled-looking Neil and an equally bedraggled, but nevertheless rather stunning girl.

'Hi, Dad,' Neil said blithely.

'Er, yes . . . hallo.' Malcolm still did not open the door.

'This is Judy.' Neil touched the girl's arm and she turned towards him slightly, as if familiar with the gesture.

'Well? Can we come in or can't we?' Neil's tone was beginning to sound a little peeved.

Malcolm opened the door, clutching the raincoat self-consciously to him.

Neil and the girl looked at each other. 'Well, you certainly know how to keep your marriage interesting,' he commented drily. 'What's Mum wearing?'

Malcolm could hear them laughing – a private, shared laugh – as he ran back upstairs to tell Maddie of their arrival.

Neil led Judy into the kitchen and hung her anorak with his on the back of the kitchen door. He put on the kettle and looked to see what was in the biscuit tin. She stood awkwardly looking out of the window.

'Nice place,' she said after a while.

'I told you, didn't I?' he responded. Coming up behind her and lifting her hair to kiss the back of her neck.

'Your dad, though . . .' she began, not responding.

'I told you that, too,' he laughed.

'It's your mum I'm dying to meet,' she said, turning now to face him. She caught hold of his face in her hands.

'I love you,' she began quietly, but was interrupted by the sight of Malcolm, now fully dressed and standing awkwardly in the doorway.

Neil broke away, but without embarrassment. 'Where's Mum?' he asked.

Malcolm said she would soon be down, and sat rather awkwardly at the table. Judy joined him.

'Shall I pour you a cup?' she asked, indicating the pot of tea.

'Please. Please do,' said Malcolm. She poured the tea and handed it to him, smiling. There was no doubt, thought Malcolm, she had a great smile.

'So,' he said, 'what's the plan? Home for Christmas?'

'Yeah,' said Neil.

'And Judy?' asked Malcolm, knowing the answer before he asked.

'I wondered if Judy could stay with us,' Neil began. 'We've got the room . . . I mean she can share my—'

'Yes, of course we have, but your own family, won't they expect you?' Malcolm asked.

Judy grimaced.

'Doesn't get on with her parents,' Neil explained.

Malcolm nodded. 'Well,' he said, 'If Judy thinks it'll be all right about *her* family, then she's welcome to stay.'

At that moment the door opened to reveal Maddie, dressed as if she were about to go out to lunch at the Savoy rather than have a cup of tea in her own kitchen. She wore an ice-blue jersey suit with a matching scarf, suede high-heeled shoes, faultless make-up. He hair was arranged with even more elegance and considerably more precision than usual.

Neil and Judy stood up to greet her. Neil immediately took in the details of her impeccable appearance and wondered what it might signify, while Judy made conscious of her own bedraggled hair and crumpled jeans instantly felt ill-at-ease and out-of-place.

'Eggs and bacon?' she enquired, her voice as cool and precise as her appearance.

Neil nodded.

'No, I'll do it, Mrs Laurie, if you'll just tell me where everything is,' volunteered Judy, suddenly anxious to do all the right things. But Maddie turned to her with a smile of icy sweetness and declined her offer. Judy sank awkwardly back into her chair.

What an incredible woman, she thought – even more grim than she imagined. She looked as if she'd stepped off the front cover of *Woman's Own*, complete with fixed grin and a frying pan at the ready. Not surprising Neil had been in a hurry to leave the nest! With a mother like that, it was a wonder he'd turned out so well.

'You *sure* I can't help you?' she reiterated, but Maddie

turned to her with a look that would have caused the Sahara to freeze over.

'Quite sure,' she said and continued, in all her finery, to prepare the feast for the homecoming of her beloved son.

Judy sighed; it was going to be worse than she had expected.

But Judy was not a girl who was easily defeated. When she saw a problem, she liked to grab it by the horns, and try to master it. It was not in her nature to be the passive victim of circumstances, nor for that matter the passive victim of Maddie Laurie.

The next morning she found Maddie alone in the conservatory. She was wearing the clothes she had arrived in, but Maddie was attired in another faultless ensemble from her wardrobe. Judy took in the details of Maddie's strained and too-perfect appearance, and knew that one of them must break the ice even if it required dynamite to do it.

'Will you and I be friends?' she asked, standing in the doorway, making no movement towards Maddie.

Maddie looked up from her gardening magazine. 'Why ever not?' she asked.

'Because I'm stealing your favourite son away,' replied Judy bluntly.

Maddie had been quite unprepared for Judy's aggressive approach, had expected perhaps tears, pleading or shy acquiescence. But this girl was a different kettle of fish altogether. 'Yes, yes, so you are,' she said with deceptive casualness, 'but I knew somebody would, some day. So why not you?'

Judy could feel a sort of anger bubbling up inside her. 'I do happen to—' she began, but Maddie interrupted her quickly.

'If you tell me you love him I'll scream. How *can* you? You're nothing but a girl, yourself.'

'We ought to get a few things straight, Maddie,' Judy began.

'Maddie?'

'It's your name, isn't it?'

Maddie laid aside the magazine and leant towards the girl. 'I'd like you to know one thing for your own safety,' she said, 'I'm surprised at how malevolent I feel towards you. Not because it's *you* in particular, but towards any person who presumes to take my place.'

Judy looked at Maddie with a new sympathy. It must be hard, giving up somebody you had clung to for so long. Especially knowing that it was all more or less inevitable, that you had no alternative.

'It's quite all right,' she said softly.

But that was not the response Maddie wanted. 'You mean I've lost the power to frighten usurpers?' she asked.

'I just think it's fabulous that you understand yourself so well,' said Judy, and she meant it.

'But surely,' said Maddie, 'the next step from that must be to use that understanding and retire gracefully from the scene.'

'It'll happen, I'm sure,' said Judy with a slight smile.

Maddie got up. It was bad enough to have the wretched girl in the house at all, without having to put up with her blessed sympathy and understanding into the bargain.

'Well, at this moment,' she said, hoping to put an end to the discussion, 'I am blind with jealousy and I have no plans to suppress my feelings.' She turned and walked towards the door, pausing only to pull aggressively at a dead leaf on one of the geraniums.

Judy watched her with a curious mixture of resentment and pity. 'I'll watch out then,' she said pleasantly, but added, 'I did expect it.'

Maddie turned. Why?'

'Oh, things Neil said about you: how possessive you were, concerning him. How the others could go hang as long as he was all right, even Malcolm.' Maddie did not show any reaction, so Judy continued, 'Yes, he told me quite a bit about you – enough to make me feel I know you, anyway.'

'How boring that must have been,' said Maddie laughingly lightly, 'and eventually how annoying – listening to a boy spend so much time talking about his mother when the attention might have been on you.'

'Oh, not every day,' Judy corrected her. 'Just when the subject came up.'

'Yet you feel you know me.' Maddie shook her head, her hand on the handle of the door. 'Hardly think so ... dear,' she added, before sweeping out of the room leaving Judy, battered but far from defeated, to prepare herself for the next round.

Malcolm was watching the two women from a discreet distance, feeling rather like a field observer in a dangerous and unpredictable battle. It was, he felt, an extremely unfortunate set of circumstances that had brought Judy to Denton on this particular occasion. He had often quailed at the thought of Maddie's reaction when Neil showed his first signs of really growing up. They had talked about it in the past, joked about it, even. But somehow he had chosen the wrong moment, without being aware of how wrong it was. Maddie was feeling at her most vulnerable and would have found it hard to cope with *any* girl friend, let alone a rather unusual, individual and obviously threatening young woman such as Judy. Now, if he'd come home with a naïve, sweet little seventeen-year-old in tow that would have been a different matter, but Judy was no seventeen-year-old and, Malcolm thought wryly, she was neither sweet nor little and definitely far from naïve. He would have to say something to Neil before it was too late.

His opportunity came the next afternoon as he watched Neil working with considerable expertise on the ever-troublesome car. If Neil was good for nothing else, he thought, he certainly knew a thing or two about distributors. Pity he hadn't decided to be a garage mechanic, it could have saved them all a lot of money.

'Gordon wrote to me the other day,' Neil remarked, replacing the distributor cap and wiping his greasy hands on his jeans.

Malcolm looked up. 'Oh yes?'

'First time in his life,' said Neil, fiddling around with the hose. 'Sent me a cheque to help me with University. He begged me to finish my course, no matter what. Has anything happened to him?'

Malcolm shook his head, playing for time. 'Say anything else?' he asked.

'No,' replied Neil, 'Oh ... See you Christmas, that's all.' He continued to mess about with the car. Malcolm, though taken aback by the news of Gordon's unprecedented generosity, had something else on his mind. 'I'm not sure how to put this,' he began tentatively, picking up an oily rag and rubbing away at a door handle with it.

Neil lifted his head, knowing what was coming.

'About Judy,' Malcolm went on. 'Don't let her put your mum's nose out of joint.'

'Right,' said Neil agreeably and busied himself once more with spanners and bolts.

'You don't know what I'm talking about,' Malcolm persisted. 'She knows everything about you: what you like for breakfast, what brings you out in spots ... She darns your socks, washes your underwear. But worst of all, she talks about it. Neil, does this ... Neil does that ...'

Neil looked up sharply. 'Like Mum and you,' he said.

'But you're only playing at it,' Malcolm said. 'I know you've *left* us, but don't flaunt the fact in Maddie's face.'

Neil became inordinately interested in something deep in the bowels of the car's engine.

'She thinks you're the greatest thing on earth, Neil,' said Malcolm sharply.

'And she's jealous. What can I do?' Neil retorted.

'Stop pretending you're cruel,' said Malcolm and added softly, 'Hurt her and I'll kill you.'

Neil continued his work on the car and did not reply.

In the kitchen, Maddie, still immaculate under her apron, was making a huge batch of mince-pies. The door opened and she glanced up to see Judy, smiling that annoying smile of hers. She began, aggressively, to cut shapes in the pastry using the rim of a glass, bringing it down on the table each time with a loud bang. Judy watched her.

'Can I help you, Maddie?' she asked after a while.

'Not thank you, dear,' Maddie replied coldly and banged the glass down sending up a cloud of flour like gunsmoke.

Judy laughed as the image suggested itself. 'Somehow we've got ourselves a battle without even firing a shot,' she said. 'That's why I'm leaving, before the invisible blood begins to flow.'

Maddie continued to attack the pastry, with an awful ferocity. Then suddenly, she stopped, and, looking straight at Judy, asked her sharply. 'How old are you?'

'Twenty-five,' Judy answered.

'He's only nineteen,' Maddie shouted, as if that fact, in itself, were enough to settle the issue.

The two women faced each other. Judy, who had wanted, from the start, to make allowances, to try to be tolerant of Maddie's extraordinary behaviour, found herself closer to hating another woman than she would have believed possible. Maddie, not bothering any longer to hide what she felt or to control her emotions, began to lash out with every weapon she could muster.

'He's not a kid and I'm not a senile vulture,' began Judy.

'No,' retorted Maddie, 'but you've been around. It shows, dear, in the face – in everything you do.'

'So?' asked Judy.

'So pick on someone your own size,' Maddie returned to the mince-pies.

Judy drew in her breath sharply. She had not wanted to fight, but Maddie was offering her very little alternative.

'I won't offend you by using the word love,' she began quietly, 'but I'd give up a lot for Neil. As much as you.'

Maddie licked the mincemeat off her fingers. 'That would be your mistake. I never gave up a thing. I didn't need to,' she said smugly.

'Why didn't you choke him at birth! You would have saved yourself a lot of agony.' Judy could hear her own voice rising to an ugly pitch, but could see no way of retreating from the fray.

Maddie wiped her hands elaborately on her apron. 'Not really,' she said. 'You see, you're going to win him in the end, I know. Not by any skill you have, not by any natural progression the male of our species follows when looking for his second mother . . .'

'But by the fact that he gets pissed off with your teeth marks in his neck!' Judy abandoned all attempts at restraint.

'No,' said Maddie very casually, 'more simple that that . . . I haven't got long to live, you see.'

'Some people use *ANYTHING* when the chips are

down,' she retorted and clapped her hands in a facetious display of admiration for Maddie's devious skill.

'But it's true . . . it's absolutely true!' Maddie pleaded, jolted into some urgent sense of reality by Judy's reaction.

'Oh for God's sake!' Judy turned to leave the room.

'Judy . . .'

Suddenly, Judy turned and without warning began to shout, her voice rising to drown Maddie's pleading. 'Yes, yes,' she began, 'well here *is* something true . . . me, married at seventeen, turned inside out by a local boy who went screaming to *his* mum the day I divorced him. Yes, I've been around and it shows. But your Neil isn't like that boy. He's kind for a start. He *loves* me. On top of which, the time is coming when he won't rush to his mum when the going gets tough. He'll turn to me. And that is because he's growing up, Maddie. Horrible, isn't it? I've been around and it shows, specially from my side, and I'm not looking to be kicked again. But Neil won't do that, for by some miracle you've brought him up in a way I entirely approve of. Fluke! Must've been. No . . .' Suddenly her voice softened a little. 'Sorry – it was the cherry on top. But not as bad as you telling me you're dying.' And she turned and walked out of the kitchen.

Maddie watched her go. She was so overwhelmed by conflicting emotions that she could neither speak nor move. On the one hand, she was filled with a mixture of shame and regret at what she had allowed to pass between them, while at the same time she was amazed by the fact that Judy had not taken her revelation seriously at all.

She stood for a moment, uncertain what to do next, then, grateful for some simple mechanical task to take the place of the drama and confusion, turned again to the mince-pies.

It was some time later that the door opened and Neil

walked into the kitchen. Maddie looked up and knew, without asking, that Malcolm had told him the news. She held out her arms to him but he walked past her, his face a mask, without expression.

'He says you're going to die,' he said, nodding in the direction of the garden.

Maddie came towards him, but he backed away round the table.

'I wanted to tell you myself. I'm sorry I'll be leaving you to fend for yourself . . .'

Neil took a pie and bit into it. 'It's all right,' he said, his mouth full. 'It obviously can't be helped!'

Maddie watched him with growing disbelief. Malcolm had said that he was tough, a natural survivor, but she had never in all her imaginings, expected such a display of cold indifference.

'Neil,' she began reaching out to touch him, her hands still covered with flour.

'Don't,' he said, backing away sharply and vigorously rubbing at the mark she had left on his jacket.

'Why are you being so cold?' she asked, confused. 'It's the opposite of everything you are.'

Neil turned almost angrily. 'What do you expect of me?' he snarled.

'More than I'm getting, you selfish little sod,' Maddie replied, her hurt incomprehension erupting now into simple anger.

'Oh, that's guaranteed to bring me to heel in floods of tears,' he jibed sarcastically.

'Look,' said Maddie, searching for some reasonable, if unpalatable explanation for Neil's behaviour. 'If you're afraid to show your feelings because of *her*—'

'*Her*?' Neil quickly seized on what she had said. 'The shorthand for anyone you've taken a dislike to? Where is "*she*"?'

'Upstairs, packing,' said Maddie. 'She took umbrage at the fact that I'm dying and decided to leave.'

'You told her?' Neil began accusingly. 'Told *her* before me?' He turned and made for the door.

'My God,' said Maddie with feeling. 'we thought Gordon would be difficult. He was a pushover compared to you. Even your father said so.'

'Then sink your teeth in him, make *him* your favourite. I've had enough,' he said and stomped out of the kitchen. On the stairs he stopped, drew in his breath, hearing Maddie's voice calling his name. He waited, listening for her to call again.

'Neil,' she called, and again, 'Neil'. He hesitated, swallowed painfully, then ran upstairs to his bedroom.

In the kitchen, Maddie stood absolutely still listening to the sound of her own agitated breathing. Suddenly, she grew afraid. Carefully, gingerly, she put down the tray of pies she had been holding and sat down by the table. In her ears she could hear a sound like a rushing wind, a terrifyingly familiar, unmistakable sound. Quickly she slid off the chair onto the floor, pies and baking-tins clattering around her as she brushed past them in her haste. The wind was a roar now and she began to fling her head from side to side, grunting, till at last, mercifully almost, her jaw snapped shut and her body juddered to a halt in the grips of a powerful and shattering convulsion.

Neil found Judy lying on his bed idly flicking through an old copy of *Punch*.

She looked up when he came in, knowing at once from his expression, that something was wrong. "What is it?' she asked.

'I thought you were leaving,' said Neil.

128

'Not without you,' Judy replied, and asked again, 'What is it?'

'Things I've just said to my mother,' he muttered barely audibly, and wandered over to the window. The garden looked bleak in the misty half-light of the December afternoon. The apple tree which every summer, for as far back as he could remember had creaked with its burden of apples, stood idle now, stripped of both fruit and leaves. In the driveway he could see his father tinkering with the car, pathetically ill-at-ease with any machine, trying to make it look as if he knew what he was doing, but hopelessly out of his depth. Rather like himself, in fact. He turned away to look at Judy.

'She *is* dying, Judy . . . truly,' he said.

She put aside the magazine ready to deny his statement, but he did not give her the chance. '

'I've known for weeks,' he said.

Judy shook her head slowly. 'Why didn't you *say*?' she asked.

Neil shrugged and turned away from her to look once more out of the window onto the garden. How many times, he thought, had he stood there as a child, on summer evenings, long after he should have been asleep, watching his mother working. She used to tie her hair up in an old scarf, put on a disgusting old jacket and wellington boots, but somehow she had always seemed beautiful to him, mysterious, unobtainable, weaving her way amongst the lupins and wallflowers, standing under the apple tree as the light faded, walking away from him across the shadowed lawn. It was like being under a spell, a spell which she had woven so subtly but with his total complicity. He had known all along that it must be broken – the enchantment – that he must free himself from the intricate web they had both woven. But he had hoped to do it slowly, imperceptibly almost, so as to cause them both the minimum of pain. But now there was no alternative. She was leaving him before he even had the chance to leave her. He swallowed hard.

'In a way,' he said, his eyes still fixed on the distant apple tree, 'I'll be immensely relieved when she dies.' Then he walked abruptly from the window and sat down next to Judy on the bed. Lightly, without speaking, she began to stroke the nape of his neck until he turned and caught her up in his arms in a fierce and almost desperate embrace. It was less complicated than thinking.

Though Malcolm felt little empathy with machines and in particular with car engines, there were times, he thought, when they could be curiously soothing. He knew he had bungled breaking the news to Neil. He had ended up sounding like a cross between a policeman and a missionary, mealy-mouthed and patronising. But that was no reason why Neil should have reacted with such appalling casualness, such cool detachment. Thank goodness Maddie had not been there to see it. Still, he was sure Neil would have his reasons, just the same as Gordon had his. Everyone must cope as best they can. It was just that sometimes one's children were so bloody peculiar it made you wonder whether you knew them at all!

He heard the back door open and looked up to see who it was.

In the door, as pale as stone and shaking visibly, stood a very frightened-looking Maddie.

'What is it?' He ran towards her.

'I've had a fit,' she said.

He motioned her to sit down on an upturned box outside the garage, and watched with relief as a little colour gradually seeped back into her drained face. Then he took off his jacket and placed it gently round her shoulders, feeling her shiver as he did so. Her make-up was all streaked where she had, in her distress, rubbed her eyes and cheeks with her hands. He took out his oily handkerchief and handed it to her, his eyes never leaving her.

'Just like that, you had a fit?' he asked when he was satisfied that she had stopped shaking.

'It was Neil,' she said very quietly, 'cold and cruel when he spoke to me.'

Malcolm took a deep breath. He eased the handkerchief out of Maddie's hands and began gently to wipe her forehead with it.

'Why's he suddenly turned on me?' she asked, her voice close to tears.

'Put it this way,' said Malcolm, pulling his jacket tighter around her, 'you don't want him to stay a baby if you're going to die ...'

'What has that got to do with him turning on me?' she asked.

'He's just spreading his wings in the only way he knows how. This Judy,' Maddie grimaced, but he continued, 'she's meant to be proof for all to see that he doesn't need us any more.'

'But she's been married before. And she's older than he is,' Maddie objected.

'Not good enough for your little boy – that's what you mean, isn't it?' Malcolm began to stroke Maddie's hair. She looked up and caught his hand.

'What did he say to you?' he asked after a while.

She shrugged. 'It was so unlike him ... defending her against me!' She paused, then added with a wry smile, 'I had a go at *her* and all! She bites back.'

'Busy morning you've had,' Malcolm laughed, but Maddie did not feel like joking.

'Poor girl,' she said. 'Something very sad about her and I picked on it.'

'Quite easy to go in there and apologize,' said Malcolm. Maddie nodded.

'And what about Neil?' she asked. 'I don't want him under my wing. I just want . . . a bit of love, that's all.'

'I'll sort him out,' said Malcolm and helped her to her feet. 'He's been getting on my nerves anyway. I'll take him aside and have a word, but in the meantime you can square it with Judy.'

'Don't hurt him,' said Maddie anxiously. 'Don't tell him about my fit.'

'Bring him back in time for tea, don't get his feet wet, blow his nose every half hour and, if anyone looks askance at him, kill!' Malcolm parrotted, as if talking of a three-year-old.

Maddie laughed, and, handing him his jacket and handkerchief, walked back to the house. Malcolm was right. It would not be *so* difficult to apologize. But first she would have to tidy herself up a little.

When Neil heard Malcolm call his name, he extricated himself from Judy's arms and hurried to answer. There was something about his father's tone which did not encourage him to argue.

Judy shook her head angrily. They said, 'Jump!' and he jumped. She was angry with herself as much as with him, angry for getting involved in such a stupid set-up. As if she didn't know any better. Angry at allowing herself to be dragged into a real old-fashioned family drama when she'd vowed never to get into that scene again. She'd have to move on, that's all there was to it, Christmas or no Christmas. The rucksack was there, waiting. All she had to do was chuck in her toothbrush, cut her losses and get out . . . just as she always did.

There was a gentle knock on the door.

'Can I come in?' It was Maddie's voice, but sounding more tentative than usual.

'It's your house,' she mumbled.

The door opened and Maddie, looking, Judy noted, more than a little nervous, came in.

'Stupid to fight really,' Maddie began, 'when the truth is I need your help . . .' She glanced towards the rucksack. 'Not going, are you?'

'Might.' Judy did not look up. She was not sure to react to this new velvet-glove treatment.

'I really *could* use your help. There's a lot of cooking still to do for Christmas.' Maddie smiled encouragingly.

But Judy was still suspicious. 'I've given you enough chances,' she said. 'Like most women of your age, you start to backtrack only when the damage is done.'

'I didn't mean to hurt you. Honestly.' Maddie stretched out her hand towards Judy, but the girl did not take it.

'It's *you* that will be hurt,' she retorted scornfully 'I spent the worst years of my life with a possessive mother. And when I got the chance, I was off. And *she's* the one who regretted it, cos I never went back . . .'

'I'm not like that,' Maddie protested.

'That's what *she* said,' said Judy.

'Truly I'm not.'

'That's what *she* said,' Judy repeated, her face hard.

'Stop being so clever and please look at me,' Maddie said firmly. 'I want you to stay for Christmas. We will have a wonderful time and you'll wish it never had to stop.'

Judy's face softened. 'Stay on as an assistant cook?' she asked.

'It's a tall order, I know,' Maddie laughed. 'It's a male-dominated dining-room.'

'Who washes up?' as if this might be the crucial and decisive factor.

133

'Everyone but us,' Maddie assured her. 'We sit by the fire and knit!' Then, as if suddenly struck by a brilliant idea, she asked, 'Do you knit at all?'

Judy did not answer but reached into her rucksack and produced an intricate and delicate shawl.

Maddie took it admiringly. 'It's lovely!' she exclaimed. 'I have this baby's dress which I . . .' she stopped herself, laughing. 'No, I can't!'

Judy smiled: 'You just have!'

'It's beige,' said Maddie, 'with never-ending patterns . . . and I'm stuck.'

Judy touched Maddie's arm. 'Peace in our time, Maddie,' she said quietly.

Maddie sat on the bed and, at last, the two women began to talk easily, without reserve or malice. And having once disposed of the barriers they had erected against each other, they were able to make a new start in their relationship, based not on fear, but on a kind of understanding, and on their mutual concern for Neil. And Maddie began to see that Judy, far from being viewed as a threat, should be welcomed by her as her very necessary, if somewhat surprising successor.

'Do I hand him over officially, then?' she asked eventually.

'Break a bottle over his head?' Judy joked, then became serious again for a moment. 'No, in the circumstances, he should try and get as much from you as he can, for old times sake. By way of thanking you,' she paused, 'maybe I *should* go.'

'No, please,' Maddie said and was surprised to find how much she meant it, 'I'd like him to see us become good friends. It'll help him when I die.'

Neil had found Malcolm waiting impatiently by the car, the door open.

'Get in,' he said roughly.

Neil was about to protest but something in his father's face made him decide against it.

'I've been less than kind to my mother,' he said pedantically, climbing into the passenger seat, then added, 'I'll put it right.'

'Thought you would,' said Malcolm with frightening coldness, climbing in beside him. Then he turned. 'I don't know what you said to her, but for the first time in your life you hurt her.'

'I had to start somehow,' said Neil looking out of the car window.

'You ignorant *git*,' his father exploded.

Neil had had enough. 'Can I go now, *sir*?' he asked insolently, but Malcolm started up the engine.

'We're going for a ride,' he said.

They drove in grim silence for several miles. Malcolm did not trust himself to speak while angry, knowing that it would be all to easy to pull down the carefully constructed barrier behind which Neil was hiding his feelings. He looked at him quickly from time to time, but the boy stared doggedly ahead, his face giving nothing away.

They came to a pub that Malcolm sometimes visited with Maddie. It had once been a quaint country inn, but had recently changed hands and the new landlord, in his wisdom, had seen fit to pull out all the old timber in favour of chrome fittings, a vivid red carpet and the occasional imitation brass carriage lamp. It seemed, thought Malcolm, a very suitable setting for Neil in his present frame of mind.

He bought two whiskys and set one down in front of his son. Neil sipped it and smiled appreciatively.

'This really *is* a new generation, Dad,' he said. 'Let's

face it, we've been brought up on death, thanks to *your* generation – war, coronaries, cancer ... we thank you heartily for them and all the fear they've sharpened our wits with.' He paused to take another sip of his drink, then added, in much the same tone as before, 'And everyone's mother dies.'

Malcolm looked at him in frank disbelief, not sure whether to shout, laugh or cry, in an attempt to break through this absurd barrier of logic and intellect.

'You're a thoroughly modern man, are you?' he asked, 'Slicker, faster, tougher?'

Neil shuffled about a little in his seat, searching, almost visibly in his intellectual bag of tricks for his next card. 'I don't want you to think I can take all this in my stride,' he began.

Malcolm sighed inwardly, wondering just how long it would take.

'It's a big effort to come to terms with ... well ... the complex mass of reactions one has to a thing like this.'

'Take it in your own time,' said Malcolm quietly, hoping that it would soon be over.

'And, fortunately, that effort prevents you from reacting in a so-called natural way, clouding the issue,' Neil went on, rather as if he were addressing an international convention on the subject. 'One has a part to play and usefulness is better than howling your head off,' he added sagely.

Malcolm waited to allow the next few platitudes to be aired, then decided that enough was enough. If Neil would not, of his own accord, break out from behind the pathetically fragile wall behind which he was cowering, then *he* would have to smash his way in, using a pickaxe if necessary.

'I used to think young men of your age had nothing new to tell us; that they talked the kind of balls you've just spouted – utter nonsense – and its purpose was to hide their fear that the older generation might be right after all. But listening to you just now, maybe I'm wrong.' He paused and prepared himself for his final onslaught. 'Like I said, we're asking you to grow up awfully fast, but I didn't expect you to disappear up your own arse in the attempt. *Specifically* you, that was! As for the "modern man" in general, well ...' He mimicked the callous and impersonal tone of Neil's earlier remarks, 'His mother dies, or a hundred years from now the incubator falls apart ... but for now his mother dies, and he doesn't turn a hair. The disgusting, heartless bugger! Wouldn't you agree?' He paused, then added more quietly, 'I think you've been having me on.'

He saw the boy's face begin to crumple, disintegrate as if someone had trodden all over it with heavy boots. Which in a sense, he had. Then, laying his head down on the table Neil, at last, burst into tears. He cried noisily for a moment or two as Malcolm watched in relieved silence.

'Oh Dad,' he said, at last, between sobs, 'what am I going to do?'

Malcolm took from his pocket the same oily handkerchief he had offered to Maddie and handed it to him. 'You're going to set up your own life,' he said quietly, 'maybe with Judy, maybe someone else. But you're going to do it gradually, not desperately. And along the way you're going to preserve the memories worthy of it, not wipe them out.'

Neil scrubbed at his eyes with the grimy handkerchief and nodded gratefully.

Back home, he found Maddie where he knew she would be – sitting in the rocking-chair, waiting. He crept into the room, stood quietly by the door, watching her.

'Mum!' he whispered.

She did not look up 'Mm?'

'If I say I love you now, will you believe me?'

Maddie nodded.

'Gonna miss you . . .' He was still standing some distance away from her, his tone as casual as he could make it.

'Now don't start me off,' she began, half-reproachfully.

Neil turned to go but Maddie called. 'Hey! Where are you going?'

'I was just passing through,' he said.

'Give us a kiss then,' said Maddie.

'Or what?' he enquired in mock-belligerence.

'Or I'll sulk,' she retorted.

He pecked her dutifully on the cheek.

'Of course you're going to miss me,' she murmured, and added, mostly to herself, 'It's lucky that Judy will be staying for Christmas after all.'

Chapter 9

That year, Christmas Day fell on a Tuesday, which was exactly as Maddie would have planned it. After weeks of hectic arrangements, of shopping and cooking, of baking and wrapping, of mysterious conspiring and secret journeys, they would have two days to prepare for the onslaught of Christmas Eve. Whereas in previous years, Maddie had sometimes almost longed for Christmas to be over, just so that she could gain some relief from the frantic preparations, this year she positively welcomed them as a necessary and timely diversion for her and the rest of the family.

While she was so busy arranging and preparing, there was little time to think about her illness, and, she convinced herself, while she was constantly surrounded by flurry and bustle, no one would notice that each day the mere process of surviving from morning to night was becoming more and more of an ordeal.

In fact, Malcolm had, more than once, caught her unawares as she clutched at the edge of the table in sudden pain. And Neil, silent and unobserved, had watched her descend the stairs with exaggerated precision as if weighing each step.

Yet caring for her as they did, and knowing that there was no alternative, they all joined together in unspoken complicity, a loving but painful pretence that everything was quite normal.

The house was bursting at the seams, humming with industry.

Maddie, delighted with her enlarged and willing work force, strode purposefully about, directing operations, looking for all the world like a rather diminutive general on the eve of a vital battle.

Malcolm, surveying her iron rule with a mixture of fierce pride and barely concealed amusement, wandered aimlessly from room to room, trailing balloons and tinsel, sampling titbits and engaged in the extremely pleasant and rewarding task of watching everyone else at work.

And *how* they worked! Judy, having once made the decision to stay, threw herself with flair and enthusiasm into the job of cook, emerging from time to time with flour in her hair, to issue orders for more supplies. Neil found himself in charge of the Christmas tree, while Sue, taking over in the cleaning department, chased around the house hoovering up holly berries, bits of fallen tinsel and drawing pins.

Gordon was allocated the task of stringing up Christmas cards. Maddie watched him, precariously balanced on an armchair, as he juggled with a vast collection of cards. It was, she realized suddenly, the first time in several years that the whole family had been together for Christmas. She was loving every frenetic minute of it.

It was just a couple of months since her illness had been diagnosed, but it seemed like years. So much had happened since then, not just to her, though she knew herself to be at the centre of it, but to all of them. It was not that they had changed, for that word implied too drastic, too dramatic a reversal. It was more as if each one of them had come more sharply into focus, like figures drawn in magic ink, gradually becoming visible. She used to think that she knew them, but she realised now that she had only known them in part. She had learnt more about them in the last few months than in the rest of their lives. It was just ironical that it had been the shared knowledge that she was about to die that had brought them all closer together. But this, she told herself sharply, was no time for such gloomy thoughts. This Christmas, come hell or high water, she was determined to enjoy herself. Nothing and nobody was going to spoil it. The children and Malcolm seemed only too happy to go along with this. Her main problem was Angela Burrows ...

They had not seen Jack Burrows since the day he had stormed out of the house clutching his principles, nor had Malcolm been able to bring himself to discuss the matter. But Maddie and Angela, who had struck up an acquaintance before the incident, had gradually become closer after it. Maddie had been surprised and pleased to discover something in common with the fifth of Jack's wives, since her relationships with the previous four had been tenuous to say the least. Angela was different somehow; she had a mind of her own, and was not content to fit neatly into her husband's scheme of things like her predecessors. The two women met quite frequently for lunch or coffee, and soon established an easy, unstrained relationship. Until Angela raised the subject of religion.

Maddie had always found Angela a surprising woman – what Malcolm called a 'bit of a character' – but one surprise for which she was ill-prepared was the discovery that Jack's new wife was a Christian. Not an 'Easter Sunday, weddings, funerals and the occasional midnight mass' kind of Christian, but a believer, a fully paid-up, card-carrying member of the Church.

Maddie had nothing against religion. It had just never figured large in her scheme of things. It was somehow all bound up with the memory of school assemblies – standing in a mass of shuffling, untidy schoolgirls, nudging and pinching each other whenever the reading referred to 'loins', 'wombs', 'breasts' or – horror of horrors – 'begat'. True, she was still officially C of E; and there was the old embarrassed imprecation when things got particularly tough, the muttered mild oath, aimed at whatever deity might be unfortunate enough to hear it, and the occasional forgivable, but mercifully temporary lapse into sentiment at weddings, christenings and of course, funerals. But that, Maddie thought emphatically, was enough.

However, Angela was after her immortal soul, pursuing her with all the zeal and fervour of an old-style missionary, until Maddie began to feel a great deal of sympathy for that one black sheep, harmlessly minding its own blighted business, nibbling away at forbidden hedgerows, while the immensely worthy shepherd kept trying to drag him back to the fold.

Ever since Angela had first broached the subject, Maddie had been strenuously avoiding a second encounter. She had even pretended to be out when she called, but Angela's commitment was too strong to be that easily daunted. If Maddie could use tricks and subterfuge, then she could use them too. Eventually, she bluffed her way into the house and managed to engage not just Maddie, but also Malcolm in serious discussion.

It was just as well she was a tough lady, thought Maddie, as Malcolm, with his special blend of heavy sarcasm, acidity and low wit, proceeded to attempt to demolish her arguments. It was the 'jargon', as Malcolm succinctly put it, that 'got up his nose'. They made it all seem like a fairy tale – Noddy in Toytown, God in Heaven and Bob's your Uncle. Just like that! The sheer presumption of it made him scream.

'Listen to you,' he said to Angela, 'is like watching a

stained glass window. It's all there in primary colours: Hell, Fire, Damnation, Glory. You can still see through it, though.'

Angela wouldn't be put down that easily. She'd got a point she wanted to make and it would take more than a bit of leg-pulling to deter her.

'Faith in God, and in Christian fellowship, will bear you up, support you,' she said, her eyes on Maddie. 'Death's an unknown quantity. You must be afraid of it.'

'No, I'm not any more,' replied Maddie with confidence, and was almost surprised by the realization that it was true.

She *had* been afraid, at the beginning, had been consumed by fear, eroded by it, made incapable of action or reasonable thought. Fear had lurked behind her like a thief, stalking her in the dark places of her mind, hoping to catch her alone, waiting always for the moment to strike. But somehow, almost imperceptibly, she had built up her own resources, and, when fear found her, she had been able to battle with it, until, having proved herself to be the stronger, she knew that it could never threaten her again. But she had done it not through any divine intervention of 'Christian fellowship', but through the discovery of some fund of strength within herself, hitherto untapped – and of course, through the love and support of her own family. And that, for her, was as good as any religion.

Suddenly Malcolm felt that the discussion could go no further. 'You either do or you don't believe,' he pointed out reasonably. 'Conversion, like charity, begins at home, from an overwhelming need. Maddie and I tend to rely on ourselves and each other, take responsibility for our own destiny, albeit that your God has seen fit to call her number.'

'But it isn't *her* life,' Angela protested. 'It's *His*. What right have you to take it?' As soon as the words were spoken, Angela regretted them.

'It's all right,' said Malcolm calmly. 'Jack obviously told you. Jack would. He could never bear the weight of any secret on his own. *His* life? What right have we to take it?' He paused, then continued passionately. 'I won't insult you with starving millions, the basic malevolence of mankind to our Earth, the sick, the old, the lonely, all of them *His* lives . . . and you've heard it all before and the more you hear it, the less of a punch it packs. Christianity may have eased some of the pain, but it's done sweet fanny adams to root out the disease . . . the one described by our own stupidity, selfishness, greed.'

'Our fall from Grace,' Angela added, still not defeated.

Maddie, who had listened quietly to Angela's protestation and Malcolm's outburst intervened quietly, 'What right have we to take it? The right to spare those around the grief of watching me decay at snail's pace.' She paused, then asked, 'what would *you* do in my position?'

There was a long silence. Angela looked first at Malcolm, then at Maddie.

'Possibly even the same,' she admitted eventually, 'but with a lot less assurance. The important thing is to recognize the issue.'

'But I thought you were a Christian,' said Malcolm.

'I am,' said Angela, 'even on a bad day. And I also firmly believe that we should go up the pub and join the others.'

Malcolm nodded, smiling. 'Revelations. First line,' he said.

But that, as Maddie pointed out, was only half of the 'Burrows problem'. The other half, the long-standing and bitter silence between Malcolm and his friend, Jack, might well prove more difficult.

Ever since the quarrel, it had been impossible to mention Jack's name in the Laurie household. Malcolm, hurt and bewildered by Jack's apparent betrayal, could find no way to forgive him, no means to explain away what he considered to be a grave breach of their friendship. The man was a fool, a pompous hypocrite, and, he convinced himself, he didn't care if he never set foot in the house again.

But Maddie *did* care, for several reasons, not all of them easy to present to Malcolm. Firstly, the men had been friends for years. Surely, she reasoned, there must be *something* to be salvaged, even in spite of Jack's behaviour. Malcolm, she thought, was adamant *now*, but what about afterwards, when he could no longer rely on *her* companionship and support? How could he afford to lose a friend who, in spite of everything, knew him almost as well as she did?

And it was, after all, Christmas, when everybody swallowed their pride along with the mince pies; the traditional time for hatchet-burying. She decided to invite Jack and Angela to dinner on Christmas Eve.

Christmas Eve came, at last. Maddie, wearing a dark-blue kaftan and antique earrings Malcolm had given her on their last anniversary, wandered through the house in a pleasant daze. The rooms were a blaze of colour, every wall hung with tinsel and streamers, every corner filled with glossy green holly. The Christmas tree, standing massive in the corner of the living-room, was resplendent with coloured lights, golden bells and intriguing parcels.

In the dining-room, Judy had laid the table with a white lace cloth and arranged red and green candles around an old white tea-pot filled with holly.

From the kitchen came the tempting smell of roasting meat and the hissing and bubbling of vegetables.

Maddie felt like the queen of some prosperous and flourishing empire. The house looked beautiful and the family justly proud of their efforts. Only one thing was needed to make it a *perfect* Christmas.

When the doorbell rang, Maddie hurried to answer it. On the doorstep she found an embarrassed and somewhat contrite Angela, but no sign of Jack.

'Bit of a problem, dear,' Angela began, walking past Maddie into the hall. 'Jack's not here,' she said, fingering the elaborate confection of crepe paper and bells suspended from the hall ceiling. Maddie looked out of the window and was surprised to see Jack's car parked in the drive.

'But the . . .' she began, puzzled.

'Oh, *I* drove the car here,' explained Angela. 'I couldn't wait any longer. I hoped against hope he might be here.'

'Come in and see,' said Maddie, leading the way into the dining-room.

Angela took off her coat and followed. He eyes ran over the beautifully arranged table, the heavily decorated room, the huge logs roaring and spluttering in the grate.

'You've gone to a lot of trouble,' she remarked. Then, wandering over to the sofa, which was drawn up invitingly close to the fire, she leaned over and whispered, 'Malcolm? Come out, come out, you heathen!'

Maddie appeared behind her, cleared her throat theatrically, and offered her a gin and tonic. 'Slight problem, Angela,' she said.

'Oh?' said Angela.

'No Malcolm!'

Malcolm had gone to fetch Uncle Sidney. He found him waiting impatiently on the doorstep; there was no sign of a suitcase, but in his hand was a huge sack.

Sidney climbed eagerly into the car, dragging the sack after him.

'What have you *got* in there?' Malcolm asked, starting the car.

Sidney did not answer the question. 'This is the nearest I've come to being excited since the war broke out,' he chuckled, rubbing his hands with anticipation.

He settled into his seat and waited for Malcolm to begin talking. He knew, since Malcolm had come alone, it would be because he *needed* to talk. Just like his last visit in fact. The only trouble was it took him such a time to get started.

'You've come on your own then,' he said, trying to get the ball rolling.

Malcolm nodded at the sack occupying the entire back seat. 'It's as well,' he muttered.

Sidney tried again. 'If you can drive and talk, so be it. If you can't, pull in.'

'Stop seeing through me,' said Malcolm gratefully.

There was a pause while he wondered how to begin. There was so much he wanted to say. And somehow because it was easier to say it to Uncle Sidney than to anyone else, he had almost consciously been storing it up until just such an opportunity arose.

'What happens to me when she's gone, Uncle?' he asked, his eyes on the road; then, not waiting for an answer, added almost to himself: 'I had thoughts of joining her.'

'Well *you* would,' Sidney replied drily, 'seeing as you're such a miserable sod.'

Malcolm looked out, his eye caught a couple standing at a bus-stop. Their coat collars were turned up and the

147

woman was blowing on her fingers, laughing between blows, as the man hugged her tightly from behind in an attempt to keep them both warm. He looked away.

'I can see myself now without her,' he said. 'I'll be frightened,' Malcolm went on quietly. 'I can feel it now. Nothing will be familiar, not even the kids. They grow away and onwards. Imagine the house with no Maddie, bed with no Maddie, rocker, table ... I'm going to go quietly mad, aren't I?'

Sidney sighed. What the boy needed was a sharp kick up the backside, followed by a friendly pat in the same region to send him in the direction he was going in, anyway.

'I've an idea you've your whole future mapped out: remarriage, new house, new job, if they'll have you at your age. New country maybe,' he said looking at Malcolm out of the corner of his eye.

'No,' Malcolm's reply was adamant.

'So why are we sitting here talking about *you*?' Sidney asked, then provided his own answer. 'Because you feel guilty and want me to give you the OK.'

Malcolm looked more than a little confused. 'Some thoughts, yes ... general plans,' he muttered.

'General plans, eh? Oh well, there's nothing evil about them! Though why you have to call me in to buff up your soul I've no idea.'

'Because *you* don't count either,' retorted Malcolm, vastly relieved. 'Another miserable old sod!'

But he still had one other matter on his mind. 'Dinner at our house tonight,' he began after a while. 'The friend I told you about will be there. The one who'll rat on me if I kill her. We haven't spoken for months.'

Sidney shrugged. 'Could've changed his mind,' he said. Malcolm shook his head.

'He frightens you, doesn't he?' said Sidney. 'But not

half as much as the thought of her coming to you, open hand, open heart, and you funking it . . .'

'Right on the nose, mate,' Malcolm replied. There was a long pause.

Then Sidney turned to his nephew and said firmly, 'You won't.' It was a cross between a definitive statement and an order.

'Why not?'

'Because I'll be right behind you, expecting great things, a private display of supreme courage,' said Sidney grandly, then added, more in character, 'I'll tan your arse if you let me down.'

'But Jack?'

Sidney broke in impatiently. 'So you fell out! Maybe he's sorry too.'

'He has strong feelings about euthanasia.'

The old man waved his hand dismissively, as if to sweep Jack and his arguments out of the window and get on to more serious topics.

'Me an' all,' he said, irreverently, 'What's for dinner?'

Christmas, thought Jack Burrows, is a load of humbug. He was sure he'd heard that somewhere before, but couldn't think where.

The house messed up with holly berries and bits of tinsel; the wretched Christmas tree dropping pine-needles all over the carpet; everyone stuffing themselves with food till they got indigestion or drowning themselves in drink till they got a hangover. And the presents! Pretending to be delighted when somebody gave you an after-shave which smelled of liquorice; clapping your hands with glee at a silly little pack of hankies and a miniature screwdriver. It was all a waste of money. But by far the worst of it was the season-of-goodwill-to-all-men clause. How many Christmases when he was a child had he grimaced while long-lost aunties buried the hatchet for the day, simply to avoid shedding blood into the brussel sprouts? How many times had he heard people say, 'Well, it *is* Christmas . . .' as if that, in itself, were enough to counteract all the acrimony and ill-feeling engendered on the other 364 days of the year.

Angela had tried that one on, of course. 'Well, it *is* Christmas, dear!' She never called him dear unless asking him to do something she knew he was going to hate. Like making it up with Malcolm Laurie . . .

The pub, he noted, was full of idiots, falling about, toasting each other in anything from orange juice to brandy, making so much row you could hardly hear yourself think. Young people, mostly – some pretty girls, but all of them hanging on to scruffy, loud-mouthed student types . . . He looked up and saw Neil Laurie, beaming triumphantly.

'Drinking alone?' Neil asked.

'No. With the ghost of Hamlet's father,' Jack replied sarcastically, indicating the seat opposite him.

'How are you keeping?' Neil asked, not deterred. 'I homed in on you, specially. You know me; always a kind word for the disabled.'

Burrows sighed. This was *all* he needed. Wasn't it bad enough that it was Christmas Eve without having to endure this irritating young idiot with his excuse for a moustache and big mouth to make up for it. Still, might as well get it over with!

'You're working your way round to something, Neil,' he said.

'There was talk of you and yours having dinner with Dad and his. What happened?'

Jack looked up sharply. 'We fell out. Months ago,' he said. 'Buzz off, Neil, you're getting on my nerves.'

150

But Neil had no intention of leaving. Patting Jack's imaginary companion on the head, he sat down. 'Are you really going to let her die, knowing that the pair of you wouldn't even nod across the grave?'

Jack looked up, then looked away, quickly. 'I used to save you all my my foreign stamps,' he laughed. 'All of a sudden you're telling me how to run my life.'

Neil continued, undaunted, 'Even if the least you did was shelve it till after she's gone—'

'Shut up, Neil!' Jack exploded angrily.

'It's all right,' said Neil calmly, 'feel free to emote. We know all about you and her, the pride and the passion ...'

Neil, watching Jack closely, saw emotion spread across his face, uncontrollably, like a stain, then he played his best card. 'She asked me to come and get you,' he said quietly. 'Maddie.'

'I don't believe you.'

'On my mother's life,' Neil's expression did not change.

'Don't do that,' said Jack angrily. 'It's in very poor taste.'

'Oh,' said Neil, 'So maybe you *do* know how my father feels.'

'Of course I do,' Jack replied. 'Is he there?'

Neil nodded. 'You were the one friend he had, and you left him high and dry. We won't forget that.'

'You don't know all the facts; we fell out for good reasons.'

'Now's your chance to make nothing of them,' said Neil.

There was a slight pause. Burrows looked at Neil with surprise which gradually became a sort of affectionate gratitude. 'But you do know the main one? Stupidity,' he said, and putting down his glass, smiled across the table.

He would have to get a move on if he did not want to be late for dinner.

However, when, full of good intentions, he arrived at the Lauries' house, he was greeted not by Malcolm, but by Maddie and Angela. Malcolm was nowhere in sight. Suddenly, he wondered whether it had been such a wonderful idea after all, this game of kiss-and-make-up. Here he was, all ready to eat humble-pie and the blessed man wasn't even there. He wandered irritably from room to room, cursing and muttering while Maddie watched him with amusement.

Suddenly, there was a sharp tapping on the window. Jack stopped mid-sentence.

'It's Malcolm isn't it,' he said. 'He's been listening to every word I've said about him just to have the edge on me. Well, tough,' he called out. 'Go round the other way!'

He went to the window and, flinging back the curtains, revealed not Malcolm, but Father Christmas, furry hood, wellington boots, cotton-wool beard, sack and all, grimacing and making signs to be let in.

'It's Uncle Sidney,' Maddie exclaimed, and ran, full of excitement to meet him.

They greeted each other with all the genuine pleasure of great friends who seldom meet. Then, seeing Jack lurking in the background, Sidney pronounced, 'And *this* must be the high-principled big-mouth who plans to rat on young Malcolm come the day.'

Maddie smiled affably, as if she regarded that as a perfectly normal introduction. 'And this is his wife Angela,' she said brightly.

'Will dinner be soon, Maddie?' asked Jack. 'I can't stay long . . .'

'Be quiet, Burrows,' growled Angela. 'Follow me.'

She drew him, appearing for all the world like a rather well-dressed pig led unwillingly to market, into the living-room. And there, looking just as unwilling, stood Malcolm, with Maddie murmuring encouragement, at his side.

'Right, you two,' she said, swinging into action, 'We're going to leave you alone together for five minutes and when we come back we want everything to be over and done with.' Then, pulling Sidney by the sleeve of his scarlet tunic, she and Angela left the room.

The two men stood looking at each other for a moment. Then Malcolm, without speaking, went and poured two whiskys. Jack sat down on the sofa, warming his hands at the fire.

'You're looking old,' Malcolm said softly.

'Must be all that Scotch you're going to pour down my throat . . . yes please!'

Malcolm handed Jack the glass and looked down into his face. 'As a matter of fact,' he said, 'you look well . . .'

The first words were the hardest. After that, it was surprisingly easy. Malcolm had been prepared for awkwardness at least, or even further argument, but surprisingly he found Jack eager to revise his position. It was as if, having done that, he no longer had any patience with the views he had so forcibly propounded at their last meeting. Nor did he want there to be any other secrets between them, not that there was so little time left.

'You know I've fancied her rotten, as Neil put it, ever since I met her,' he said suddenly, 'She's one of the reasons I've been married so many times. They never compared to Maddie.'

Malcolm was genuinely surprised. But on reflection, it made sense – the missing link in the Jack Burrows story, you might say. He held out his hand. 'Are we friends again?' he asked.

'Suppose so,' said Jack and, reaching out, gripped Mal-

153

colm's hand. 'Put it this way,' he said smiling, 'my new accountant refuses to represent me.'

There was only one more matter to be settled between them.

'She *is* still dying?' Jack asked.

Malcolm nodded.

'And you still intend to . . .?'

'And you still intend to sound the alarm?' Malcolm asked.

Jack shook his head. 'No,' he said, 'You have my word on that.'

Malcolm raised his eyebrows. It was the last thing he had expected. After all, an apology was one thing, but Burrows had been *so* adamant – so convinced of his viewpoint.

Jack explained. 'I've just put myself in your position more and more each day . . .' He paused, then added with a wry smile, 'Apart from which Angela said she'd leave me, and I must get *some* continuity in my life.'

'Angela?' said Malcolm. 'I thought she was dead set against it.'

'She changed her mind.'

But, even if a peace treaty *had* been signed between Jack and Malcolm, Uncle Sidney was not prepared to leave any loopholes through which Burrows could slip. It was just a feeling he had, the way you sometimes get a feeling about a dog or another animal. It seems friendly enough; it licks your hand, fetches nicely; but somewhere in its eyes you see the possibility that one day it could turn and bite.

They had enjoyed an excellent dinner: cold cucumber soup, followed by roast-lamb with roast-potatoes, parsnips, carrots and peas. Uncle Sidney, still attired as

Father Christmas, had eaten well, but had insisted on needling Jack between mouthfuls, in spite of Malcolm's protestations that the row was over.

Eventually, as they finished up the last of a delicious chocolate mousse, he would be restrained no longer and launched into an emotional attack on Burrows which was, in effect, also a passionate defence of Malcolm and the way in which he planned to help Maddie end her life.

'He's going to help her,' he said, 'to spare her, himself, his kids . . . and me . . . the agony.'

Maddie tried to stop him from going on, but he waved her away, determined to say what was on his mind.

'So he does that . . . saves us all the agony, her the degradation. Maybe it offends your widely researched and privileged view of love,' he said, glancing first at Jack, then at Angela, 'and that's where your mouth jingles and you say, "I'll tell on you." To what end? Trouble for him? Miserable last days for her, bad liver for me?' He paused, then glared straight at Jack. 'You breathe a word,' he said fiercely, 'and I swear blind it was *me* who killed her, and I've nothing to lose.'

There was a moment in which everyone absorbed what he had said.

'If only we all had such an Uncle,' said Jack quietly.

After that it was time for it to be simply Christmas. The children arrived back from the pub and were amused to find Father Christmas waiting for them, complete with presents of amazing appropriateness.

Neil, tired of jokes about his slow-growing moustache, was delighted to receive an electric razor; Sue loved her silk scarf; Judy found it hard to understand how Uncle Sidney had known that the old enamelled brooch would be so exactly what she might have chosen herself.

Maddie waited till last for her present. It was wrapped, as the others had been, in a particularly non-festive brown paper bag. Sidney, she thought affectionately, knew all about priorities. She opened the bag and peeping inside, gasped with pleasure and surprise.

It was a lovely old dressing-gown, made of fine lawn, deeply edged in lace and threaded through at the neck with satin ribbon.

'It's beautiful,' she exclaimed.

'It was my mother's,' said Sidney.

Maddie turned the dressing-gown over and over in her hands, admiring its fine workmanship, delighting in its soft, yet simple luxury. She knew that Uncle Sidney had given her the most beautiful and precious gift he could think of. He was, she thought, an amazing man – a surprising man – someone who knew how to offer comfort and support without ever indulging in sentimentality. She was very glad that when 'the time', as he called it, came, Uncle Sidney would be there with them.

Afterwards, when the others had gone to bed, Malcolm found Maddie alone in the conservatory. He caught his breath. The day's exertions had obviously exhausted her. Suddenly he saw how very frail she looked, fragile even, her eyes burning with uncustomary fierceness in her pale face.

She looked up and smiled as he came in.

'This is our twenty-seventh Christmas,' she said.

'And not one of them was white,' he joked.

'And you still love me, don't you?' she asked.

'No more than usual.'

'Seriously . . .'

He came and sat on the floor at her feet; her hands rested gently on his shoulders, lightly stroking.

'You aren't . . . happy by any chance, are you?' she asked. 'Right this moment?'

156

'Hate to admit it,' he said. 'Yes.'

'Happy Christmas,' said Maddie.

He turned and, very gently, tried to pull her to her feet. 'Stand up.'

'No,' she laughed, protesting. 'You want the chair. It's an old trick.'

But he pulled her up all the same, drawing her to him.

'Can you hear the surf? Can you hear the surf booming?'

She laughed and shook her head.

'Nightjars?'

She shook her head again.

'Parakeets snoring?'

'Must be going deaf,' she giggled.

'In five seconds from now you'll hear it all,' he promised, and wrapped his arms around her.

Chapter 10

In spite of everything, or was it because of everything, it had been a truly *Happy* Christmas, thought Maddie. But New Year was proving more difficult.

She had never really liked New Year's Eve anyway, finding it even in normal circumstances a rather desperate attempt to sustain the jollifications just when everybody was beginning to wilt.

She had escaped upstairs to the bedroom where she was methodically smoothing out the creases in pieces of wrapping paper so that they could be reused next year. Malcolm always laughed at this, calling it her own private 'Save the Tree Campaign'. But she could see no reason to throw something away just because it had been used once, and next year, as usual, they would all enjoy trying to discover the origins of each parcel. She stopped, reminding herself. There was no need for her to worry about next year – perhaps even next month ... She finished folding the paper and placed it carefully in the wardrobe. She must remember to tell Malcolm where she had put it.

She could hear his voice now, exhorting the others to join in yet another game. What was it to be this time? A quiz or a treasure hunt, perhaps – or just a quick round of carpet bowls, an hour or two of Monopoly, a knock-out Scrabble competition. It was typically Malcolm, this frenetic burst of almost childish activity. It was safer than thinking, easier than doing nothing, and, while he could persuade everybody else to join him in his tireless pursuit of 'fun', then the party could not end.

Maddie smiled sadly. *She* did not want it to end either, but she knew that it must, and perhaps sooner than even he realised. After all, she had promised herself.

It was her eyes that bothered her most. Sometimes she could hardly see objects right in front of her face, sometimes she saw them in double vision, twin images, mocking her; sometimes only a blur of colours, vaguely moving shapes. And looking from the window, nothing – just the dim outlines of what she knew from memory to be apple trees, and beyond that, a total and terrifying blackness.

Even familiar faces now became indistinct – fluid, like pictures seen in water. She wanted to reach out and hold them, fix them with her hand, but they kept shifting, slipping from her grasp.

She sat down at her dressing-table and, reaching out to her own reflection, traced its contours with her index finger, carefully, like a child drawing on a frosty window. At least *that* face remained familiar – the same nose, the same mouth, the same imperfections and blemishes. Nothing had changed. But even as she looked she was forced to acknowledge a strange new tautness about the mouth, some new tension in the forehead, and, in the eyes, caught unawares, a sudden glimpse of the fear she thought she had conquered.

Shakily, she got up and went downstairs to join the others. Malcolm, as she had feared, had no intention of bringing the party to a close. He was wound up like a clockwork toy, tight as a coiled spring. It was impossible to talk to him as he rushed about the house and garden, distributing clues, plotting and scheming, dragging everyone else after him like some manic Pied Piper. And the .

others, only too aware of his reasons, did not dare object or defect.

Eventually, Maddie decided to intervene. Drawing Sue to one side, she asked her to help put an end to the frantic merrymaking.

'You see,' she explained, 'Malcolm doesn't want it to end because when it does everyone goes home and he's left with – well, a pretty grim prospect.'

Sue asked what she could do to stop him.

'You can be the first one who's brave enough to go to bed,' Maddie replied.

The plan was a success. Malcolm, busily announcing the rules of yet another game, suddenly realised that he had lost all his competitors. Sue and Judy had retired to bed; Sidney was fast asleep in a chair; Gordon was nowhere to be seen. Even Neil refused to be coerced. The party, as Malcolm was forced reluctantly to admit, seemed to be over.

He looked at his watch. It was 12.45. The New Year had come in as quietly as he had intended – no toasts, no kisses, not a single line of 'Auld Lang Syne'; they had not even listened to the chimes of Big Ben.

He found Maddie in the kitchen eating a huge jam sandwich. The sight of her struggling to fit the wedge of brown bread oozing with jam into her mouth was almost comic, but Malcolm was in no mood for laughing. Instead, he sat down heavily next to her.

'That's it, then.'

'That's what, then?' asked Maddie, humouring him.

'Christmas over,' said Malcolm.

'Been a nice Christmas ... nice New Year,' said Maddie, ladling another spoonful of jam onto her remaining crust of bread. Knowing how she always watched what she ate, he raised his eyebrows. She shrugged.

'That's one good thing about it,' she laughed, then reached out to stroke his arm. 'Thank you for making it all work – for frightening everyone into being cheerful.'

'Tomorrow they all go except Sidney,' he remarked miserably.

'I won't be sorry.' Malcolm saw that she meant it.

'I will.'

He watched her finish the remains of the sandwich, licking jam off her fingers with evident relish, then she reached out and began to cut herself another hunk of bread.

'Lovely bread,' she murmured ladling butter onto it with complete abandon.

'I don't know how you've managed to keep a brave face for a week,' he said, marvelling at her.

She looked up. 'No effort at all. I've enjoyed it.'

'Really?'

'Well, apart from the odd worry about you. Now are you going to cheer up or do you need beating over the head?'

He looked at her steadily for a moment. 'That sandwich . . .' he began at last.

'Want one?' She reached out for the bread.

He nodded, then saw that she was cutting two. One for him, she explained, and just one last little one for herself.

The next day, Uncle Sidney decided to plant some daffodils. He got up early, as usual, and went for a gentle stroll round the garden. It was hardly light and the grass was wet, sparkling with heavy dew. He found the box of bulbs, forgotten, in the garden shed and went inside to harangue Malcolm and Maddie. Did they, he asked, or did they not want a show of daffodils in the spring? He seemed to find nothing incongruous in the question.

Perhaps, thought Maddie, he was right. There *would* be a Spring, even if she was not there to see it. And if daffodils were to bloom, why should they not bloom in the Laurie's garden, as they had done every April for as long as she could remember.

She and Malcolm had got up late and were still in dressing-gowns, enjoying a leisurely breakfast of toast and tea, when Angela and Jack arrived. Angela took off her coat and made a beeline for the tea-pot.

'We come to prevent you both jumping off a cliff,' she said bluntly.

Malcolm laughed. He appreciated the sentiment even if the expression of it were a little crude.

'Kind of you,' he said.

'And yet now we're here, I don't feel terribly jolly,' Angela remarked. She gave Jack a none-too-gentle dig in the ribs. 'Cheer me up, Burrows. Make a fool of yourself.'

'Why don't you two boys buzz off somewhere?' said Maddie. Malcolm looked up almost too quickly.

'Go on,' said Angela. 'Don't hang about.'

Jack followed Malcolm into the study. They stood for a moment by the window watching Sidney, on his hands and knees, busy with his trowel.

'Should be a lovely show,' said Jack after a while. 'The daffodils.'

Malcolm turned abruptly.

'As far as I'm concerned, they can go rot,' he said. He walked over to his desk and began to tidy an already-neat pile of papers. Burrows watched him anxiously.

'A fit in the night,' Malcolm muttered. '*She* doesn't know about it, even. She fell out of bed.'

Jack nodded. 'Pearson could stop that, you know. Dammit, *I* could stop it.'

'Can either of you cure double vision as well?' said Malcolm sharply.

Burrows shook his head, then turned to face his friend.

'Look, I don't mind joining you in the gloom, but you must begin to think of yourself . . . and I'm the expert on that subject.'

Malcolm sat down behind his desk, and began to sharpen an already-sharp pencil. 'I've never thought about myself like that,' he said. 'It's always been *us* – with absolutely everything. She knows it too. It frightens her.'

'Never made any plans on your own?' Jack asked.

Malcolm shook his head. Perhaps it was hard for a man like Jack to believe, but it was true nevertheless. Jack had seen four wives come and go, and in all that time, he, Malcolm, had, without effort, remained faithful to, and utterly dependant on one woman. Everything he had ever planned or dreamed of, he had shared with her.

He looked at Jack, knowing how hard it must be for him to understand so single-minded an affection. 'God knows what I'll do when she's gone, Jack,' he said. 'Sidney threatens me with normality. What do you threaten me with?'

'My extensive personality and the fact that you'll go mad if you don't become more selfish. Take yourself back twenty years. When the kids were snapping round your heels, money was tight and she had less time for you than you're willing to admit.'

'It was never like that.'

'Of course it was!' Jack insisted. 'But not in hindsight. Because she's going to die it was all wonderful, it was all flute music and daisy-chains.'

Malcolm tried to protest but Jack would not be interrupted. 'No one reaches another person as fully as that. Human beings aren't made to blend into each other. You're kidding yourself. Twenty years ago there were times you could've gladly walked out on her.'

Malcolm shook his head slowly. 'She was, and is, everything I ever dreamed of. When she goes, I don't think much of me will be left behind.'

'Stop that! Always the romantic image of yourself, your marriage, your kids . . .' Burrows spoke sharply.

'Come on Jack,' Malcolm reasoned. 'You felt exactly the same way about her. Everything you ever dreamed of . . . How the hell do I kill her, that's what I want to know?'

Sometimes, in those long days and even longer nights, Malcolm felt sure that he was going mad. His nerves, stretched taut like violin strings, reverberated at the slightest pressure; his senses, made acute by constant watchfulness, plagued him with distorted messages. Everything was twice as large as life, poignant with an extraordinary and acute agony. He walked like a sleep-walker through a nightmare world, a landscape of harsh, discordant colours which burnt the eye, where there was no respite, no peace, only the constant reminder of pain.

And nobody could help him – not Jack with his strong words and tranquillisers, or Sidney with his simple wisdom; not Angela with her religion; nor even Maddie with her love. It was his own personal and particular hell and he would walk in it, lonely and terrified, till the day she died, and many days after.

But just as, in those days, Malcolm watched Maddie, constantly alert to the signs of her illness, all too conscious that each day brought with it a greater and more unbearable onslaught of pain, a greater sense that time was running out, so she watched him, but more secretly, reluctant to let him see how fearful she was for him.

And she reproached herself for allowing him to

depend on her so completely. As each day brought her a new awareness of her body's deterioration, she grew more anxious at the thought of leaving him, more determined to make some sort of provision for his well-being after her death.

For that reason, if for no other, she was grateful for the presence of Jack and Angela – Jack, because he was Malcolm's oldest friend, a relationship which seemed to have been strengthened by their disagreement and reconciliation, and Angela, because something in her independent, robust personality made her a not-too-sentimental leaning-post, a shoulder to cry on which would move discreetly away before it became too sodden.

When Maddie broached the subject, Angela accepted the responsibility gladly, knowing that it was important for Maddie to have at least the small comfort of knowing that Malcolm would not be lonely when she was gone. She could see how Maddie was struggling to convince herself that he would survive, even though she feared that he would not.

Maddie found herself strangely relieved to be able to talk to someone other than Malcolm. There was a growing tension between them, even in their most mundane conversations, a constant awareness that each thing they did might be for the last time. It was becoming increasingly difficult for them to really relax in each other's company, as if the knowledge of her impending death was a third presence, a silent intruder in every conversation.

Malcolm, surrounded as he was by all this caring, all this solicitous and affectionate concern for his well-being both present and future, found it difficult to accept so much overt kindness. He felt as if he was being swaddled in cotton-wool just when he most wanted to be exposed to the elements. His only hope, he believed, was somehow to live through the agony, to experience it with every nerve in his body. Like an athlete training for a marathon, he could not afford to become soft, to forget how to weather pain.

Late that morning, Maddie made herself a mug of coffee and went to sit in the conservatory. Her head was troubling her, as it did most of the time now, making it impossible to concentrate on conversation. Everything kept fading in and out rather like a badly tuned radio, so that it was really much easier to be alone and to focus on just one thing at a time, to think her own thoughts. Soon after, Malcolm observed, Jack got up, muttered something about looking for a book, and excused himself. Malcolm glanced at Angela, but she showed no sign of any reaction; instead, she continued to help herself enthusiastically to the remains of a large ham which was to be their improvised lunch. Ten minutes, he decided. He would give them ten minutes. Long enough for Burrows to say what he had to say, declare his undying love and all that stuff. Long enough for Maddie to pat his head kindly and send him on his way . . .

'So you wanted to tell me, you love me . . . before I go . . .' said Maddie, her eyes on Jack's face. They had disposed of the jokes, the laughing reminiscences, the half-expressed regrets. Now nothing was left except the unvarnished truth. 'Just in case I've not been aware of it all these years.' She added, smiling, 'well, I have. You're not very good at keeping a secret. It's been both comforting to my ego and a blight on my conscience.'

Jack sighed with a sort of relief. 'So now you know, and I know you know, and you know I know you know! But I still never *said* it, in twenty-six years! I love you, Maddie. So simple isn't it? To me, you're the most beautiful woman I've ever known, and one of the few people who understood and tolerated me.' Then, as if embarassed by his own declaration, he added, lightly, 'You're also a superb cook.'

Maddie was not yet prepared to let him take refuge in joking. 'Did it ever occur to you why I never gave you a reason to hate me?'

Jack shook his head.

'You never thought that a part of me ... a small part ... felt the same way about you?' she asked.

He looked at her with genuine surprise. 'No! How small?'

'Oh I can't give you a quantity, Jack,' she smiled, 'but rest assured that it was ... is ... still there. Every woman loves more than one man, even if the second is a figment of her imagination. She's lying if she tells you any different. The choice is so wide – husbands, sons, lovers ... in that order.'

'Why on earth did you never say?'

'Because I love Malcolm more than anyone else in the world,' she replied simply.

'But you carved your initials in me somewhere.'

She smiled. 'How foolish it seems at our age, and now that it's over ...'

'No,' said Jack emphatically, 'if you weren't dying I'd never have known, and, selfish as it may seem, that's one good thing to come out of all this.' He stood up, took both Maddie's hands in his. 'You're not kidding me are you? You wouldn't do that ...'

'Ask yourself,' she said softly.

'No ...' He pulled her very gently from her chair and drew her to him. How many times had he imagined this moment? How many other women had he held in this way without it meaning anything at all!

'I am your aging lover, and I claim my prize,' he whispered, 'I've waited some time.'

They kissed with the passion of those who know that their first kiss will almost certainly be their last, and broke away from each other only as they became aware of Angela and Malcolm watching them from the open doorway.

'The one and only time . . . I swear it,' babbled Jack.

Maddie sat down again, saying nothing.

Malcolm, showing no sign of any anger, shrugged his shoulders. 'It's me who should apologise for butting in. I'm sorry.'

Slowly Jack realised that there was to be no trouble – no tantrums, no tears, no recriminations.

'Malcolm,' he said 'let's you and me go and have a drink in a dark corner somewhere.'

Malcolm smiled. 'If you've loved Maddie too, then nothing but good can have come from that. Right now she needs all the love she can get. All I can say is that I've never felt your presence in my marriage and I thank you for that. Both of you. But whatever joy you managed to give her from a distance, I thank you for that too.'

'Thank *her* that I didn't try stealing her away,' said Jack.

'No need to thank her. She was just playing by the rules. Like I've done.'

Maddie was watching Angela, forgotten for a moment by all three of them. 'Angela? Are you all right?'

'Anything you say,' Angela replied, her voice icy, 'I'm just a beginner.'

'Come on,' said Malcolm, taking hold of her hand, 'Let's go and have some lunch,' and turning to Jack, added mischeviously, 'I hope to God Sidney didn't see you kissing. He'll plant you with those daffodils!'

*　　　*　　　*

'Malcolm . . .?'

'Mmm?'

'Oh, nothing . . .'

Maddie lay on her side, in bed, watching him. His arms were folded behind his head, his jaw clenched tight in defiance. He was determined not to show any emotion, but, incapable, as ever, of hiding it.

'You're not sulking are you?'

'No.' He continued to stare straight ahead.

'Well, it's just not on, is it,' she said gently. 'I mean Jack Burrows, hardly a mate for life as his record proves only too well . . .'

'Don't slander him now,' Malcolm said, tight lipped. 'It's unworthy of you.'

She sighed. 'You're making me feel guilty at every turn of the way . . . and you're enjoying it!'

'Don't slander me, either. Anyway, I was thinking of something rather different . . .'

'What?' she propped herself up on one elbow.

'That my self-confidence, where our love's concerned, is irrelevant.' He turned to look at her. 'I'd sooner you had a dozen lovers than an incurable disease.'

The words, even as he spoke them, surprised him with their truth. Just as he had been surprised by his own reaction on finding Maddie in Jack's arms. He had spent a lifetime controlling his jealousy, taking care never to reveal how deeply she could hurt him if she so chose, holding back sentiment for fear of seeming self-indulgent, using jokes and games to hide the depth of his feelings. But in that split-second he had been shaken by an emotion so primitive in its intensity that it had both terrified and amazed him. But more than that, it had shown him that he could still feel, that he had not been transformed into an emotionless zombie by pain and fear.

Love, thought Malcolm, was one of those things you never really analysed until it appeared to be in jeopardy. Yet, for the lucky ones, it seemed an infinite commodity: the more you gave, the more you found to give. Maddie had obviously loved Jack, after a fashion, for years, and yet that love had in no way diminished her total commitment to him.

And he, in spite of his truthful protestations of total fidelity, had still found room in his affections for others. For he too, as she had gently pointed out, had loved Jack, in his own way, as he had loved Uncle Sidney too, allowing both of them glimpses into his soul that even *she* had been denied. And then, of course, there was Gilly . . .

Yet, in spite of the love they had both found to share with others, or was it, perhaps he wondered, because of it, their love for each other had been inexhaustible, had survived everything – jealousy, anger, argument, absence, the passing of time; even the sombre threat of her death had not proved strong enough to destroy it.

He looked at her, suddenly discovering the words. 'I love you,' he said quietly. 'You're everything I ever dreamed of come true.'

'Right . . . Good night.'

She had not heard, or else had not believed her ears.

'Good night.'

Disappointed, he turned out the light. They lay a second or two in the darkness, silent, not touching. Then Maddie stretched up and, turning on the light, reached out for him.

'What a beautiful thing to say,' she whispered.

Chapter 11

Soon, Maddie began to think about saying goodbye to the children. It was not a question of *when,* for it seemed daily more apparent to her that she had very little time to spare. If she had ever been tempted to forget, with each day came a fresh reminder that her death was not simply a possibility but an even more imminent reality. She could tie her belt a little more tightly; she could apply a little more colour to her cheeks; but she could not hold back the waves of pain which seemed to grow even more intense, more ruthless till they threatened to dominate everything and exclude every rational thought. And there was still so much left to do. She was concerned as to *how* to leave the children, so that the parting not only contained as little pain as possible, but also so that each one of them was given the means to go on living after her death. Of course she had tangible mementoes she could pass on to them but they were somehow not enough; she wanted each one of them to inherit something of herself – some strength, some insight, some lesson learnt from her experience, so that she could feel that her death carried with it at least some positive aspect, some hopeful invest-ment in the future.

At first she had considered writing each one of them a letter, but that, on reflection, seemed too cold, too formal and calculating. Then she toyed with the idea of calling them all together and making a farewell speech, but that, even to her, had its comic potential. Somehow she could not see herself playing a Shakespearian death-bed scene without someone breaking down, and into tears of laughter rather than grief.

No, there was only one way to do it: face to face with each one of them alone, just talking quietly – no melodrama, no contrived speeches. And it seemed quite plain that Gilly must be the first.

It was a blustery day early in January. Maddie stood in the conservatory looking out of the window. Uncle Sidney and Malcolm were arguing about whether or not to fell the huge elm which for years had stood guard over the garden, and now, riddled with disease, threatened them with its fragility. A pair of magpies, oblivious of any insecurity in their position, perched high in its branches. She knew that they were magpies because they visited the garden each winter, but, in spite of the morning light and what she knew to be their sharply etched harlequin markings, they appeared to her now only as blurred shapes, a sudden flash of black and white which was then lost in the branches of the dying tree.

She turned away from the window, fingering the chain which she wore around her neck. It was fine silver, and on it hung a delicate oval locket finely wrought with a design of bows and studded with tiny rubies. Inside, there was a lock of hair, not fair like her own, but more tawny-coloured. It had belonged to her mother – a trinket which she wore on special occasions, on weddings and christenings, at Christmas time and on her birthday. Maddie had loved to play with it as a child, opening the tiny clasp to take out the silken coil of hair, stroking it gently, holding it against her cheek.

One evening, her mother had called her to her bedroom. She was folding away piles of silky underwear, laying sheets of tissue paper between the garments, placing lavender bags at the bottom of each neatly arranged drawer. Maddie had gasped with surprise, a sort of intuitive fear. The only underwear she had ever known her mother to wear were shapeless and utilitarian vests, a fierce-looking corset and armoured brassiere, oyster-pink voluminous pants, lisle stockings. And now this secret cache, this private hoard of finery, hardly worn, probably never seen or admired, took her breath away. She had said nothing, sensing something more profound beyond the systematic arrangement of the surprising garments. Her mother, too, was silent, finishing her task. Then, when the last garment had been laid in its drawer, she sighed deeply, as if with relief at a job well done, and, turning to Maddie, unclasped the pendant, which, surprisingly, since it had been no special occasion, she was wearing around her neck. She handed it to her, without speaking, and, silently, Maddie put it on.

A week later her mother had died, and Maddie had worn the pendant ever since. But today, she had decided, she would give it to Gilly.

Maddie had asked Gilly to come alone that morning, but on reflection, perhaps it had been an unnecessary request. All too often these days Gilly appeared, Beatrice Matilda in tow, with no mention of Nick's whereabouts. And, when they *were* together, Maddie, with her customary acuteness, had noticed a certain formality between them, as if it was an effort for them to relate to each other in front of others, difficult to maintain an air of happiness, of unforced intimacy.

The Christmas festivities had, of course, provided a useful diversion from any problems, real or imaginary. They had joined in all the preparations, all the fun and games, but she was sure that from time to time she had intercepted a glance, overheard a muttered comment, in-

173

dications of the fact that for her daughter and her husband Christmas was simply a breathing-space – that their problems were still pressing and unresolved.

There had been other men before Nick, of course. Not that any of them ever had much chance. Malcolm had jealously seen to that. But with Nick it had been different – a hundred times worse. For months before the wedding Malcolm had dragged himself around the house in an agony of silent but all too apparent misery. When she questioned him, he muttered something about Nick not being good enough, the old escape clause, but she had not allowed him much opportunity to elaborate on it. In fact, she had left him severely alone to grapple with his own emotions; there was nothing she could do to help him.

Perhaps she had been wrong; perhaps it would have been better to bring it all to the surface then, to challenge him with his own unresolved feelings of jealousy and rejection, to clear the air for once and for all. For everyone's sake. But she had been a coward: she knew that now. Gilly had married Nick with her father's public blessing, but in private he had never let her go. And she, entering into marriage with her father still hanging around her neck like the proverbial albatross, had simply regarded it as an extension of her cosseted and protected childhood. She said she loved Nick, whatever that was supposed to mean, but all her allegiance, her respect, her admiration was not for him, but for Malcolm, and, safe in the knowledge that in his eyes at least she could do no wrong, she was saved from the adult chore of taking any real responsibility for her actions. 'Hello, Mum.'

Maddie turned to see Gilly framed in the doorway. She was not, as Maddie immediately noted, looking her best. Her hair, usually her finest feature, looked as if it had lost touch with the hairbrush; she was dressed, not in her usual motley-but-effective style, but rather as if she had simply thrown off her clothes the night before and thrown them on again that morning.

Maddie had been preparing herself to be tough, outspoken, to give Gilly a piece of her mind before it was too late, but seeing her now, Gilly did not seem aggressive and prickly as usual, but slightly abject and vulnerable. She was surprised to find herself experiencing a novel reaction towards her daughter: not irritation or frustration, but a sudden surge of what she could only identify as compassion, and a surprising feeling of resentment towards Nick for allowing her to be unhappy.

They stood together for a while without saying anything of consequence, watching the men struggling with the chain saw. Gilly, who believed she knew why Maddie had sent for her, waited. Suddenly she caught her mother's eyes on her face.

'What are you looking at?' she asked.

'He should take more care of you,' said Maddie fiercely. 'You're a good girl – the best daughter I could have wished for and—'

'You sound as if you're about to say goodbye,' said Gilly.

Maddie turned sharply. 'Good heavens, no.'

'Good heavens, yes, Mum.'

Maddie shook her head, smiling now at having been discovered. Of course, she should have known better than to have tried to pull the wool over her eyes – Gilly was far too clever for that. Not that she let it show, of course. But that was one of the things she'd wanted to say. Putting her arm loosely around Gilly's shoulder, she led her into the living-room.

'So the problem is,' she said, as they sat down, 'how to say goodbye without really doing so.'

Looking at Gilly now, Maddie knew why it was that she had wanted to say goodbye to her before the others.

She had always thought that they were quite unalike – physically, emotionally, temperamentally, and that had created a sense of distance in her mind, which was only enhanced by the close liaison – some might call it conspiracy – between Gilly and Malcolm. But now she saw that there was a link between them that transcended all differences, for in her daughter she could see all the hopes and ambitions she had once had for herself before she had settled into married life with Malcolm.

She looked up at Gilly. 'You're the nearest thing to me I've ever met. You hold in trust all my old hopes for myself, all the ambition *I* once had.'

'Really?' Gilly was surprised.

'I wanted to be ... a teacher. Just like you,' said Maddie, watching Gilly's reaction.

'What's funny about that?' Gilly asked.

'And when you decided on it for yourself I was so pleased. Envious, as well,' Maddie paused, then added quietly, 'Don't chuck it away, kid.'

Gilly sighed deeply and began to rock herself to and fro in the rocking-chair. Her mother's mood had taken her by surprise, caught her off-guard. She had expected questions, challenges, recriminations even. But this new intimacy made everything so much harder. She had seen Maddie watching herself and Nick, had avoided her enquiring gaze on many occasions. But now that Maddie had come out openly on *her* side, as it were, perhaps it was time to speak of her *own* plans.

'Mum ...' she began softly.

'Yes, what is it?'

'Mum, I am going back to work again.'

So that was it. Or probably just the tip of the iceberg. Three years Gilly had waited for that baby – three years of longing and doubts, of tears and disappointments, and now, just months after the birth, she was talking of going back to work.

'I thought you'd be pleased,' Gilly said defensively, sensing her displeasure.

'What does Nick say?' Maddie asked.

'Nick doesn't know.'

It was exactly as Maddie had feared. It was not just a simple decision to go back to work but a much more complex assertion of independence. Gilly was not going back to teaching because of the money, or even because of the stimulation it would give her, but as an act of defiance against a husband who had somehow failed to measure up to her expectations.

She felt a sudden surge of anger at Gilly, an almost uncontrollable desire to catch hold of the girl and shake her till she saw reason. She had called Gilly to her to say goodbye, to give her a memento she could cherish, but it was not going to be as simple as that. Sweet words and reassurances were not what Gilly needed now – though obviously they were what she would have liked to receive. How could she stand by and watch her beloved – yes, beloved daughter ruin not only her own life, but that of Nick and Beatrice Matilda too knowing that she had had it in her power to avert the crisis. And how, when her own life had so short a time to run, could she allow Gilly to wilfully throw away time, love, self-respect, all in one unreasoned and unreasonable act of childish rebellion?

'You know your trouble?' Maddie's voice rose; Gilly looked up, startled. 'You've been ruined, not by me ... by your father.'

She saw Gilly swallow hard, shocked, uncertain how to respond, but now there was no going back.

'You're a bad-tempered, inflammable, ungrateful little bitch.'

'The best daughter you could have had, I thought – not ten minutes ago.'

Maddie jumped up and walked rapidly to the door.

'You going somewhere?'

'Well, I'm not going to stand by and watch you ruin your life.' Maddie flung open the door with an almost theatrical gesture.

'I should keep out of it if I were you,' Gilly's voice was thick with resentment.

'Then why did you tell me about it?'

'Because I thought you'd understand.'

'Understand? I understand that you ask too much of everyone around you and if you don't get it, you tear their ears off.'

'Then if I'm such a cow,' Gilly shouted, 'spare Nick the rest of his life with me!'

'I'm just going to see if he can do what your father should have done twenty years ago,' retorted Maddie, and stalked angrily from the room. She glanced in the hall mirror as she passed, and was surprised to see her eyes alive with suppressed anger, her cheeks flushed with a sort of excitement.

She found Malcolm and Sidney in the garage still grappling with the recalcitrant chain saw.

'Malcolm,' she snapped her fingers. 'Keys!'

'They're in it,' said Malcolm, not knowing what to make of her manner. She opened the car door and jumped in, starting the engine with a roar of the accelerator.

'Maddie, where are you going?' he asked, utterly bewildered.

'Ask Gill! Ask your kamikaze daughter. She's planning to leave Nick. I'm blaming you.'

'Really?'

'Is that all you can say?' Maddie began, somewhat recklessly, to back the car out into the drive.

178

'Given time I could say an awful lot—'

'Well, you're obviously hell-bent on doing nothing about it!'

'Again, given time I could do quite a lot.'

'Yes! Sympathise with her. Instead of putting her across your knee . . .'

'Always thought of you as such a calm girl,' murmured Uncle Sidney.

'Well, I'm finding my feet aren't I?' Maddie laughed. 'Cutting it a bit fine, yes, but better late than never!'

'Three clichés in a row,' said Malcolm. 'She *must* be upset.'

'Stop being such a clever dick and get in there and talk to your daughter,' Maddie growled and drove off at high speed.

'Drive carefully,' said Malcolm, almost to himself.

Uncle Sidney looked distinctly ill-at-ease.

'I'd better check up,' said Malcolm uncomfortably.

'Oh, something and nothing, boy,' said Sidney. 'She's trying to put the world to rights before she goes. That's the annoying thing about dying.'

Malcolm sighed heavily. 'Well, maybe I should anyway . . .'

Sidney nodded. 'Yes. You go on in and look after your favourite,' he said.

Malcolm looked up sharply, then, shaking his head, walked quickly into the house.

Maddie quickly covered the distance to Gilly's house, her mind racing. She knew it was very dangerous to drive in her condition, but this was important. Once there, she parked the car untidily outside the gate and ran up the drive. She knocked and rang at the bell simultaneously but there was no reply, although she could see lights burning at random all over the house. The back door was, as usual, unlocked. She let herself in and went looking for Nick.

She found him soon enough, draped untidily over an easy-chair in the living-room. His eyes were bleary; he had obviously not shaved for a week and his clothes looked as if he had slept in them. In his hand was a bottle of brandy, much of which had obviously already found its way down his throat.

'Well, Jesus Christ!' said Maddie, taking in the scene in all its unpretty detail.

Nick looked up unapologetically.

'How long have you been on this?' asked Maddie contemptuously.

'Month . . . two . . . Who knows? And you've come to straighten me out!' Maddie shook her head in disbelief as Nick continued: 'One thing I should warn you about: I used to be a pleasant drunk, but there seemed to be so little call for it in this house, I turned nasty all of a sudden. Understand?'

'Perfectly,' said Maddie with icy precision. 'And so have I.'

And she stretched out her leg and quite forcibly pushed him off his chair and onto the floor, where he lay looking up at her in injured surprise.

'Make as much as a little move, Nick, and I'll crack your head open,' she threatened.

'And she wonders why I say it's like living in a boxing-ring. Your daughter . . .'

'She's leaving you,' said Maddie sharply, before he could go on. 'I called her a fool. Remind me to apologise to her.'

Nick struggled to his feet. Maddie watched, exasperated, as he walked unsteadily to where she had placed the brandy bottle and poured himself a generous drink.

'Do you *love* her?' she asked angrily. 'Yes or no?'

'The unanswerable question, Maddie. If I say yes, you say then how can you bear to let her go. If I say no, you ask why and I have to invent reasons which have nothing to do with the truth.'

'I know the truth,' said Maddie harshly, interrupting him. 'You're an idle, feckless, irresponsible bastard.'

'I'm none of those things, Maddie, none,' he protested. 'I don't blame it all on her. Don't you blame it all on me.'

Maddie sat down heavily. This was proving more complex than she had imagined. It was not just a simple case of Gilly's thwarted romanticism or Nick's feckleness. Somehow the pair of them had found themselves land-locked in a situation where they could not support or communicate with each other, only grind against each other painfully, using their individual weaknesses as weapons which scarred not only the wounded but also the wounder.

It was, of course, a fatal combination: Gilly fending off her hurt with a barrage of insults, sheltering behind a wall of toughness; Nick, meanwhile, determined to bleed to death in full view of the whole world, using the drink as an easy means of justifying his misery, parading his own weakness like a banner, taking any escape route rather than meet Gilly full-face.

She let him talk, more than he had perhaps ever said before, admitted more, even to himself, than he had previously admitted. And as he talked, she again experienced the sensation, as she had more than once in the past months, that things were coming gradually into focus; and, not for the first time since she had realised that she was dying, she wondered whether that in itself served to heighten her perceptions of people and situations or whether it was simply a case of concentrating all her efforts on those things which she most wanted to be sure of before the end came.

Eventually, of course, the conversation turned to Malcolm. This was, for Nick, the hardest part of all, but Maddie knew that painful as it was, unless he could be encouraged to vent his feelings on the subject there would be no hope.

'It's *him* you should be onto about what's happening,' he exploded angrily. 'It's him that's deceived her ... cushioned her. She thought marriage would be peaches and cream all day long. And if it turned out rough, well no doubt he could help her out of it and into the next disaster.'

In spite of everything, Maddie was surprised at the vehemence of Nick's attack on Malcolm. Suddenly she saw quite clearly what she must do to save the situation.

'Do you or don't you love her? Tell me, Nick,' she challenged him.

At first he was reluctant to answer, sensing a trap.

'I won't tell. Promise I won't,' she urged.

'I bet,' he muttered.

'I can't prove it to you, can I? If you don't trust me, that's the end of it, of course.'

'I do,' he said very quietly.

'Trust me or love her?'

'I don't trust you but I love her,' he replied.

'Right,' said Maddie, turning and walking purposefully to the door, 'brace yourself for a very eventful week.'

'It's all over,' Nick protested.

'Over my dead body,' said Maddie.

Maddie felt reasonably proud of her success so far. She had forced Nick to open out and admit to his true feelings; she had presented Gilly with a few unpalatable home-truths. Now all that remained was to confront Malcolm with the sobering fact that his indiscriminate and overpowering love for his daughter had slowly undermined her marriage, and to convince him that the only way to demonstrate his love for her in future would be by letting her go, as he should have done long before.

But helping to rebuild a shaky relationship was not something one could easily achieve in a few minutes. It would take time; and time was the one thing she had in very short supply. If only there was someone she could entrust with the responsibility of continuing what she had begun. Then she could die happy in the knowledge that she had done everything possible to safeguard her daughter's future happiness.

It was then that she thought of Peter Harrison. Looking back over the confused and somewhat bizarre events of that day in November – Nick falling about the place pretending to be drunk, Gilly crying her eyes out one minute and ranting and raving the next, Malcolm utterly bemused by the whole thing – Harrison seemed to emerge in her mind like a rock, an island of sanity, calm and quiet dependability.

And so she decided to make Peter Harrison the guardian of Gilly's happiness, knowing that she could entrust him without any fear that he would neglect it, and feeling confident that his special brand of unemotional but firm support would be help and a comfort to both Nick and Gilly, should they ever need it, after her death.

While Nick was reluctantly revealing himself to Maddie, Gilly had been pouring her heart out to Malcolm, but with somewhat more predictable results.

For every bad word she had to say about Nick, Malcolm added two or three of his own. Yet somehow Gilly failed to derive comfort from this litany of criticism; instead she was surprised to find herself defending Nick with one breath, while deriding him with the next.

'So you aren't happy?' Uncle Sidney asked from the doorway, where he had been listening unnoticed.

'I *am*,' she protested, wondering with an unaccountable sense of having betrayed something, how much of their exchange he had overheard.

'No you're not,' Sidney contradicted her.

Malcolm, furious at Sidney's intrusion into their cosy private world, walked angrily from the room. Sidney followed him, not to be deterred.

'I think it's time you went home, Uncle,' said Malcolm, making no attempt to hide his anger.

Sidney was unmoved. 'I'll ignore that remark in case you think you meant it,' he said.

'You've become the complete ruin of privacy in this house,' said Malcolm bitterly. 'You're everywhere. The face at the window, the ear at the keyhole ...'

'Guardianship, that's all it is,' said Sidney, quite undeterred by Malcolm's tone.

Malcolm turned in disgust and was about to march out of the kitchen, but Sidney caught him by the sleeve.

Malcolm shook his arm free. 'Let go of me!'

'You've verged on the wicked, boy,' said Sidney, his voice low. 'Do you know that? Not a word I use lightly.' Malcolm looked up sharply, about to defend himself, but Sidney carried on remorselessly. 'Gilly came to you because this time she wanted to hear the opposite version to her own. Couldn't you see that? She wanted you to contradict her, in the nicest possible way, but you agreed with her as you've done for twenty-five years. So he's a jobless drunk! That doesn't make him the lowest form of life. But you went to town on him, and she didn't want that. Stood out a mile to an impartial observer, even through a keyhole!'

Malcolm shook his head, but said nothing, knowing his Uncle well enough to realise that he was in no mood for being argued with.

'So now she's left in a right quandary,' Sidney continued. 'Her own feelings versus Father's opinion. And up till now, Father's always won.'

There was a pause while Malcolm eyed his Uncle sullenly without speaking.

'Better set it right,' said Sidney quietly.

'I'm going to, I'm going to,' said Malcolm rattily.

He found Gilly alone in the spare bedroom. She was sitting awkwardly on the narrow bed, gazing out of the window, but seeing nothing.

It was a poky room, he thought, looking round as he entered, though once, when it had been Gilly's bedroom, he had thought it pretty and cosy. He remembered it as it had been when she was a child: candy-striped wall-paper a pink duvet and her collection of shells and interesting stones arranged on the window-ledge. Now it was full of empty boxes, piles of books, bags of clothes collected for jumble, and the wall-paper, once fresh and vivid, had faded noticeably.

'It's a joke isn't it,' he said as lightly as he could. 'Girls return to their old bedrooms to find them full of junk.'

Gilly looked around her and smiled weakly.

'Gill, I've done a dreadful thing,' Malcolm began . . .

Maddie had called into the police station to see Pete Harrison on her way home and had, without undue fuss or ceremony, assigned to him the responsibility of keeping an eye on Nick and Gilly after her death. He, as she had known he would, had accepted the brief in the same spirit as it was given.

Then, feeling somewhat more at peace with herself, she had returned to fit the final piece into the jigsaw.

She found Uncle Sidney sitting calmly in the rocking-chair flicking through the pages of *Country Life*.

'Got it sorted, then?' he asked, not looking up.

'Do you have the whole country bugged or just this house?' asked Maddie, not sure whether to be pleased or dismayed at the old man's omniscience, then added, by way of explanation, 'I've recruited some help.'

'It may not be necessary,' he answered, pointing towards the ceiling. 'Malcolm's with her now ... explaining that young Nick isn't a bad example of the species. But will he point out the crucial thing about Gill? No. *You'll* have to do that.'

'Just point me in the right direction,' said Maddie.

'Few outsiders know that underneath that vicious tongue of hers lies a rather nice young woman,' said Sidney.

'You think so?'

'I know so. But I'd still like her to prove me right.'

Maddie made her way upstairs and found Gilly where Malcolm had left her. She sat down next to her on the narrow bed.

There was no need for her to ask what had passed between her and her father. For whatever had been said, it had left Gilly both chastened and strangely quiet – calm almost, as if she had been buffetted by a long and terrible storm and now felt at once battered and yet relieved to find that somehow she had survived.

'You *are* ... you really *are* everything I could have wished from a daughter,' said Maddie.

Gilly looked up, shook her head, bewildered. 'I get this

feeling that everyone's being worked by Uncle Sidney,' she said.

'He says you've got a sharp tongue which hides the rest of you from us. Is that true?'

'Does anyone think well of me today?' Gilly asked, her voice almost pleading.

'Yes,' said Maddie. 'Nick. He loves you.'

'You asked him?'

'Of course. Try asking him yourself.'

'Since there's nowhere else for me to go I shall probably have to,' said Gilly and she breathed out with something which seemed to Maddie to be akin to relief.

Maddie stood up and undid the clasp on her locket. 'I wanted to say goodbye to you, you were right about that. But I also wanted to give you something, not for what it is, but because it's mine. And my mother gave it to me in rather similar circumstances.' She held the locket out to Gilly. 'Will you have it?'

Gilly took it, her eyes never leaving her mother's face.

'You've been good to us, Mum,' she began. 'You've done everything we could have wished ... but you did it twice as passionately, twice as lovingly as anyone else ...'

Suddenly, without speaking, Maddie reached out and gripped Gilly's hand hard, holding it firmly between her own. It was a strange, uncharacteristic gesture, but one which was far more expressive than any words she might have chosen – a token of compassion, of understanding, of mutual support, of strength, and of the unique and strenuous love which each had demanded of and received from the other.

'Now I think it's time you were going home,' she said.

Chapter 12

At first, in those short wintry days, Malcolm found it hard to accept that Maddie was really dying.

He watched her constantly, but in secret, afraid to seem over-anxious in his solicitude, trying to convince himself that he could see no outward sign of any further physical deterioration. He could not detect in her her mood any obvious note of depression or hopelessness. She seemed to him to be the same Maddie, but perhaps even *more so* – *more* beautiful, *more* full of energy and wit, *more* aware of the needs of others – in short, more compassionately and vibrantly *alive* than he had ever known her.

Then came the fit. Oh, there had been others, of course, but never one to approach this in either duration or intensity.

They had gone to bed early, as they often did, and, after reading, chatting and dozing, had dropped gently off to sleep. Malcolm was awoken, as he had been before, by that terrifying hoarse grunting.

'Maddie,' he urged, 'Maddie, stop it! Maddie ... please! Please stop it!'

But he could not reach her. The grunting continued on and on, accompanied by the rhythmic thrashing; finally, before he could do anything to save her, she had fallen out of bed onto the floor, where she lay, comatose, completely still, beyond his reach.

He would, he told himself, make little of it, as usual – try to turn it into some kind of poor joke, hiding from her his own terror. But he knew that this time it was worse. The comfort he had derived from convincing himself of her apparent normality vanished in an instant; it had been, after all, an illusion – a hollow comfort he had been stupid enough to allow himself. Now he was forced, whether willing or not, to accept the cold reality of her impending and unavoidable death.

But there was, as it happened, no opportunity for any deception. When she began to recover consciousness, it was with an almost instinctive awareness that this time she had weathered a major crisis. She felt depleted, spent, as if she had been physically battered by an unknown and merciless assailant.

She could see nothing clearly – either with her actual or inward eye. Everything was blurred, broken up into absurdly recurring images, present and past merged together, in a jumble of distorted and hazy pictures, double exposures, as if someone had opened a box of bad old photographs and scattered them at random before her eyes, asking her to impose some order on their chaos.

Unknown to Maddie, Neil and Judy had arrived that night, soon after she had suffered the fit, having driven from Keele on their newly acquired motor-bike.

Malcolm, not wishing to induce panic in others, as well as in himself, had omitted to mention what had happened, hoping that, by the time they saw her, she would have recovered sufficiently for it not to be too apparent.

In the morning, he told them that she was tired and wanted to lie in. But Neil, vaguely suspicious at his mother's unprecedented indolence, insisted on seeing her.

'Mum, Mum, are you awake?' he called, pushing open the bedroom door.

Maddie sat up quickly and made a frantic attempt to pull her hair into place.

She looked terrible – worse than Neil had ever seen her look before, sort of crumpled, unnaturally pale, disordered, as if someone had tried, with a certain measure of success, to erase her features.

He said nothing, allowing himself, instead, to be harangued about the dangers of motor-bikes. It was easier than talking about her. Certainly easier than saying goodbye, which he knew instinctively she was preparing to do.

Over the next few days Maddie tried on several occasions to speak seriously to Neil, but somehow it never worked. She formed the words in her head, rehearsing them in their every inflection, waiting for the right moment. But just as she thought she had acquired sufficient courage to begin, she would look at Neil and see, not a reasonably self-possessed young man of twenty, but that hurt and bewildered child with the grazed knee, the little boy on whom bigger boys picked at school. He was still her *child*, her protected and much-loved youngest, and she simply could not bring herself to leave him.

Uncle Sidney, in his self-appointed role as guardian of the family, was keeping a weather-eye on everybody's mood and, in particular, on Maddie. He had been watching her for several days now, and was only too aware of her inner struggle. Finally, realising that it was not a problem she would ever be able to solve alone, he decided to intervene and solve it for her. If she could not bring herself to confront Neil and say what had to be said, then he would have to speak to Judy and ask for her help . . .

Judy found Maddie sitting up in bed, still looking pale

190

and drained, but sufficiently recovered to be glad of a visitor to relieve the monotony of being alone.

She sat down on the end of the bed, noting with some surprise how relaxed she felt in Maddie's company. Maddie, for her part, pushed away the uncomfortable memory of their earlier exchanges, and looking now at this young woman whom she had made the object of so much resentment, found herself facing someone whom she was positively glad to be able to regard as a friend and an ally.

Suddenly it seemed to her that perhaps the easiest and kindest way to say goodbye to Neil was by *not* saying it, that the best gift she could give him would be a sort of tacit and long overdue acceptance of his adult status. Perhaps the idea of a farewell scene was, after all, rather self-indulgent – for *her* benefit, rather than his.

She turned to Judy, voicing her thoughts aloud, 'I wanted to say so much to him. You know the kind of thing. About how much joy he'd given me, how much he'd made me laugh, how much he'd made me feel so ... worthwhile. He does that to people. Treats them with respect until they feel a sort of pride in their existence. But maybe it's best not said – a heavy load of sentimental rubbish to chuck at a twenty-year-old ...man.'

Judy smiled, reading between the lines.

'So I chuck it at you,' said Maddie. 'Look after him for me. Look after yourself. Drive carefully ...'

She could not permit herself to say much more, but just as Judy was about to leave the room, she called her back. 'Judy, I wanted to give him this ... Neil I mean. Will you make sure he gets it? I can't do it, myself.'

'What is it?'

With a brave attempt at casualness, Maddie drew a ring from her finger and handed it to her. 'Just this. A ring my father had. I put it aside for Neil the day he was born,

Judy took the ring and examined it in silence.

'And there's a brooch on the dressing table,' said Maddie. 'That's for you. You stood him on his feet. I'll always be grateful for that. Or would . . .' she added, her voice tailing away.

Judy took the brooch, holding it together with the ring in the palm of her hand. Still, she said nothing. Then, as if surprised at her own intensity of feeling, she pushed both gifts unceremoniously into the back pocket of her jeans, and hurriedly left the room, in search of Neil.

Uncle Sidney had been engaging in secret machinations. It was Judy who had first given him the idea. What everyone *really* needed in his opinion was something to raise their spirits – a bit of glamour and excitement to lift them out of the state of despondency into which Maddie's rapidly-deteriorating health had suddenly plunged them. Farewell speeches and presents were all very well, in their own way, but they were nobody's idea of fun. What would do them all a lot more good was to get dressed up in all their finery – to get out of the house and have a jolly good feed, something to drink, a bit of a laugh, and blow the expense! He would pay, himself.

That evening, the house closely resembled the dressing-rooms of a theatre before a gala performance: Malcolm, without a murmur of his customary reluctance to get dressed up, emerged in his best suit, sporting a rather jazzy tie, like a banner proclaiming a change of mood; Judy made this what she described as the 'annual appearance' of her legs, complete with high-heeled shoes. Neil, rummaging in his wardrobe, discovered both a jacket and a white shirt, and decided to surprise everyone by wearing them.

Even Uncle Sidney, delighted with his role as the protagonist of this pleasing little drama, appeared at seven o'clock, immaculate and amazingly dapper in a well-pressed pair of trousers, a *proper* jacket, and a collar and tie.

Maddie had at first protested that she was not well enough to go out, but had been persuaded into changing her mind by a combination of her reluctance to disappoint Sidney and a desire to see the family enjoy themselves in spite of everything.

She was sitting at her dressing-table, carefully applying make-up when she saw, in the mirror, the reflection of a remarkably suave and sophisticated-looking Neil. At first she thought she was imagining things again, summoning up apparitions from her overworked imagination. Then he moved towards her, holding up his ring finger to enable her to see that he was wearing the ring she had given him.

She turned, surprised. 'I didn't mean you to have it now . . .' she began, but he cut across her, his voice full of an unaccustomed authority.

'*You* may find it difficult to say goodbye,' he said. '*I* don't . . . Or rather I'd like to say it however much it costs.'

Maddie caught her breath, and returned to applying her make-up with a sort of desperate precision.

'Shall we start at the beginning?' Neil asked, then, without pausing, answered his own question. 'Yes, why not! Thanks for the beginning; thanks for the feeling that I'm someone, not just anyone. I'm sorry I put the frog in your coat pocket in 1968. It seemed funny at the time. Not really sorry for much else . . . I couldn't have had a better mother. You've been in my mind more than anyone else I've known. I'm sure it'll continue that way ...'

He held out his hand to her and she took it, allowing him to draw her to her feet. Then he kissed her, and she held on to him tightly, knowing as she did so, that she was saying a last goodbye to the child and greeting, for the first time, the man who was her son.

'My favourite,' she murmured, half-seriously, half in play, 'my favourite in all the world. Only please, please, never tell a soul ...'

He went downstairs to meet the others, waiting expectantly, in the hallway. Uncle Sidney, impatient as ever, consulted his watch and despaired of them ever reaching the restaurant at all.

There was an air of tension, a high-pitched excitement at the audacity of their action. For Maddie was dying ... and they were somehow flying in the face of it.

Then, as if at a secret signal, everyone fell silent, following Sidney's eyes as he looked upwards. There at the top of the stairs stood Maddie. She had dressed carefully, choosing an outfit which in some way disguised her palour, and her face seemed to glow with a new, and special vitality. She paused for a moment, as if for greater effect, as if letting them see and believe what they all most dearly wanted to see and believe – that not only was she still alive, but that she was still somehow miraculously and triumphantly beautiful.

Then slowly, but with great confidence, she descended the stairs to join them.

The telegram from Gordon arrived a few days later. It read: 'PLEASE BE IN HERNE BAY FRIDAY 21 STOP BRING SID STOP STAY WEEKEND STOP'.

Malcolm read it several times before exploding angrily.

After all that had passed between him and Gordon, nothing had changed. He wondered what on earth had allowed him to persuade himself that things could be different, that Gordon could ever be anything but a pompous, selfish, egotistical . . .

Maddie listened to his rantings with a mixture of irritation and amusement, as they packed for the weekend. She had to admit that the telegram *was* terse, that Gordon had offered no explanation for his request. But something which she could not explain with logic told her that what lay in store for them at the end of their journey to Herne Bay, might well prove to be a pleasant surprise – an end which would somehow justify the typically uncompromising means by which Gordon had summoned them to his presence.

They set off very early in the morning. It was a cold, bleak day, a day on which the sun made no attempt to penetrate the heavy barrier of grey cloud which threatened snow. But Maddie, ensconced in her warmest coat and fur-lined boots, was charged with the anticipation she had often felt when, as a child, she had embarked on mysterious journeys, knowing that some delightful and lovingly prepared treat lay in store at the other end. And she hoped, as she did now with increasingly regularity, that today would be one of her better days, with sufficient respite from pain to enable her to enjoy whatever awaited her.

They arrived at Herne Bay to find their hosts obviously not long out of bed and still attired in pyjamas and dressing-gowns. This, of course, only served to increase Malcolm's irritation.

'You know what they've been doing while we've been flogging it down slippery roads, don't you?' he remarked caustically to Maddie, when Gordon and Sue had hurried off to get dressed.

'Yes I do,' said Maddie, smiling.

'What?' asked Uncle Sidney, all innocence.

'And you know, too,' Malcolm snapped. 'Oh God, it's another age! He tells us what time to be here and when we arrive almost on the dot, he's not bloody ready for us. Would I have done that to *my* father?'

'Why are you whispering?' asked Sidney. 'You're frightened he'll hear you, aren't you?'

'I'm not frightened of him, mate, I can tell you. I shall have to have a word with him,' said Malcolm threateningly.

Maddie sighed in desperation. Sometimes Malcolm could be so obtuse.

'If it isn't obvious to you why we're here, then I despair,' she said.

Malcolm jumped. 'He's told you? Well, he would. Tell me, though? That's quite a different matter ... that'd be *polite.*'

'He hasn't told me,' said Maddie as patiently as she could, 'but I haven't been boiling inside since I left Oxford, so I'm a little more receptive to details.'

'You'd better fill us in then,' said Malcolm.

'No. You owe it to yourselves to work it out.'

Malcolm shook his head, completely puzzled. Maddie, taking pity on him, stretched out to the table and picked up Sue's handbag: it was brand new. Under the table were a pair of matching shoes, also brand new.

'There'll be a new dress too.' She watched with vast amusement as realisation slowly spread across Malcolm's face.

'Oh no,' he said.

'What?' Sidney was a little slower to catch on.

'They're getting married,' said Malcolm. It was not, he

thought with sudden and unexpected satisfaction, going to be such a bad day, after all.

But if Malcolm was pleased at the thought of a wedding, Maddie was absolutely delighted.

She found Gordon in his bedroom putting the finishing touches to his already smart and festive appearance. Coming up close behind him she reached out to touch his cheek.

'Oh Gordon,' she said, 'what a kind man you are. I know you wouldn't marry her if you didn't love her, but to make it so soon . . . for me . . .'

'My way of saying goodbye,' he said.

'Yes,' said Maddie quietly. 'Will you live here, in this flat?' she asked, then answered her own question, 'No, I suppose you can't, not if you plan to have kids. Well, *I* plan you to have kids! Where, then? Are there any nice houses round here?'

Gordon stopped combing his hair.

'There are nice houses in Oxford, too,' he said without undue emphasis.

'You're coming back?' Her voice rose with excitement. 'For him?'

Gordon nodded. 'I'm chucking it in here because I want to be near the old man. And Sue . . . she's got no family but this one, God help her! It's for our sake as much as his. One forgets how nice it can be, how stabilising to turn to your old man for advice, listen to him spout a stream of rubbish, then go and do the opposite. Comforting. He may need me, too, more than he thinks. They all might . . . we'll see. But my guess is he'll be the first.'

Maddie was delighted with the news of Gordon's decision. If he had wracked his brains to think of the one gesture which would give her the greatest pleasure and peace of mind, he could hardly have thought of anything more appropriate.

Not only did it comfort her immensely to feel that Malcolm could rely on the support of his elder son when he would, she knew, most need it; it was also an immense relief to her to be able to feel that the life-long battle which had been waged between Malcolm and Gordon had, at last, found a peaceful resolution, in an arrangement which would be of immense benefit to them both.

'So where's my present then?' said Gordon, holding out his hand. 'Neil and Gilly got a present . . .'

Maddie smiled and reached into her handbag. In the excitement of the moment, she had almost forgotten.

She took out a small leather pouch and handed it to him. Intrigued, he opened it and drew out a gold watch on a chain. He looked at it admiringly.

'For those days in court when you fancy strutting around a bit,' said Maddie. 'It's terribly corny, but it was my father's and therefore goes to you. I hope it will help you remember me on this particular day, how happy I was.'

Gordon looked up.

'Don't need a watch to remember you,' he said. 'Does it do for weddings?'

'That's just about all it's known for the last fifty years. And funerals.'

He looked at her sharply.

'Sorry,' she said lightly, 'forget I said that.'

He reached out and took her hand. 'You're looking good,' he said softly, hoping that he sounded convincing, 'a space flight away from *anyone's* funeral.'

'Nevertheless,' said Maddie, 'We'd better say goodbye.'

He lifted her hand to his lips and kissed it. 'Goodbye,' he said, very softly.

*   *   *

It was a quiet wedding, but that was exactly what Gordon and Sue had planned, and as Maddie, given the particular circumstances, would have wished it. There were no formal speeches, only Malcolm's gruff, but nevertheless sincere congratulations, and Sue, looking confident and relaxed in an informal dress, was still as happy as any bride complete with veil and white gown.

Uncle Sidney, who had to admit a sneaking delight in all special occasions, insisted on appearing in every one of the many photographs, as if the event could somehow only be sealed by the eternal proof of his smiling presence. Malcolm, watching his antics as he gladly made an utter fool of himself for everyone's benefit, wondered how they would have been able to survive the events of the last months, had it not been for Uncle Sidney. For, by being himself at all times, by refusing to do anything to modify his eccentric, uncompromising, busybodying behaviour, even in the face of Maddie's illness, his uncle had somehow given them all a sense of proportion and helped to keep them if not sane, then at least as sane as he was.

Malcolm smiled to himself, wondering if he would ever be able to convey his appreciation to the old man, knowing that the last thing Sidney wanted was to be involved in sentimental demonstrations of gratitude, however, heartfelt. He had tried thanking him on various occasions, but without success. Perhaps, like so many aspects of family life, it was simply one of those things which would have to be taken as read, accepted but never commented upon.

And, at that moment, looking first at Gordon, then at Sue and, finally, at Maddie herself, he saw that there were simply no words adequate to describe the incredible and mysterious blend of love, fear, pain and delight with which each family gathering had been charged since they had learnt that Maddie was about to die.

They left the registry office and made their way to the restaurant where they were to have lunch.

Malcolm was amused to find that it was the very same place where he had caused such a furore on the day on which they had broken the news to Gordon.

They settled themselves at their table and began to study the menu. The waiter hovered solicitously nearby. Malcolm was feeling particularly hungry, which was hardly surprising as he had eaten nothing since he had grabbed a slice of toast at the crack of dawn. He decided on fillet steak, preceded by avacado with prawns. It seemed a suitably extravagant choice for the occasion.

He was just settling down to his pre-lunch drink, when he caught sight of Simon Anstey.

Ever since their first meeting in that very room, Malcolm had regarded Anstey as one of his least favourite characters. He still smarted at the memory of the man's slippery 'charm', his sarcasm and his unendearing egotism. He had hoped that their paths would never cross again but here he was, turning up to spoil what should have been a perfectly happy occasion.

Anstey slid up to their table, and smiled ingratiatingly but without warmth.

Gordon looked up unenthusiastically. 'Morning, Simon. How's business?'

'Good and dirty,' Simon replied with relish. 'How's the law? Still ruled by the letter?'

Gordon controlled an impulse to grab the man by his impeccable cravat and pull hard. 'No,' he said levelly, 'not even you can spoil today for me.'

'Why not?' asked Anstey, his voice harsh, 'you spoiled several for me.'

'Because I've just got married,' said Gordon. 'Wish me luck and we'll call it quits.'

'To Sue?' Anstey exclaimed. 'Your secretary? Who was it accused me of inhabiting a small world? Congratulations! Both of you.' He bent and kissed Sue, adding, 'I hope you'll be as happy as I am in my marriage. Do have a drink with me.'

'No thanks,' said Gordon. 'We're going in to eat.'

Hardly trusting himself to resist attacking Anstey in one way or another if he stayed, Gorden led Sue away to the dining area.

Anstey was not a man to be deterred that easily. Gordon had caused him a lot of bother when he had backed out of that deal and he was damned if he was going to let him walk away scot-free.

He beckoned to the waiter. 'I'd like to buy a drink for the happy couple,' he said.

'They *all* seem so happy,' said the waiter, still somewhat mystified by everything concerning the Lauries.

'Gordon Laurie and the girl,' said Simon impatiently. 'I'd like to send a little note with it.'

They were just finishing their hors d'oeuvres when the waiter appeared, smiling hugely, at their table, carrying a tray on which stood one glass of orange and two straws. He handed it to Gordon, together with the card with Anstey's message.

With mounting fury, Gordon read it aloud:

'Start as you mean to go on.'

'That's it!' he exploded, and was about to jump up when Sue restrained him.

'No, don't! What does it matter? It's Simon Anstey, a penniless wide-mouth. Ignore him.'

Gordon was pleased to agree. He had never hit anyone in his life and did not propose to begin on his wedding day. He would content himself instead with a sharp reply to Anstey's note. He took out his pen and wrote, 'Sorry that was all you could afford, but thanks all the same.'

He handed it to the waiter, who bore the message back.

That, as far as Gordon was concerned, would have been the end of the matter. But Malcolm, conscious of some strange and undefined sense of excitement, had some unfinished business with Simon Anstey.

He found him leaning against the bar.

'Why, Mr Anstey,' he exclaimed, 'what an unconfined joy to see you ... struggling.'

Anstey turned to him, his face breaking into a supercilious smile. 'People like me annoy people like you,' he said, 'because we always win in the end. Isn't that so? We refuse to go down under the weight of your moral iron. We make money, we screw the helpless for every penny they have, we crawl as low as we need to gain favour. And we never despise ourselves. This also confuses and vexes you ... just as it does your prig of a son.'

'I have a side which vexes me too,' said Malcolm rather quietly. 'It's the part of me which, in spite of everything I do, rears its ugly head under the name of revenge. I always put the boot in last.'

The waiter brought him the wine he had ordered and, as he picked it up, he allowed his hand to nudge Simon's drink, spilling it onto the bar.

'I'm so sorry,' he said, and, taking the crisp handkerchief from Anstey's top pocket, used it to mop the bar, before putting it, crumpled and wet, back into the same pocket.

Anstey clenched his fists in anger. 'You—'

'Please, please take a poke at me,' Malcolm urged. 'You'll have the shock of your life.' Then he added with a note of something approaching menace, 'Don't ever take the piss out of me or mine.'

He turned to go, would still have left the other man

202

unharmed, except by the verbal lashing, if Anstey had himself been able to resist a final jab.

'She's still alive, I see,' he called. 'How much longer?'

Malcolm spun round, his face white, his eyes blazing. Suddenly it all showed, the long months of anguish and frustration, the painful, drawn-out days, the lonely and watchful nights, the bitterness, the incomprehenion, all the fear and all the anger.

Blindly, he lashed out at the bewildered Anstey with a force and a fury which surprised them both. It was only one punch, but it left Anstey on the floor.

Then, amazed at what he had done, but filled with exhilaration and a strange and almost primitive sense of power, Malcolm turned and walked quickly back to join the others.

In Malcolm's absence, Uncle Sidney had been entertaining the others with one of his famous stories. Maddie, who had dutifully, and, not without enjoyment, followed all the ramifications of the plot, suddenly lost interest in its outcome as she caught sight of Malcolm, returning with the wine.

Even at a distance, something in his manner disturbed her, but, when he actually reached the table, she could almost *see* the tension, like static electricity, sparking off him.

'All right, dear?' she asked, although she already knew the answer.

'Yes, thanks,' he muttered, making himself exceedingly busy uncorking the bottle and pouring wine for them all.

She looked at him knowingly.

'I said "Yes, thanks",' he repeated with a certain irritation.

At the rear of the restaurant, Gordon could see their waiter engaged in earnest conversation with the manager. He glanced at Sue, hoping that his father had not done anything silly, today of all days. The two men ended their conference and the waiter made his way straight to their table, as if on an important and somewhat dangerous mission.

'Mr Laurie,' he said, leaning over Malcolm's shoulder, 'Your bill, sir.'

'I didn't ask for it,' said Malcolm, ignoring him completely.

'I think you did, sir.'

'I say no,' Malcolm repeated angrily.

The waiter's voice was reasonable but firm. 'It's either that or the police.'

Maddie jumped up.

'Where are you going?' Malcolm asked, but she brushed aside his question and walked purposefully to the bar, where, if she had judged the situation correctly, she knew that she would find Simon Anstey.

Anstey rose to greet her.

'What happened?' she asked tersely.

'He hit me with something a good deal harder than his rhythm stick,' said Anstey.

'I don't believe you,' Maddie replied.

Anstey smiled infuriatingly. 'Such is the nature of true love,' he murmured. 'A glass of something?'

Maddie shook her head.

'I like the local peasantry to think of me as sweetly forgiving, generous to the point where I offer the other cheek!'

'You provoked him, without a doubt,' said Maddie.

'Oh, without a doubt,' he replied smugly. 'But he hit me as if he were hitting the whole world, not just because I insulted him but because they're stealing you away. Is that about right?'

'He's been looking for someone to thump for a long time,' she said and got up to go.

But Anstey was not a man to resist hitting back and at a target as far below the belt as possible.

'I'll tell you something you want to hear,' he said quickly. 'I'm glad Gordon is leaving Herne Bay, for your sake. It's already getting to him. He treats other people as if they were there to be used. He sees life in the only way possible – himself as a thousand men in a straight and ordered line, the rest of us as one single idiot to be kicked.'

'You couldn't be further from the truth,' said Maddie.

Disturbed, in spite of herself, by Anstey's cruel analysis of her elder son, she walked back to join the others.

Gordon, who had watched the exchange from a distance, and had judged something of its content, looked across and caught Anstey's eye, thus provoking a further outburst.

'Gordon,' Anstey shouted across the bar, 'don't get lost in the mediocrity which is your father. He's forced your hand for twenty-five years!'

Maddie tugged at Malcolm's sleeve. 'Let's go,' she pleaded.

They all got up to leave.

'I guarantee your life, your marriage, your mind will all be in shreds within a year,' said Anstey with controlled viciousness, as Gordon helped Sue into her coat. Then, satisfied that he had wrought sufficient havoc, at least for one day, he turned from them and ordered himself another drink.

Chapter 13

As they drove back from the restaurant to Gordon's flat, the day, which had begun with so much laughter and optimism, seemed transformed into some sort of painful ordeal which must somehow be endured by them all.

Restricted within the confines of the car, they sat at first in heavy and uncomfortable silence, as each one of them went over the events in the restaurant, trying to make some sense out of what had happened.

Maddie, losing the control which had prevented her from attacking Anstey himself, now turned on Malcolm, blaming him for provoking the whole ugly incident.

They argued bitterly for several minutes, until Sue, who had, up to that moment, refused to become too involved, burst out angrily, 'And what about my marriage, eh? What about my wedding day? Nobody thinks about that! It's *my* day, no one else's. Not Maddie's. Mine!'

'I'll kill him,' shouted Gordon, invited to sudden fury by Sue's unaccustomed lack of control. 'I will! Look what he's doing to us!'

Malcolm accelerated to a breakneck speed as if he could somehow physically drive them all out of their present mood, but this only made matters worse.

'Slow down,' screamed Sue. 'For God's sake, slow down! I don't want to be married and dead on the same day.'

There was a terrible silence as if something unthinkable had been said.

'What's that supposed to mean?' asked Maddie, her voice icy.

'Death isn't your sole prerogative!' Sue retorted.

Suddenly Uncle Sidney, caught in the crossfire, could stand it no longer. 'Shut up!' he bellowed. 'Just shut up all of you!'

Surprised and intimidated by the sheer volume and authority of his tone, their voices died away, caught in mid-sentence.

'Stop the car,' he ordered. 'Stop it.'

'For God's sake,' Malcolm protested, but Sidney refused to brook any argument.

'Pull in there! Pull in!' he shouted, indicating an approaching lay-by.

Malcolm, who knew when it was wisest not to argue, conceded. He drove into the lay-by and the car, with almost audible relief, juddered to a halt. They waited, in some embarrassment, for Uncle Sidney's lecture.

'What now, oh master?' asked Malcolm in a last-ditch attempt at flippancy.

'We don't want a Sermon on the Mount,' said Gordon, trying in vain to catch Sue's eye.

But Uncle Sidney was in no mood for joking. It was all very well, this elder statesman role he had found himself cast in of late, but sometimes a man had to stop everything and shout, 'Enough!' as much for his own peace of mind as for those around him.

The last few months had been hard. Ever since the day he had first learnt of Maddie's illness, he had felt like a juggler who has to keep twenty plates spinning all at the same time and who runs from one to the next trying to avert disaster. Malcolm and Jack – now that had been bad enough; but Gilly's so-called divorce had been even worse; and now, just to cap it all, the entire family had gone completely to pieces just because of a jumped-up whippersnapper like Simon Anstey.

'One man,' he exploded, 'one stuffed piece of expensive tailoring has thrown the whole world into a corkscrew. Shall I tell you how it happened?'

They all looked at him.

'*He* didn't do it! Your world has shrunk to the size of a marble. We know why that is. We close ranks in a disaster. Fine! *But not so close you don't realise when your chain is being pulled.*'

Afterwards, Sidney felt very tired. Oh, they had listened to his remonstration, all of them. Perhaps they had even taken some notice. But it was a bit like walking through a muddy ploughed field wearing shoes that were too light for the job. You ended up feeling as if your legs weighed a ton and you couldn't put one foot in front of the other.

And what was the use when you really came down to it? You told them a few home-truths perhaps, but nothing really changed. People didn't learn; they just carried on in their own sweet way, doing what they felt like doing, messing up their own lives and everyone else's and there he was stuck in the middle of it all, like it or lump it, dispensing his pearls of wisdom, like some all-year-round Father Christmas. Thinking of Christmas reminded him how long he had been away from his own house, his home-brewed wine, his woods, his pheasants, and he was filled with a strange and potent longing which was almost like loneliness.

That evening, Malcolm, Maddie and Sidney returned to Oxford. Sidney spent the journey uncomfortably dozing in the back of the car, never sleeping properly but simply hovering on the edge of consciousness, half-listening to snippets of conversation, shielding his eyes from the lights of passing cars.

When they arrived home, the house seemed cold and unwelcoming and it was too late to think of cooking dinner. Malcolm volunteered to go out and get some fish and chips if Sidney would light a fire for the evening.

He quickly agreed, glad to have something practical to do. He fetched logs and coal, then busied himself with newspaper and kindling-wood, twisting the paper into neat spirals, constructing a fragile tower which would burst into flames with a single match.

He was convinced that Maddie was watching him, felt sure that she must sense his change of mood and detect in it some kind of subtle betrayal.

'Uncle . . .'

He did not look up but continued to balance small pieces of coal on the struts of his precarious edifice.

'Still love us?' she asked, lightly touching his arm as if to convey sympathy for him in whatever battles he was silently waging.

'Fair bit . . .'

He turned from the thriving fire to look up at her.

'It's soon, isn't it?' he asked.

She nodded . . .

Afterwards, he lay on his bed, staring at the ceiling as if its cracks and contours were a map which might lead him to an easy solution. He had wanted to comfort Maddie, but lately he felt damn all use or comfort to anyone, least of all himself.

In spite of his hermit-like existence, Sidney was not a man normally given to introspection and self-analysis. He got on with life, finding strength and meaning in a variety of simple routines. Protected in some way by this satisfying and private ritual, he had always found it easy enough to offer himself, at least on a temporary basis, as a source of strength to his family and, in particular to Malcolm.

But he had come to realise that his particular strength sprang from and, in some strange way, depended upon his independence.

In these last weeks, he had hardly set foot in his own cottage, had not walked once in the woods. His home-made brew bubbled away unattended; his own hearth still contained the uncleared ashes of a long-cold fire. He knew that he had had no choice – he had stayed where he was most needed. But nevertheless he found himself suddenly fighting back a wave of resentment at the events which had made him a prisoner of his own conscience.

He was, after all, the only member of the family who had not been allowed the indulgence of showing his own feelings. They had all been so busy leaning on him, letting him offer his rough but immensely steady shoulder to whoever might feel the need of it, that they had somehow overlooked the fact that he too had needs, felt grief, wanted reassurance.

Later that night, when Sidney had gone to bed, Maddie sat in her favourite rocking-chair gazing into the fast-dying fire. Malcolm sat at her feet. Gently, she stroked the ever-spreading bald patch which he no longer made any attempt to conceal.

'Ruddy Indians,' she murmured.

'I was going to have a message tattooed on it. I've heard all the jokes there ever were about baldness,' he said, smiling.

'Even from behind,' Maddie said softly, 'you're the best husband I've ever had.'

'Now she tells me,' he joked.

'How could I know till now?'

Silently they watched the fire as the last flames subsided.

'Soon, is it?' Malcolm asked.

'Yep!'

He leant forward to poke ineffectually at a fragment of wood which still glowed red, but it refused to be coaxed back into flames.

'Have you really . . . really loved me . . . all the way? In spite of the trouble I've caused?' he asked eventually.

'Really,' she replied.

'I love you, too,' he said.

They sat in silence. The room, without the light of the fire, had grown dark and cold.

'What's the date tomorrow?' Maddie asked suddenly.

'Sixteenth.'

She nodded.

'Soon be spring.'

'Crocusses are through already!'

She prodded him very gently in the back. 'You go on up to bed. I won't be long.'

First, she went to the conservatory. Her favourite room, her 'private place', wasn't that what Malcolm had always called it? Along the window-ledges, in a variety of pots and bowls, crocusses and daffodils were already forcing their way through the dense brown earth. She ran her fingers over the sharp green tips, imagining them as they would be when they burst out into their profusion of vivid colour. Daffodils had never failed to surprise her – so perfect in their symmetry, so utterly blatant in their brazen yellowness.

She wandered from room to room, touching, looking

211

... And in each room, some familiar object, some particular angle of chair and table, some trick of light on a certain ornament, each thing served to remind her of other times, other occasions. In these places, with these commonplace objects, she had lived her life, and the rooms themselves vibrated still with the memories.

In the kitchen, the old table, scene of so many childish meal-time tantrums, where so many cups of tea had been consumed over so many family debates, crises, quarrels ...

'Malcolm,' she heard her own voice from the past, 'I'm going to die ...'

She heard his voice come back at her, 'I know, I know.'

In the hallway, she paused by the telephone. So many requests, messages, so much news, good, bad or indifferent ...

She heard it ring, saw Malcolm pick it up in a delirium of excitement, heard her own voice rise to a fever of anticipation

'It's a boy! I just know it's a boy!'

And Nick's proud reply, 'It's a girl ... it's a big girl!'

Last of all, she walked into the lounge, saw the rocking-chair still moving very slightly in the deserted room. She pushed it gently with her foot, watching its rhythmic motion ...

She saw herself sitting in it, easing it gently to and fro ... and Neil, leaning over her shoulder with a large mug of tea, before coming to sit at her feet.

'Sorry ... got off on the wrong foot ... nerves, you see. I came home knowing I was fighting a losing battle ...'

She saw herself lean over to ruffle his hair. 'So, you puffed out your chest, stamped your feet. You're not a shrimp, you're a frog ...'

She watched as the chair, empty now, continued in its

silent, but eloquent motion, then turned and very slowly made her way upstairs.

Malcolm, who was lying in bed apparently reading, looked up as she came in, but asked no questions.

She undressed and got into bed beside him.

'Once upon a time,' he began, 'there was this princess, see . . . lived in a castle at the top of our road . . .'

He knew that she was going to ask him to do it soon – and he knew that he would have no option but to fulfill his promise. He had expected it to be hard, and it was – confronting the actual reality of what he must do, the stark mechanics of how, and where, and when. But it was harder still, watching her grow weaker day by day, watching her struggle to retain at least a surface appearance of normality, fighting the pain and losing. And each day he saw in her some new evidence that she could not go on, that he must not let her go on – some reminder that there is a limit of endurance beyond which no one human being can ever ask another to pass, not if they had the means to prevent it within their grasp.

'You don't expect me to go to sleep tonight, do you?' he asked eventually.

'No,' she said, leaning up on her elbow. 'I want you to tell me the things you remember best.'

'About you, of course!'

'Who else?'

He thought long and hard.

'Your cold feet,' he volunteered. 'You've always had cold feet. Except when you were pregnant.'

'Fancy being remembered, after twenty-six years, for your feet,' said Maddie, laughing.

'Me?' Malcolm asked.

'You were always going to give up smoking, but you never quite made it . . .'

'So,' he shrugged, 'you married a weakling.'

'Don't think *I* shall sleep much either,' said Maddie after a while.

'Well then?'

'You can get up and make me a cup of tea,' she suggested.

'Thanks very much,' he joked, but began to climb out of bed.

'Then I want us to start at the beginning,' said Maddie.

'Yes . . .'

'The day you first saw me . . .'

Chapter 14

The next morning, Malcolm woke early. Maddie was still sleeping peacefully, her face blurred in the half-light of the darkened room. For a moment, he studied its familiar contours as if hoping to draw some strength from their tranquillity, then he leapt from the bed, drew back the curtains, and seeing no possible alternative, allowed the day to begin.

He dressed quickly, choosing a checked shirt which Maddie had bought him last Christmas and which he had never worn, thinking it too garish.

Suddenly he was struck by the fact that the room seemed extremely untidy, and so, with something verging on relief, he began industriously to tidy things away, opening and shutting drawers with gusto, dusting surfaces with whatever came to hand, even folding several discarded shirts, which for weeks had lain in a heap at the bottom of his wardrobe. And, all the while, fired by an almost manic energy, a refusal to be still or silent, he whistled tunelessly between his teeth, snatches of 'West Side Story', bits and pieces of the 'Hallelujah Chorus', the Esso jingle.

Maddie, climbing slowly and painfully into consciousness, watched him, not knowing how to break into his perpetual motion.

He looked up and saw her.

'Malcolm . . .'

'Tea?' He spoke quickly, before she could finish. She

stretched out to catch his arm, but he dodged out of her grasp, sweeping up last night's cups from beside the bed and walking hurriedly to the door.

'No time for idle chatter. Tea to be made, uncles to be fed and watered . . .'

His hand was on the door handle, ready to effect his escape.

'Malcolm,' she almost pleaded. 'Slow down, will you?'

He paused for a moment, turning to look at her.

'How do you feel?' In spite of himself, he could not prevent a note of hopefulness from intruding.

'Rotten.' Her voice was light, giving no special emphasis to the word.

'You don't look it,' he replied brightly, then, not waiting for any further discussion, he fled from the room.

He closed the door, leaning gratefully for a moment against it, his heart pounding.

'Morning,' the Uncle Sidney said brightly as they met on the landing.

'Just going down to make tea. Everything all right?'

Malcolm looked up, his eyes blazing. 'Oh yeah! Everything's wonderful! You silly bastard! What a question'

'All right, so I won't talk to you. Does that suit?'

'No,' said Malcolm, his voice softening.

'Well then,' said Sidney, walking downstairs.

Malcolm paused for a while, as if bracing himself to go on, then followed.

In the kitchen, Sidney busied himself making tea. Malcolm watched, finding some comfort in the familiar ritual.

'It is today, isn't it?' Sidney's tone was conversational as he continued to pour milk into mugs and hunt for the ever-elusive sugar bowl.

'Stop pushing it! How do *I* know?' Malcolm exploded, glad of an outlet for his pent-up emotions.

'Just asking, nothing more,' Sidney shrugged, unmoved.

The tea made, Malcolm carried two mugs upstairs to the bedroom.

Maddie was sitting up in bed, her hair brushed, looking extremely calm. She reached for the tea, smiling. But it was not, he realised, an open smile; there was something in her eyes that said, 'Touch me not,' something which said, 'I have decided . . . let me go.'

'Breakfast!' he exclaimed brightly. 'What do you want for breakfast? I'll shout down the dumb waiter, at the dumb uncle, and tell him to stick the eggs on. Go on, what's for breakfast?'

Maddie forced him to look at her. 'Nothing.'

But still he pushed on, relentless, terrified. 'Now, why not! Big breakfast, middle-sized lunch, small tea, that's what you've always said . . .'

'It's today, Malcolm.' Maddie's voice was quiet but sharp, cutting through his chatter like a knife.

He knew that during the last long months – through all the waiting, all the agonised watching, he had been preparing himself for those words yet hoping daily that he would never hear them spoken. Oh yes, he had made the decision, had entered into an agreement with Maddie which bound him to her more firmly than any promise he had ever made before. Yet, somewhere in his mind he had believed that there would be an alternative, that something would save him from the actual act. He looked down at her face with its now unmistakable marks of pain.

'Right,' he said softly, knowing there was no need to fight any more. 'If you say so.'

'By which I mean right now,' said Maddie, refusing to lose the advantage she had gained.

'No!' Malcolm was appalled at her calmness.

If he had known it would be like this . . . but what could he have done? Was there any way of making it easier?

He must have been crazy to have agreed in the first place, mad to have even thought that he would be able to bring himself.

'Go on,' she urged. 'Go and get it. Don't tell me you can't remember where you put it . . .'

He sat down on the end of the bed, feeling the energy drain out of him. 'We never talked about today,' he said, his voice subdued.

'No need. I'll tell you exactly what's going to happen. I'll have it in orange juice.'

'No orange juice,' said Malcolm absurdly relieved, as if its absence might be the deciding factor.

'Then you squeeze an orange . . . or even two,' explained Maddie patiently.

'Give me your hand.'

She put out her hand, palm upward, as if surrendering it to him.

He took it and held it firmly in his own. 'I won't mess you about . . . orange juice it is.'

Maddie smiled, relieved that there were to be no more jokes, no more games, no more running.

'When I've taken it,' she said, 'you'll stay with me, yes?'

He nodded.

'When I've gone, you clear everything up, you call the doctor, and you say I woke up feeling dreadful, pains in my head and in my chest, you went down to get me a cup of tea . . .'

He was listening to her voice, but not the words, letting the sound wash over him. She sensed his inattention and jerked his still-captive hand, so that he was instantly alert again.

'... you went down to get me a cup of tea, and when you got back I was dead.'

She paused while he absorbed the word – the word so often thought of in the past months, but never before so bald, so irrevocable.

'Got all that?'

He nodded, 'Yeah.'

'Go on then,' she said very softly.

Reluctantly releasing his hand from her grasp, he got up.

Slowly, like a sleep-walker, like a man walking under water, he went to the study, opened his desk and unlocked the top left-hand drawer. Then carefully, as if dealing with something immensely fragile, he pulled out the drawer, and, taking out a small cash-box, opened it to reveal the small, brown bottle. Then he replaced the cash-box, slid the drawer back into place, and locked it again.

Turning to leave the room, his eye was caught by the portrait of Maddie, staring down at him with what seemed to be a kind of mocking amusement.

'I'll wake up in a minute, won't I?' he said wryly, addressing the painting. 'And you'll crash to the floor, tear yourself into shreds and leave a message saying, "Fooled you!" So it's all a dream. I'll surface to the sound of voices saying in amazement, 'You didn't *really* think she was dying!'

He pushed open the door to be met by wreaths of smoke from Uncle Sidney's pipe.

'I put the oranges on the table,' Sidney murmured.

'What oranges?' Malcolm began angrily. 'Stop listening at keyholes will you?'

Sidney shrugged and walked off in the direction of the living-room.

Malcolm made his way to the kitchen. There on the table were two oranges, a knife to cut them with, a glass to pour the juice into, an orange-squeezer and the morning paper. The old man had forgotten nothing.

He looked at the oranges for a moment, found himself gazing absent-mindedly at the morning's headlines.

'PETROL FAMINE HITS SOUTH!' he read, and 'BREAD PRICES UP AGAIN!'

He picked up one orange and cut it in half before squeezing its juice into the waiting glass.

He heard the phone ring twice only before Sidney reached it, listened while his uncle reassured Neil with a few well-chosen platitudes, before replacing the receiver. Then, he cut the second orange in half and added its juice to that of the first. Then, wiping his sticky fingers on a piece of kitchen-paper, he drew the brown bottle from his pocket, shook it fiercely, removed the cap, and poured its colourless contents into the glass where it immediately blended innocuously with the juice.

He swilled it around a little, then dipped his forefinger into the mixture. Shaking it in the air to remove most of its moisture, he tasted it quickly. Convinced that it tasted of nothing but oranges, he turned to go upstairs.

In the hallway, the telephone stared at him in silent accusation. He removed it gently from its hook, laying the receiver on one side.

Slowly, carrying the glass gingerly as if it might explode, he began to climb the stairs, pausing only to turn and catch a glimpse of Sidney, arms folded, pipe in mouth, watching his ascent.

He pushed open the bedroom door; Maddie was waiting.

She smiled when she saw him and beckoned him to come in, watching him as he approached, her eyes on the glass.

'Two oranges,' he said.

'What a waste of vitamin C,' she joked.

'Don't, please.' It was too late for joking.

'I want to be buried, not cremated,' she said, her eyes never leaving the glass.

He nodded.

'Put it down,' she said.

He placed it slightly out of her reach.

'No. Where I can reach it!'

He moved it a little closer to her.

'Thank you,' she said. 'Sit down.'

He sat on the bed. Maddie took off her wedding-ring and handed it to him.

'For Malcolm,' she said. 'You tell the doctor I always took it off at night, if he asks.'

'You've thought of everything,' he said.

He weighed the ring in the palm of his hand, but put it on his little finger.

'Uncle Sidney all right?' Maddie asked.

'I think so,' said Malcolm.

'You realise he's right outside the door,' she said, somewhat amused at the old man's constant vigil.

He was about to jump up and reprimand his uncle, but Maddie restrained him.

'Uncle Sidney,' she called softly.

There was a clatter and Sidney practically fell in through the doorway.

'What is it? What's wrong?' he asked.

'Caught you,' Maddie smiled.

'Yes, well, I was hanging around in case I—'

'No need to,' said Maddie, her voice authoritative. 'You go downstairs and wait. Promise me you'll do that?'

'Promise.'

'Goodbye, Uncle,' Maddie said softly.

He made as if to come towards her. 'Are you sure I can't—'

'Goodbye, Uncle,' she repeated sharply, then added, more gently, 'Thank you ...'

Reluctantly, but knowing that he had been given un-equivocal instructions, he left the room.

Malcolm watched him go, then turned again to Maddie.

'You're everything I ever dreamed of come true,' she said, taking his hand. 'That's all I want to say.'

'It's been such ... good fun,' he said, surprising him-self with this description of their life together.

Gently, she withdrew her hand from his as if wishing to retreat into some private space.

' 'Bye Malcolm,' she said.

' 'Bye Maddie,' he answered.

She took the glass and, without hesitating, drank its contents. Then she handed it back to him. He looked at it, saw that it was completely empty, and replaced it on the bedside table.

'Quite exciting, really!' she smiled. 'Quite an adventure ... make me comfortable, will you?'

Malcolm stood up and looked down at her for a moment, then he plumped up the pillows behind her head and straighted the duvet. She lay back.

On the bedside table, beside the empty glass, lay Maddie's hair-brush. Malcolm picked it up, running his fingers along the smooth contours of its handle and its soft bristle. Then gravely, and with great gentleness, he began to brush her hair.

Downstairs, in the kitchen, Uncle Sidney looked at his watch, opened the newspaper and closed it again, began to drum his fingers on the table in an agitated and rhyth-mic beat.

Maddie slept, breathing heavily, her head laid back on the pillow. Malcolm put down the hair-brush, quietly, as if fearing he would wake her.

'Maddie . . . Maddie . . .' he whispered.

He found her hand beneath the quilt and took it in his, fingered the white band where the wedding-ring had been, then raising it to his lips, touched it very lightly with his lips.

In the kitchen, Sidney's fingers continued to drum on the table, then gradually faded to the rhythm of a slow heart-beat, growing slower, more indistinct, till suddenly, abruptly, the beat stopped and he leapt to his feet, listening.

Now Malcolm, his eyes on Maddie's face, saw her breathing grow fainter, sensed that all motion had ceased in her, as if in one instance she was there with him and in the next, without warning or dramatic change, she was not

He knew that she was dead.

He stood up, still holding her hand. Then, gently, conscious of relinquishing his last contact with her, he placed it by her side, before leaning to kiss her lightly on her forehead.

He turned to walk to the door, and had made his way halfway across the room, before the full realisation of it came to him. He stopped, turned back, and like a man who meets himself in a dream, heard his own voice, but strange and as if from a great distance, cry out her name over and over.

'Maddie . . . Maddie . . . oh, Maddie . . .'

He stood, immobilised by grief, his arms spread wide in utter disbelief and desolation.

Sidney, standing at the kitchen door, strained to catch every sound from upstairs, while forcing himself to honour his promise to Maddie to keep his distance. He heard Malcolm cry out, and ran up the stairs two at a time, to meet him as he emerged, distraught and sobbing, from the bedroom.

Sidney held out his arms, just as he had done on that other day, so long ago, and pulled him to him in a firm embrace.

Malcolm could not tell how long he stood there. But slowly, like a man emerging from a fevered sleep, he clambered back to the surface of his consciousness, became vaguely aware of the rough texture of his uncle's jacket, damp where his own tears had fallen, smelling as ever, of dogs and pipe tobacco.

Carefully, as if mistrusting his own limbs, he made his way downstairs. Even the stair carpet looked unfamiliar and each room seemed full of hostile and alien objects, mocking him with their refusal to be changed by what had happened.

He wandered into the living-room, and collapsed into Maddie's rocking-chair.

Sidney stood beside him, watching.

'I never thought I'd make it,' Malcolm said after a while. 'Even now I'm not sure what I've done.'

He saw Sidney glance surreptitiously at his wrist.

'Will you stop looking at your watch?' he said.

'Must have things running smoothly. No mistakes!' said Sidney. 'Maddie would not have liked mistakes.'

Malcolm looked up, surprised at his uncle's ability to be practical.

'She *is* dead, isn't she?' he asked suddenly.

Sidney nodded.

'Maddie wouldn't have stood for any slip-ups,' Malcolm continued. 'Maddie would have ... Everything changes tense. Maddie *was* ... because Maddie no longer *is*.'

Sidney put his hand lightly on Malcolm's shoulder.

'I killed her,' said Malcolm.

'*We* killed her,' Sidney corrected. 'All three of us.'

Suddenly Malcolm shivered. 'It's cold in here!'

'Pull up to the fire.'

Malcolm shook his head. 'Things to clear up . . .'

He made as if to stand up, but Sidney restrained him. 'I'll see to it. All of it . . .'

'Do you know what needs doing?' Malcolm asked.

'I heard. Give me the bottle.' He held out his hand.

Malcolm seemed to hesitate. 'Mm?'

'In your pocket.'

Malcolm took the bottle from his pocket and passed it to Sidney.

'People should be told, I suppose.'

'I'll see to that an' all,' Sidney assured him. 'Kids?'

Malcolm nodded.

'Jack . . . Michael Pearson – he's in my book – asked me to tell him. Tell him first, will you?' And his voice became remote, as if remembering the cold mechanics of what he had so recently done. 'He gave me the stuff . . .'

Sidney left Malcolm and went back to the bedroom. Moving quietly, reluctant even now to disturb Maddie's calm, he took a tissue from the box beside the bed and very gently wiped her lips. Then, placing the soiled paper in his pocket, he touched the mug of cold tea, as if re-assuring himself of its necessary presence, and picked up the glass which had contained the orange juice.

His tasks completed, he paused for a moment, looked down at Maddie's face, thinking it as beautiful now as he had ever seen it. Then he went to the window and drew the curtains.

He took one last look around the room in the dim half-light, then went to the door, pausing only to wave one last, almost casual goodbye, before returning downstairs.

In the kitchen, he washed the glass, dried it and placed it in the waste bin. Then, needing to be doubly sure about it, he broke it into several pieces. Next, he washed the orange-squeezer, carefully removing all evidence of its recent use.

He looked up to see Malcolm watching him.

'Everything all right?'

Malcolm nodded.

'Like to see other people work, do you?'

'I want to do something,' said Malcolm.

'Make a cup of tea, then.'

Malcolm picked up the kettle and went to fill it.

Sidney walked past him to the door.

'Where are you going?' Malcolm asked, reluctant to let the old man out of his sight.

'Phone,' said Sidney. 'Your friend Burrows is an obvious boy to sign the certificate.'

'No,' Malcolm said firmly. 'He couldn't take it.'

'Better for us,' Sidney argued.

'I said no!'

'As you wish.'

Malcolm turned on the tap, watched the water running away, then heard Sidney's voice, clear, full of quiet authority: 'We've had a death in the family. We'd like one of the doctors to come round . . . My nephew's wife, Madeline Laurie. L-A-U-R-I-E. The Old Forge, Denton . . . Thank you.'

Doctor Miller, when he arrived, was very young, suitably grave, and quite business-like. But, not, as they had expected, a total stranger. He had, it seemed, seen Maddie on several occasions in the last months.

Sidney did not allow this fact to disturb him, but led the young man upstairs.

Malcolm waited downstairs, seated again in the rocking-chair.

After what seemed a very long time, he heard the bedroom door shut and the two men coming downstairs.

The doctor came towards him, his hand outstretched.

Malcolm looked up, startled, suddenly not knowing what to expect.

'Mr Laurie, I am so sorry. Please accept my condolences.'

Malcolm nodded.

'I'll leave this with you, for the registrar,' Dr Miller handed him the certificate. 'Natural causes is hardly an *adequate* description, don't you agree?' said the Doctor.

'Depends what you mean.' Malcolm felt his heart begin to thud.

'Cancer is the obscenity of our age,' the doctor went on smoothly. 'In twenty years time it won't exist.'

Malcolm nodded, relieved.

The doctor closed his bag, did up the buttons on his jacket.

'Can I give you something?' he asked, as he turned to go. 'To blur the edges?'

Malcolm shook his head. 'No thanks.'

'Goodbye then.' Dr Miller turned towards the door.

Sidney accompanied him out of the room, thanked him for his trouble, then, with some relief, watched as he walked to his waiting car and drove away.

Gilly was the first of the children to arrive, accompanied by Nick and Beatrice. She walked straight past Uncle Sidney without saying a word and into the living-room.

Nick tried to follow but Sidney restrained him: 'Give them a minute or two . . .'

Nick nodded. 'When did she die?' he asked.

'About nine o'clock,' said Sidney.

'Poor old Malcolm,' Nick murmured.

Gilly found her father rocking himself gently to and fro in Maddie's favourite chair. She thought he looked smaller somehow, crushed almost.

She threw her arms around his neck.

'You were quick,' he said, looking up.

'We'll stay, Dad, if that's all right?' she said.

'We'll see,' Malcolm said doubtfully.

'*I'll* stay,' Gilly corrected herself. 'With Beatle ... she'll be OK. Just so long as you aren't alone ...'

'I'm not, love,' Malcolm said gently.

It was going to be difficult, this bit, but he had promised Maddie. If he could just get over these first few minutes with Gilly, then the rest would follow.

'Did Nick come with you?' he asked.

'Yes.'

'And Beatrice, then ... I'd like to see her. To remind me it was all worth it.'

'What?'

'Your mother dying, of course. What else has happened today!'

'She looked so marvellous last time I saw her. Who would have thought ... Funny that she knew!'

Gilly was thinking aloud and Malcolm let her do so, steeling himself not to over-react to what were, after all, simply natural speculations.

'Funny she knew she was going ...'

Malcolm drew in his breath, forced himself to answer calmly, 'I'm surprised she didn't tell you the day. She always had to have everything organised!' He smiled wryly. 'She won't be around to make lunch now!'

'I'll do it,' Gilly's face lit up.

'Will you?' Malcolm asked.

'Of course I will,' Gilly said, throwing her arms around his neck.

'I'll look after you. She asked me to do that.'

Gently, Malcolm extricated himself from Gilly's grasp.

'And what about old Nick?' he asked.

'What about him?'

228

'Won't he have something to say?'

'He'll understand,' said Gilly.

Malcolm took her head in his hands. 'I don't want you to stay, Gilly,' he said softly but firmly. 'You can't replace her ... no one can.'

He released her slowly and she stood away from him, hurt but unwilling to argue.

'I'll stay a bit,' she said, compromising.

Malcolm looked up and saw Nick watching the scene from the doorway, Beatrice in his arms.

'Come on in, Nick,' he said.

'There's nothing I can say, Malcolm—' Nick began, but Malcolm interrupted him.

'That's right. Now, where's that Beatrice?'

He held out his arms to receive the smiling child.

Angela and Jack Burrows arrived soon afterwards. Malcolm stood up as Jack approached and the two friends embraced, long and hard, in silence.

'Anything I can do ... anything!' said Jack, his voice hardly more than a whisper.

'I'd ask. I promise,' Malcolm reassured him.

'Has anyone seen her? A doctor, I mean?'

Malcolm nodded. 'Everything's OK.'

Jack leant closer to Malcolm, conscious that Gilly, though apparently involved in amusing Beatrice, was following every word of their conversation.

'Everything went well? No pain? No slip-ups?' he inquired nervously.

'Clockwork,' said Malcolm.

Malcolm found himself surprised at the way in which Neil had reacted to the news. From him, of all the children, he had expected tears, outrage, incomprehension. Instead, though Neil was obviously deeply affected, he remained calm.

They sat quietly together in the living-room.

For the first time since Maddie had died, Malcolm found himself consciously evaluating what had happened. Having been virtually silent for hours, he found himself talking incessantly, the thoughts falling over each other.

Neil let him go on, aware of his father's need to explore every avenue before the subject could, in any way, be laid to rest.

'Your brain's working double-time,' he said gently when Malcolm finally paused for breath.

'Just my mouth,' said Malcolm, conscious of feeling a little lighter and knowing that Neil, who had burdened them all from time to time with his philosophical rumblings, had offered him the best form of support he knew: an uncritical and patient ear for his outburst.

Gordon arrived later that afternoon. Malcolm thought he seemed rather remote, but far more worrying, he was extremely curious about the manner of Maddie's death.

At first, his questions had been little more than the conditioned reflexes of a trained legal mind, but he was soon struck by something incongruous in his father's behaviour – some strange aggressiveness which seemed to have little to do with grief.

And how *suddenly* she had died! It was, after all, quite incredible to think that only two days previously she had been at his wedding, looking, he had thought, as good as ever – looking in no way like a woman who had only two days to live . . .

Gordon climbed the stairs to the bedroom.

The room was in partial darkness. He could make out the outlines of familiar objects: his father's wardrobe, his mother's dressing-table. But even in the half-light, everything seemed strangely tidy, unnaturally still, like a stage set which has been meticulously arranged to imitate reality, but still fails to appear realistic.

Reluctantly, and with a sort of terror, he approached the bed where Maddie lay. He looked down at her, reached out to touch her face, but found that he could not. She was gone, to a place where his touch was irrelevant. And somehow, with that realisation came the knowledge that there was nothing further for him to do in that room, that the only real goodbye had long since been said.

He turned to leave, but as he did so, he caught sight of the mug of cold tea. Something about it struck him as strange. There was no ring where the wet mug made contact with the table top. Nor was there any speck of dust or stain to be found around it. Gingerly he touched it, then glancing almost quizzically at Maddie, picked it up and went downstairs.

In the kitchen, he poured the tea away down the sink and thoroughly rinsed out the mug.

Sidney, who had observed Gordon's mind at work from the moment he had entered the house, watched him, waiting for the questions to start again.

Gordon dried the mug with painstaking care before he could bring himself to say what he was thinking.

'She didn't kill herself, did she?'

Sidney suppressed a sigh of relief, having expected a different question.

'I don't think so. How would she have done it without your father knowing?'

'Perhaps he does.'

Sidney forced himself not to react excessively to

Gordon's remark. 'Her prerogative if she did, don't you think?' he said lightly.

'As a matter of fact, I do,' said Gordon.

'Well then,' Sidney shrugged.

'I'd just hate to feel that she did it . . . alone.'

'I see what you mean . . . Ask your father. He'll tell you, I'm sure.'

But in his heart, Gordon already knew the answer!

That evening, the whole family sat around the kitchen table. In the centre, Uncle Sidney's stew lay waiting. He paused, ladle in mid-air, breaking what had been a long silence.

'I don't know who believed in what around this table,' he began, 'but we all believe in today and Maddie's death . . . or rather we know it happened and we're in varying stages of belief. We'll think of her . . . just for a minute . . . May the journey have been easy.'

There was a long silence.

Neil passed his hand over his eyes, as if by so doing he could conjure Maddie up again; Nick stared into the middle-distance, probably remembering other dinners, other occasions; Gordon, tense as ever, watched his own fingers as they beat out a rhythm on the table; Jack and Angela, eyes closed, held hands as if drawing strength one from the other; Gilly stared back at him.

Malcolm looked from one to the other, and, in that instant, Maddie's death became a reality. She was not there – would never again be there with them. Everything they did, from that moment on, they would do without her.

Slowly, and still without speaking, Malcolm picked up his fork and knife and began to eat.

STARBRAT
by John Morressy

Driveships roam the starways, carrying outlaws, pirates and
slavers, for it is six centuries since the Wroblewski Drive sent
men into galactic space, far beyond the solar system. Out on the
edges of the unknown, the descendants of Old Earth have settled
down with the many races of the galaxy, from the gangling,
spidery Lixians to the furry, knee-high Quiplids. But space is a
frontier, and all too often the only law is a man with a weapon,
as it was in the Bloody Centuries on Old Earth. Slave traders
snatched Del Whitby from planet Gilead on the day he learned he
was a foundling. From the gladiatorial schools on Tarquin VII
where he learns weapon-skill, to the information banks on
Watson's Planet and the barbarities of war-torn Skorat, Del
scours the many-peopled worlds of Space for a clue to his
origins.

NEW ENGLISH LIBRARY

THE SURVIVOR
by James Herbert

A tale of
death, and of
an evil which
transcends
death

NEW ENGLISH LIBRARY

PQ 17 CONVOY TO HELL
by Lund and Ludlam

In June 1942 Convoy PQ 17 consisting of 35 merchant ships set out for Russia with an escort of cruisers and destroyers. They had a reasonable chance of success until the order came to 'Scatter!'

What followed represents one of the most terrible and tragic blunders of the Second World War.

Authors Ludlam and Lund give a first hand account of the horror and despair that faced the men left to the mercy of a cruel enemy.

NEW ENGLISH LIBRARY

Book Tokens

Give them
the pleasure of choosing

Book Tokens can be bought
and exchanged at most
bookshops in Great Britain
and Ireland.

NEL BESTSELLERS

T045 528	THE STAND	*Stephen King*	£1.75
T046 133	HOW GREEN WAS MY VALLEY	*Richard Llewellyn*	£1.00
T039 560	I BOUGHT A MOUNTAIN	*Thomas Firbank*	95p
T033 988	IN THE TEETH OF THE EVIDENCE	*Dorothy L. Sayers*	90p
T038 149	THE CARPETBAGGERS	*Harold Robbins*	£1.50
T041 719	HOW TO LIVE WITH A NEUROTIC DOG	*Stephen Baker*	75p
T040 925	THE PRIZE	*Irving Wallace*	£1.65
T034 755	THE CITADEL	*A. J. Cronin*	£1.10
T042 189	STRANGER IN A STRANGE LAND	*Robert Heinlein*	£1.25
T037 053	79 PARK AVENUE	*Harold Robbins*	£1.25
T042 308	DUNE	*Frank Herbert*	£1.50
T045 137	THE MOON IS A HARSH MISTRESS	*Robert Heinlein*	£1.25
T040 933	THE SEVEN MINUTES	*Irving Wallace*	£1.50
T038 130	THE INHERITORS	*Harold Robbins*	£1.25
T035 689	RICH MAN, POOR MAN	*Irwin Shaw*	£1.50
T043 991	EDGE 34: A RIDE IN THE SUN	*George G. Gilman*	75p
T037 541	DEVIL'S GUARD	*Robert Elford*	£1.25
T042 774	THE RATS	*James Herbert*	80p
T042 340	CARRIE	*Stephen King*	80p
T042 782	THE FOG	*James Herbert*	90p
T033 740	THE MIXED BLESSING	*Helen Van Slyke*	£1.50
T038 629	THIN AIR	*Simpson & Burger*	95p
T038 602	THE APOCALYPSE	*Jeffrey Konvitz*	95p
T046 850	WEB OF EVERYWHERE	*John Brunner*	85p

NEL P.O. BOX 11, FALMOUTH TR10 9EN, CORNWALL

Postage charge:
U.K. Customers. Please allow 30p for the first book plus 15p per copy for each additional book ordered to a maximum charge of £1.29 to cover the cost of postage and packing, in addition to cover price.

B.F.P.O. & Eire. Please allow 30p for the first book plus 15p per copy for the next 3 books, thereafter 6p per book, in addition to cover price.

Overseas Customers. Please allow 50p for the first book plus 15p per copy for each additional book, in addition to cover price.

Please send cheque or postal order (no currency).

Name...

Address ....

....

Title...

While every effort is made to keep prices steady, it is sometimes necessary to increase prices at short notice. New English Library reserve the right to show on covers and charge new retail prices which may differ from those advertised in the text or elsewhere. (3)